All of a sudden I was grateful to Jack Rawls.

He'd saved Megan from having to stake me, I thought as I felt more sunlight pour over me. He'd saved me from having to die by my own sister's hand. I looked down at my arms, sure they were starting to burn now, and for a moment I couldn't breathe.

A final wisp of smoke drifted and died in the air. The heat bubbles on my skin collapsed without bursting. Even as I watched, my skin became smooth, as if I'd imagined everything I'd seen.

Jack pulled me closer and put his mouth to my hair. "I don't kill humans, and the only reason I can think of for you not burning is that you've still got some human in you. But you and I both know you're turning, and when you do I intend to finish what I started tonight. That's a promise, vamp."

On their twenty-first birthday,
the sexy and stylish Crosse triplets discover
their mother was a vampire slayer—and that
each of them is destined to carry on their
family's legacy with the dark side.

A new miniseries from author

Harper
Allen

Follow each triplet's story:

Dressed to Slay—October 2006
Unveiled family secrets lead sophisticated
Megan Crosse into the world of
shapeshifters and slayers.

Vampaholic—November 2006
Sexy Kat Crosse fears her dark future as a vampire
until a special encounter reveals her true fate.

Dead Is the New Black—January 2007
Cursed by her own blood, wild child
Tash Crosse leaves her family, only to
learn her death might save them all.

www.SilhouetteBombshell.com

Harper
Allen

VAMPAHOLIC

Published by Silhouette Books

America's Publisher of Contemporary Romance

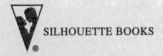

SILHOUETTE BOOKS

ISBN-13: 978-0-373-51427-4
ISBN-10:   0-373-51427-1

VAMPAHOLIC

Books by Harper Allen

Silhouette Bombshell

Payback #34
‡*Dressed to Slay* #109
‡*Vampaholic* #113

Harlequin Intrigue

The Man That Got Away #468
Twice Tempted #547
Woman Most Wanted #599
*Guarding Jane Doe #628
*Sullivan's Last Stand #632
*The Bride and the Mercenary #663
The Night in Question #680
McQueen's Heat #695
Covert Cowboy #735
†*Lone Rider Bodyguard* #754
†*Desperado Lawman* #760
†*Shotgun Daddy* #766

*The Avengers
†Men of the Double B Ranch
‡Darkheart & Crosse

HARPER ALLEN,

her husband and their menagerie of cats and dogs divide their time between a home in the country and a house in town. She grew up reading Stephen King, John D. MacDonald and John Steinbeck, among others, and has them to blame for her lifelong passion for reading and writing.

Prologue

I can't let anyone know how afraid I am.

It has to stay my secret, one that I'll die before I reveal. I probably will die, of course. Or maybe I won't, and that terrifies me more. What it really comes down to is that right now I could use a little comforting...but when a girl's let herself run out of vodka for the evening and, worse, let herself run out of men for the evening, too, she has to look for comfort where she can get it. Which sometimes means telling herself fairy stories to try to make sense of all the terrible things that have happened.

So: once upon a time there were three beautiful shop-till-they-dropped princesses named Megan, Katherine and Natashya. They were sisters—triplets, actually—who lived in a charming, upstate-New York town called

Maplesburg with their grandparents on their father's side, Grammie and Popsie Crosse.

Although their parents died when they were babies, Megan and Katherine and Tashya weren't like orphans in other stories. Grammie and Popsie spoiled them rotten and Popsie only occasionally complained about the outrageous credit card charges the girls ran up. Oh, the sisters squabbled among themselves a bit when Megan, who was the eldest by a few minutes, got a tad bossy, or when Tashya, who was the youngest by half an hour, pouted because she couldn't get her way. The middle sister, Kat, had her adorable foibles, too, if you want to get picky about it. Besides being partial to shoes, she was also partial to cocktails and men, but what girl isn't?

Anyway, except for the squabbling, the Crosse sisters' lives were perfect right up until their twenty-first year. The three most eligible bachelors in Maplesburg asked for their hands in marriage, the girls accepted, and three weddings were planned to take place that summer. Megan's Dean was a stuffy investment banker, Kat's Lance was a lawyer who would sell his own mother to get ahead, and Tash's Todd was a philandering plastic surgeon, but princesses these days don't marry for love—they marry for money and security, no? So the night before Megan's wedding, the three princesses were looking forward to becoming brides and living happily ever after.

The end.

I'm going to try to sleep now. I'm going to try not to get a splinter in my hand from the wooden stake lying beside me, to ignore the smell of the garlic hanging by the windows and doors, to convince myself that the fairy-tale version is how it really happened. Because if I can't, I have to accept that this nightmare is the reality.

In the nightmare, Lance and Todd and Dean turned into vampires and tried to kill Megan, Tashya and me. In the nightmare, we learned that our mom, Angelica, had been a vampire killer, but her skills hadn't saved our father from being slaughtered by a queen vampire, or herself from being infected by the queen. At her own request, Angelica had died at the hands of her father, Anton Dzarchertzyn, who staked her before she lost her immortal soul forever.

She left this life comforted by the belief that she'd saved her babies, at least. Again, everything comes down to needing comfort, doesn't it?

Even if comfort takes the form of a lie.

Because Angelica didn't save her daughters. As Anton, our Grandfather Darkheart, told us when he reappeared in our lives, one of Angelica's babies received the kiss of the vampire queen. That baby wasn't Megan. Grandfather Darkheart instructed us all in the ways of fighting the undead, but in the final battle between the queen vampire's army and the Crosse triplets, only Megan proved more than a match for the Mistress of Evil.

Tashya did her best, but she was out of her league. I've tried to tell myself that I was, too, but that's just another comforting lie. I killed three vamps that night... and every time I drove the stake in, I felt as if I were piercing my own heart. Although I lie here in the dark with a stake beside me, I know I'll never be able to use one again.

That's why I'm so terrified. That's why I can't share this fear—not with my sisters, not with Grandfather Darkheart. The only reason I can think of for my revulsion at killing vampires is that I'm the Crosse triplet who received the kiss of the vampire queen so long ago.

Being tipsy helps a little. Being held by a stranger pushes the nightmares away for a while. But when the cocktails have worn off and the man of the night has gone home and the bedtime stories ring hollow, I lie here in my bed and wonder when the change will come over me.

No one knows how afraid I am.

Of myself.

And of what I might be.

Chapter 1

"Abs to die for," I purred appreciatively.

On the bar stool beside me, Ramon looked up from the notepad propped on his crossed knees. "Check, boss," he said, making a tick mark on the page.

"Biceps pumped," I continued.

One of the carpenters rebuilding the club's stage began to use a nail gun, and each *thunk-whap!* seemed to go right through my pounding temples. One of the reasons I'd drifted into the Hot Box Club as late as I had was to avoid the loud construction, but I'd forgotten the double time and a half I'd promised the crew if they worked evenings this week. Of course, the other reason I'd shown up so tardily had been because when my alarm clock had gone off at noon, I'd thrown it across the room and burrowed my head under the pillows again. I took a hasty sip of the cocktail I'd concocted as a hair-of-the-dog remedy for last night's overindulgence and spoke above the noise. "Sweetie, can you give us a slow turn?"

My first order of business when I'd taken possession of the Hot Box had been to have everything inside it hauled away, most of the chairs and tables having been destroyed in a massive fight on the former strip dive's last night of operation. The replacement furnishings I'd ordered hadn't been delivered yet, so right now my new club was little more than a cavernously empty space.

Empty of furniture, that is. In addition to the carpenters working on the stage, a conga line of gorgeous males wearing hopeful expressions and not much else snaked from the vicinity of the bar to the coat check area near the main entrance. The dark-haired Adonis at the head of the line obligingly presented his rear view to Ramon and me.

"Mmm-*mmm!*" Ramon said for my ears only. "Even covered by tighty-whities, those buns look hard enough to crack nuts."

"Yours, maybe, if you get fresh with him," I enlightened him. "He's not gay, sweetie. That means I get to pick him to play on my team."

"Wanna bet, *chica?*" Ramon gave the man a sultry wink and got a faint smile in return. "Please, Kat. Some things a boy just knows," he murmured.

Instead of answering him, I raised my martini glass at the Adonis. "I think I left out an ingredient, Jean-Paul. The ones you made for me last night tasted just a tad yummier, somehow. Vodka, amaretto, orange juice, a dollop of cherry sorbet and…?"

"Crème de pêche, chérie," the dark-haired man answered, his smile broadening. *"C'est essentiel, non?* Without it you do not have a true *Baiser de Vampire*— Vampire's Kiss, as you say in English. If you wish, I can come to your place again this evening and show you more of my repertoire." He gave a glance that seemed to savor every last detail of me, taking in the way I'd pulled my hair into a silver-blond chignon, appreciating how my cream-colored Badgley Mischka slip dress skimmed my curves...and seeming to know that under my sophisticated exterior, I was wearing a deliciously trampy pink-and-black bra and panties. "My bartending repertoire, of course," he added with Gallic suavity.

"Too tempting, sweetie. Unfortunately I'm otherwise engaged," I sighed. "But I was impressed enough last night that I've decided you've got the job. Talk to Ramon before you leave and he'll go through the details with you."

"Impressed by what part of his repertoire?" Ramon asked cattily as Jean-Paul strolled out of the room in his tight briefs. "And as club manager, don't I have any input on who we hire?"

"Of course you do." I patted his hand. "But for the public to forget the guys-only reputation this place used to have when it was the Hot Box, it's vital we attract women from the start. That's the official reason for this pecs and abs beauty contest, sweetie—the fact that you and I adore looking at half-naked men is just a bonus. Trust me, having a bare-chested Jean-Paul shaking cocktails behind the bar will definitely raise female pulses."

And pulses are another must-have for our future clientele, I reminded myself as I went around the bar to freshen my drink, *seeing as how, by the Hot Box's last night of business, most of its patrons didn't possess one.*

That had been the downside of buying this establishment. Once merely a sleazy strip joint, during its final month it had been owned by the Queen of All Evil— one of the titles my sisters and I knew her by, although on the Hot Box's unpaid tax notices she'd used the name Zena Uzhasnoye, which my Grandfather Dark-heart says translates as Zena the Terrible. But whatever alias she'd gone under, she'd turned the Hot Box into a center of vamp activity…and in the process, neglected such mundane matters as paying the bills. After my sister Megan had finally staked her, it wasn't long before a notice was tacked up on the door informing anyone who was interested that the place was to be sold to pay off the creditors.

I'd seen the notice at a time when I'd been wondering what I could do with the rest of my life, and the notion of buying the Hot Box and turning it into a trendy club had seemed absolutely inspired. I like cocktails and parties and men. Clubs include all those things. Investigation agencies don't, and going to work for an investigation agency was the only other option that had presented itself since my initial life plan of becoming Mrs. Lance Zellweger had blown up in my face.

The agency idea had been Tashya's. "So we've whacked the queen *vampyr,*" she'd said to Megan and me a few days after the final battle at the Hot Box. "What about the ones that got away? We know Zena brought along a few dozen undead troops when she came to Maplesburg, and that's not counting the vamps she and her buddies created once they arrived. Strolling around at night staking any vampires we might happen to come across is better than doing nothing, but we need to get organized if we're going to clean up this town. What do you think about Darkheart & Crosse for a name?"

"A name for what?" Megan had asked, stifling a yawn—the result of her strolling around, as Tash put it, the previous night and staking whatever vamps she'd come across. Not for the first time since the battle at the Hot Box I had wondered what kind of toll being a hereditary Daughter of Lilith would take on my sister. For those who don't know, Daughter of Lilith is the correct term for what Megan is—a true descendant of Adam's first wife, the one who's gotten such bad PR over the centuries from Venus-envying men. Technically, Tash and I are daughters of Lilith, too, but the vamp-slaying destiny only gets passed down to one female descendant per family per generation.

Which makes us Megan's sidekicks, in the staking business at least. As Tash had continued, I'd suspected she wasn't totally thrilled with being a sidekick.

"A name for our agency, of course," she'd said. "Say a woman looks out her window one night and sees her boyfriend standing there, except there's no way he can be because she's in a third-story apartment with no balcony. Or some poor schmuck walking his dog after dark barely escapes being attacked by a bunch of thugs who have fangs and can fly, or a wife notices a bite mark on hubbie's neck and the next day finds him sleeping in the basement under a blanket of dirt. Who do they call?" she'd demanded. "Not the cops, unless they want to be labeled nutcases. Which is where Darkheart & Crosse comes in. We set up an office, put out some flyers—"

"And just what do you propose these flyers say, sweetie?" I drawled. "Darkheart & Crosse, Vamp Exterminators?"

Tash had given me an annoyed look. "I was thinking more along the lines of Darkheart & Crosse: Extraordinary Investigations."

"You know, Kat, I think the brat's got something," Megan had said slowly. "Grandfather Darkheart says that in the old country, everyone knows who the local Daughter of Lilith is, even if they don't talk about what she does. But this is Maplesburg. Maybe we *should* hang out a shingle."

It had snowballed from there. Mikhail, Megan's gorgeous shape-shifting main squeeze—don't ask, it's a long story—had thought the idea of an agency made sense, and although Grandfather Darkheart had been dubious at first, Megan's point about Maplesburg not being Carpathia had finally won him over.

If anyone had asked my opinion about the whole thing, I would have given it. But they hadn't, so two weeks later I had signed the papers making me the new owner of the late, unlamented Hot Box.

The acquisition had taken a big chunk out of my part of the trust funds Popsie had set up for his three granddaughters, which we'd been able to access when we'd turned twenty-one. I'd written the check without a qualm, informed Megan and Tash about my purchase, and made regretful-sounding apologies for not joining them in their Darkheart & Crosse venture.

Only then had the sick feeling that had lodged in the pit of my stomach since Tash had proposed her vampire-hunting agency idea gone away.

Which wasn't to say that I didn't still have problems, I thought now as I turned from the bar and narrowed my eyes at the crew of carpenters. I did, but they were the kind that could be solved. Cocktail in hand, I left Ramon in gay heaven interviewing the conga line of beefcake and made my way to the half-built stage on the far side of the room. The crew foreman, bulging biceps revealed by the rolled-up sleeves of his sawdusty shirt—don't you just *love* what swinging a hammer all day does for a man's muscles?—gave a grin as I approached.

"Hey, boss lady, I wondered when you'd get tired of those pretty boys prancing around in their undershorts and check out us real men." He lowered his voice and a frown replaced his grin. "Why didn't you call last night, babe? I waited around to hear from you and when you didn't phone I tried your number but I just kept getting your machine. I know you were home because when I drove by, your car was parked outside and a couple of lights were on in your apartment."

Gorgeous biceps or not, Terry was the problem I needed to solve. I took a sip of my drink and did so. "Getting my very own personal stalker wasn't what I had in mind when you and I had our fling last week, darling," I said lightly. "As spine-tingly and delicious as you made me feel during our naughty little romp, it was a one-time-only thing. *So* much more romantic that way, don't you think? You know, ships that pass in the night and all—"

"Cut the bullshit, Kat!" His tone was beginning to attract attention. I saw the dark-haired carpenter nearest to us flick a glance our way before returning to the task of reloading his nail gun as Terry went on. "I fell like a ton of bricks for you and you know it! Who the hell were you screwing senseless last night when you could have been with me?"

I sighed. I'd tried letting him down easily, but some men just can't accept it when a woman doesn't rush out to choose a china pattern after she sleeps with them. "If you must know, sweetie, one of those pretty boys over there prancing around in his underwear. His name's Jean-Paul, and to be perfectly honest, it was a toss-up as to who screwed who more senseless." I tipped back the final potent drops of my cocktail and gave Terry a wide-eyed look over the rim of the glass. "You know, it really is true what they say about the French knowing so much more about *amour.* Jean-Paul had me doing things I'd never imagined in my wickedest—"

"Spare me the fucking details," Terry said tightly. "Before I went out with you I heard stories about what a ball breaker you were, but I didn't believe them. Now I do." He grabbed a nearby toolbox. "I quit. Some other sap might have taken my place in your bed, but it won't be so easy for you to find another master carpenter to take my place on this job, lady."

Ball breaker? *Me?* I stared after his retreating back, unaccustomed anger getting the better of me. "You never *had* a place in my bed, sweetie!" I called after him. "We did it on the floor and the kitchen table and in the shower, but we never actually made it to the *bed,* remember?"

"I think we'll all remember now, sis." I turned to see Megan standing behind me, her eyebrows raised and her arms folded across her chest. She was wearing a tight-fitting sleeveless top with slim black pants, and her shoes were Chanel ballet flats. Very retro—Audrey Hepburn, right up to and including the cropped Sabrina haircut she'd recently gotten. "Didn't you used to handle breakups more…discreetly?" she asked.

I waved my hand airily. "Oh, pooh, Terry's not a breakup, he was a lapse in judgment. Although he might have a point about finding someone to replace him on the job," I admitted, my airiness fading.

"You should have thought about that before you did the floor and table and shower thing with him." Tashya joined us. In contrast to Megan's basic black, she was wearing a ribbon-belted Zac Posen bias-cut skirt topped with a cashmere shell in pale lemon that played up the strawberry-blond glints in her curls. In my bitchier moments I compare her to Shirley Temple, but most of the time I have to admit she looks like a Botticelli angel. She'd obviously entered the club with Megan but, being made of less stern stuff than a Daughter of Lilith, she'd been distracted by Ramon's conga line of hotties. She cast a last, longing look at them. "Not that I'm com-plaining, but why do they have to drop their laundry to get a job here?"

"Because the staff uniform's almost as revealing," I

told her. "Think Chippendale dancers. I want to be sure every male working at the new Hot Box is absolutely to-die-for from head to toe. Did I tell you about my idea to—"

"Kat, we didn't come here to talk about your club," Megan cut in. She frowned. "Although just as an aside, you're surely not going to keep the name Hot Box, are you?"

Even a Daughter of Lilith could be distracted, it seemed, but distractability wasn't a positive when it came in the repressive tone of voice Megan was using. I studied her, trying and failing to see the sister I'd grown up with—the one who'd rolled her eyes with me over Tash's irritating whininess, giggled with me over how dumb but fascinating boys were and later snickered with me over how dumb but fascinating men were— who'd known all my secrets and told me all hers.

Sometime in the past two months, that sister had left me. She'd been replaced by the serious-faced woman in front of me—a woman who'd sworn she wouldn't let anything stand in the way of her hereditary mission to kill vampires.

I suddenly wished I'd made my cocktail a double. I looked at the pink froth rimming my empty glass and said the first thing that came into my head. "God, no." I gave her a tiny smile. "I've decided to call the club The Vampire's Kiss. Appropriate, yes?"

Megan's gaze went flat. "Appropriate, no," she said tersely. "Not to mention tasteless. In case you've forgotten, our mother gave her life in the fight against vampires."

"And either Tash or I received the kiss of the same queen vamp who vanquished her," I drawled. "Ever notice how we don't talk about that much anymore, sis? Not since we learned you weren't the one who got vamp-marked, anyway. I guess it's a pretty delicate subject, though, with you feeling so honor-bound as a Daughter of Lilith to hunt down and stake any sister of yours who might suddenly turn undead on you."

I expected a reaction from Megan, but I wasn't prepared when Tash clamped a hand around my arm and pulled me a few feet away from the group of carpenters. She thrust her face into mine, her voice a furious whisper—furious but unnecessary, since Mr. Nail Gun was loudly at work again. "We don't talk about it because it doesn't matter anymore!" she hissed. "Megan killed the queen vamp, and when a vamp that's bitten you dies before you make your own first kill as a vampire, you're saved! You know that as well as we do, so either your memory loss is from all the alcohol you've been tossing back lately, or there really *is* something to the phrase 'screwing your brains—'"

"Congratulations, Tash," Megan ground out through gritted teeth. "We agreed before we came here that we weren't going to handle this intervention like a confrontation, and that's exactly what you've turned it into."

"Intervention?" I stared from one to the other of them. Tash looked ashamed, as she always does when she knows she's crossed the line. Megan looked upset, and just for a moment I saw my sister, not a Daughter of Lilith, behind her worried gaze. Then she nodded slowly.

"Someone has to make you see what you're doing to yourself, Kat. As usual, Tash shot her mouth off without thinking, but she's right. In the past few weeks you've gone from indulging in the occasional cocktail to downing them like water, and that scene we walked in on when we arrived just bears out the other part of what she said."

"That I screw my brains out?" I asked with icy politeness. "Because at least I do it with men, sweetie. Tell me, have you bought a dog license for Mikhail yet?"

Megan paled. I waited for her to scream at me, to insult me back, to give me an angry shove, but what she did was worse than any of those things.

She turned and walked away from me.

"On the bitch-o-meter, that one rang the bell," Tash said hotly, planting her hands on her hips and tossing back a red gold curl from her glaring blue eyes. "Mikhail might be able to shapeshift into a wolf, but that doesn't make him one. And for your information, it's not the number of men you've been seeing that has Meg worried, it's the way you treat them."

As if by some mysterious signal, the hammering that had been going on all day by the stage suddenly stopped. Then I realized that the signal hadn't been mysterious at all; the clock behind the bar showed eight o'clock, which meant the crew had put in their agreed-to overtime. On the other side of the room, both Ramon and his conga line had gone, too.

I felt like a drink. I started to push past Tash, but she stepped in front of me.

"I don't care if you don't want to hear it, I'm going

to say it anyway. You've always loved 'em and left 'em, sis, but now it's different. Your carpenter boy-toy was right—you've turned into a ball breaker. You never spend more than one or two nights with the same man, and if they can't be as casual as you are about it, you make sure you dump them as publicly and humiliatingly as possible. Megan says she can't figure it out. It's like you've got a hate on for all men. I agree. Only difference is, I *have* figured it out."

"What an exciting new experience for you, sweetie," I said acidly. "Now, if you don't mind, I really must run."

"This won't take long." Tash took a deep breath. "I know what's been eating away at you since Megan killed Zena, and why you've been acting all 'Girls Gone Wild' lately and treating men like Kleenex. It's because of what that queen bitch said about Dad just as Meg staked her—that he'd been one of her vamp servants and he'd betrayed Mom." She bit her lip. "If that were true it would mean he betrayed us, too, in a way. We grew up on Grammie and Popsie's stories about what a great son he was and how much he loved Mom and adored his darling baby daughters. When Zena realized she was going to hell, she saw how she could use our love for him as one final weapon against us, and that's exactly what she did. But it wasn't just a lie, it was a stupid lie, because Grandfather Darkheart saw our father's dead body that night twenty years ago when Zena came for Mom and us. If Dad had been a *vampyr,* he'd have been dusted, not dead."

Her words had tumbled out of her like a torrent. Now they abruptly dried up and her gaze burned into me.

I could have said a lot of things. I could have said that even if the son Grammie and Popsie remembered had once been as loving as they said, becoming a vamp would have changed him completely. I could have said that Grandfather Darkheart might well have lied about what he saw the night my mother died, to spare us pain. I could have said that it would be easy enough for a vampire to feign death to fool a desperate old man, and then to disappear into the night, never to be seen again.

I could have said any or all of these things, but seeing the shadowy fear lurking behind Tash's china-doll blue gaze, I didn't. I gave a little laugh.

"So touching of you to try out your pop psychology on me, darling, but guess what? I don't have a Daddy complex or anything complicated like that. I like delicious men. I like having a cocktail or two. Is that simple enough for you, sweetie?"

Tash's gaze hardened. "Go to hell, Kat."

"Been there, done that, courtesy of Zena, remember?" I said with a sweet smile. "Or is my little sojourn in the hot place on the night we battled her and her vamp army just another one of those things we're supposed to forget about?"

"I couldn't if I wanted to," Tash said tightly. "Because the woman who came back from there wasn't my sister anymore."

She spun on her heel, leaving me alone in the room. That's when I walked out of the club and practically into the fangs of a vampire, the perfect finishing touch to a day that had turned completely to *merde*.

Chapter 2

Thank God I was wearing Manolos. Swiftly I slipped off my left shoe and grabbed it up. By the inadequate illumination of the few parking lot lights, the vampire looked to be a teenager. He was moving so fast he almost ran into the spiked heel and staked himself, but he skidded to a halt just in time. He looked at me, astonishment on his acned face.

"Are you fucking *kidding?* That's not gonna work."

"I don't see why it fucking wouldn't, sweetie," I told him. I heard the slight fuzziness in my voice and made a mental note not to drive home if I got out of this alive, but at least the cocktails I'd downed over the course of the afternoon lent me a certain Dutch courage, I realized. The hand that was holding the Manolo against his AC/DC T-shirt was rock-steady. "And you're not so sure it won't, either," I continued. "If you were, you would have rushed me by now."

He stared at me in frustration, and then the red glow in his eyes faded a little. "Yeah," he admitted. "Guess I'll just have to use my *glamyr* on you."

The air between us seemed to shimmer. For a moment his adolescent chest took on definition under the dirty tee, his greasy brown hair looked glossy and beautiful and a wave of dark sexuality began lapping around me, drawing me to him. Even his acne-ridden skin cleared up before my very eyes.

Except for the angry red pimple on his chin. I shook my head and took a breath. "Zit-check at six o'clock," I said, feeling the *glamyr* dispel abruptly. "Sorry, sweetie, but it ruins everything."

"Shit!" he swore, his hand going self-consciously to his chin. "For a couple of weeks before I turned, my skin actually looked pretty good," he said defensively. "I was going out with this girl who worked in Hazlitt's Drugstore and she gave me these medicated pad things, you know? Then Bitsy and me broke up and I stopped using the pads. Just my crap luck to become undead when I was back in pizza-face mode."

Megan's MINI was still parked next to mine. Obviously she and Tash had been delayed in leaving the club. My plan was to keep the vamp talking until they showed up, but something he'd said puzzled me enough that I didn't have to fake interest. "Hazlitt's?" I frowned, taking care not to relax my grip on my impromptu stake. "I can remember Grammie Crosse taking me there for ice cream when I was about five or six, but they must have gone out of business at least ten years ago. When did you become a—"

Maybe he'd been trying to keep me talking, too, in the hopes I'd become distracted enough that he could risk a lunge at me. But as it had done with me, something in our conversation triggered a real response from him.

"Crosse? You're one of the Crosse sisters?" His face had been pale before, another indication that he needed to feed, but now it went so white his acne stood out like beacons. He took a step backward. "Oh, fuck, you're not *Kat,* are you?"

"Megan," I lied immediately. "If you've heard of my sister, you've heard of me, too, so you know you don't stand a chance against—"

"Nuh-uh." He took another step back, his eyes beginning to glow red again. "I can smell a Daughter of Lilith a mile away, and you're not the vamp killer. You were trying to fuck me up! You were trying to get me to *bite* you, you bitch!"

"I was trying to make you bite me?" I leaned in, astonishment momentarily overriding my fear. "Is this the undead variation of 'you know you want it, honey?' Because I don't appreciate it when human males try to pull that *merde* on me, and I'm certainly not about to let an underage, undead vampire—"

"Stay away from me!"

His words came out in a high-pitched snarl. As I stood there, my Manolo clutched in my nerveless hand and fear freezing me to the spot, he backpedalled away from me so fast that his feet got tangled up with each other and he tripped. He scrambled up again, his horror-filled red eyes still locked on mine. Then he turned to run.

I think I saw the stake before he did, but I'd swear he had time to dodge out of the way and save himself. Instead, he seemed to run deliberately into its path.

It came speeding through the near-dark parking lot with unerring accuracy, the deadly tip sinking deep into the left side of his chest, right through the *DC* part of the gothic AC/DC lettering on his tee. His hands flew to the shaft of wood sticking from him, as if he intended to pull it out.

His glowing eyes met mine again, but instead of the terror that had been in them a second ago, I saw an emotion so out of place that I knew I had to be mistaken. His hands fell away from the stake, his lips drew back from his razor-sharp canines in a death-rictus, the red glow in his eyes dimmed.

Then he turned to ash.

In the past couple of months I've seen so many vamps die that you'd think I'd be used to it. My sisters are. Megan stands over her kills grimly, as if she wants their last sight on earth to be the Daughter of Lilith who sent them to hell. Tash is the opposite; she all but does a victory dance around the ashes, and once I saw her kick them. Grandfather Darkheart caught that little performance, too, and in his heavy Carpathian accent gave her a stern lecture that I could tell Tashya tuned out before the second sentence.

I feel agonizing pain. The first time I experienced it, I was sure the vamp had somehow turned my stake against me before he'd died and I'd looked down at myself, expecting to see a yew-wood shaft protruding from my body and dark gouts of blood pouring from the wound.

I felt like that now, but I didn't bother looking for a wound I knew wasn't there. Instead, I turned to watch Megan sprinting across the parking lot toward me, Tash right behind her. I took a breath and put on my best bored manner.

"Yay, team. Chalk up another one for the good guys, and all that." Languidly I pumped the hand holding the Manolo into the air before bending to slip my shoe back onto my foot. "Impressive stake-hurling, sis. Ever think of giving up this vampire-killing gig and trying out for the Olympic javelin toss?"

Megan retrieved her stake and shoved it into the strap holster on her left bicep. "You've got a right to be pissed," she said evenly. "I shouldn't have interfered with your kill. Sorry, Kat."

"We saw you standing there like a dummy and we thought you were caught up in his *glamyr,*" Tashya explained. "Either that, or so scared you were about to wee-wee your panties. Which one was it, Kat?"

I raised my eyebrows and hoped my drawl covered the last remnants of my shakiness. "Gawd, sweeties— scared? Whatever gave you that idea? I simply hoped I wouldn't have to ruin a perfectly darling pair of Manolos by using one of them as a vamp sticker…and as it turned out, I wouldn't have had to." I gave an elaborate shrug. "Your reputation's spread, Meg. I told the little pisher I was you, and he tripped over his own feet trying to get away."

"I wondered why he was running," Megan answered. "And like Tash, I also wondered what you were playing at, standing there and talking to him instead of sending him to hell. You sure he wasn't using a little *glamyr* on you without you knowing?"

There it was in her voice again, that repressive tone that she'd seemingly inherited with her life mission of vamp killing, but now it was accentuated with a marked coolness. Not surprising, given our recent contretemps in the club, I supposed. I extracted my car keys from my purse.

"Believe it or not, sister dear, the rest of us aren't totally incapacitated when we're facing the undead. In fact, I've always suspected I'm a little less susceptible to vamp wiles than you are, but to answer your question, no, his *glamyr* didn't work on me." I turned to unlock my car, adding casually, "He seemed so inept all round it's a wonder he wasn't staked a decade or so ago. Since he was a local boy, it positively dented my civic pride."

I began to get into my MINI, but Megan's hand shot out and clamped around my arm. I stiffened. She removed it but didn't apologize. "A local vamp who's been around for decades? Not possible," she said flatly. "Maplesburg wasn't infected until Zena arrived here."

"So we believed," I answered. "Apparently we were wrong."

"*You're* wrong," Tash snapped. "That would mean Maplesburg had already turned when—"

She stopped and I finished her sentence for her. "When Daddy lived here, sweetie? Yes, that's exactly what it would mean." I looked away from her frozen face and met Megan's hard gaze. "If you don't want to take my word for it, use the resources of Darkheart & Crosse to locate a woman named Bitsy. As a teenager she worked at Hazlitt's Drugstore before it went out of business, so she'd be in her thirties now, at least. Ask her about a boyfriend she had who was into AC/DC and Clearasil."

"I will," Megan said coldly. "And if I find out you're yanking our chain over this, Kat, you'll be sorry." She strode to her car and got in. Tash was already sitting in the front passenger seat. Megan started the ignition and then rolled down the window. "Take this," she called to me, her tone expressionless. "I always keep a couple of spares in the car. You really shouldn't be out after dark without one."

I caught the stake she tossed my way. Even as my fingers closed around it, she was revving her MINI out of the parking lot. I saw the car's taillights flare red as she came to the stop before the road, and then my sisters were gone.

Ten minutes ago I hadn't trusted myself to drive. Now I was stone-cold sober. I began again to get into my MINI, and for the second time in as many minutes didn't complete the action.

From the far end of the parking lot came the growl of a car engine starting up. It caught and became a full-throated roar. I heard the solid-sounding thunk of a transmission dropping into first gear, heard the roar immediately ease into a deep rumble and then saw a pair of headlights flare to sudden life. Dazzling tunnels of light cut through the darkness and early evening ground mist as the car began slowly heading my way.

It passed under one of the lot's two feeble lights, and my heart sank. The vehicle's windows were black—not merely tinted, but blotchy black, as if someone had applied the contents of a can of matte paint to the interior of the windows. That could only mean one thing.

"Shit." I was too tired to bother translating my comment into French. "Vamp transport."

It had to be. The car had moved out of the pool of light and was now rolling through the dark again, a hulking, dated silhouette. A certain type of vamp seemed to go for vintage vehicles; probably, as Megan's Mikhail had once informed my sisters and me, because the trunks of older cars were roomy enough to make a comfortable daytime resting place if necessary. "Also," he'd added with a significant glance at the matching MINIs that had been Popsie Crosse's most recent birthday gifts to us, "because those old Detroit tanks can ram most newer vehicles off the road. At that point, sitting in a ditch in your car, you're the equivalent of a can of Dinty Moore beef stew to a hungry vamp."

"Which means that making a run for it in the MINI might be a *teensy* bit rash," I told myself out loud as the car rumbled closer. "I'll never make the three miles to town before he catches up with me, so what other options do I have?" I forced a casualness to my solitary conversation, hoping to keep my growing terror at bay. "The obvious one is to stake him. On the plus side, I was Grandfather Darkheart's star pupil when he was training Megan and Tash and me in the finer points of vamp sticking. On the negative side, when it came down to doing it for real during the battle at the Hot Box with Zena and her followers, I—"

I didn't finish my sentence, but I couldn't shut off my thoughts. I *had* been Anton's star pupil, so much so that I'd been secretly sure I was the Crosse triplet who'd inherited my mother's vamp-killing legacy and would be the next Daughter of Lilith. My first kill had ripped that fantasy from me forever.

When Zena had loosed her pack of undead on us that night, I'd taken up a fighting stance like a vampire-killing Joan of Arc, knowing I was fulfilling the destiny that had been written for me long before my birth. The first vamp that had rushed me hadn't stood a chance. I'd been so confident of my powers that I'd let him come close enough to grab me, but as he'd leaned in to slash at my throat I'd thrust my stake into his heart. In triumph I'd looked into his eyes, wanting to see him die.

Instead, I saw him being born.

It had been like watching a movie, except I wasn't watching it, I was living it. And although only a split second could have elapsed between the time I staked him and the moment he fell away into dust, I experienced his whole life. I stood in the delivery room as he came into the world. I was on the sidewalk watching him take a tumble from his trike, inside the pet shop as he pointed out the puppy he wanted, with him on his first day at school when he wet his pants and tried to hide it.

I saw him fall in love.

I saw him graduate.

I saw him being attacked in an alleyway one night by the vampire who turned him.

I saw his first kill, his final kill…and then I saw myself standing over him, my hand still on the stake lodged in his body. Terror and agony ripped through me, both overwhelmed by an agonizing sense of loss. In the moment that he turned to dust I knew the truth. His death was mine. Part of me would follow him down to hell.

I forced myself to take on the second vamp who came at me, a female, and went through the whole process all over again, but during my third kill something broke in me and Zena made her move against me. Since her move consisted of sending me to hell, I don't think it's too surprising that for the most part I've blanked out that unpleasant interlude. I don't have any trouble remembering what happened when I finally came back to full consciousness, however: the battle was over, Zena had been vanquished and Megan had proved herself to be a true Daughter of Lilith.

I'd received proof, too. I'd walked into the Hot Box wanting only to kill vampires. When I left hours later I finally understood a favorite quote of Popsie's, one he'd told me he'd read in an old cartoon: *"We have met the enemy, and he is us."*

I'd seen the enemy. I'd felt the blood tie between me and them—a blood tie forged years ago when a queen *vampyr* had marked a Daughter of Lilith's baby. I hadn't turned yet, but if Grandfather Darkheart was correct and the kiss of the vampire bore fruit in her victim's twenty-first year, I would soon.

But until I did I had to assume I was as vulnerable to being killed by a vamp as any normal human would be.

"Which brings me back to my original problem, no?" I muttered now as I steadied myself against my MINI and thrust all future problems aside to deal with my current one. "If it's a question of my survival, am I capable of staking the son of a bitch?"

I was about to find out the answer to that question. The vehicle came to a stop about twenty feet away from me, its engine idling with a heavy rumble I could feel through the spike heels of my shoes, its chrome grille glittering ominously. I waited for my gentleman caller—a car like that simply *had* to belong to a male vamp, I thought—to get out, saunter over to me and flash fangs.

The black-painted driver's window rolled down. Something projected from it and I shifted position slightly to see what it was.

Thunk-whap!

The metallic sound exploded right next to me and adrenaline kicked through me like a double shot of one-hundred-proof vodka. *I'd been set up,* I thought hollowly, appalled at my own carelessness. A second vamp had apparently landed on my MINI while I'd been watching the approach of the one in the car. Stake in hand, I whirled to face my attacker.

There was no one on the MINI. A nerve-racking possibility flashed into my mind and I dropped to my knees, stake at the ready, my gaze scanning the pavement under the car.

Thunk-whap!

Pain blazed through my right hand, and my stake clattered to the ground. Instinctively I tried to cradle my hand to my body to ease the agony, but trying to move it sent a sickening wave of fresh pain through me. In confusion I looked at my hand.

At first I didn't understand what I was staring at. My fingers were outstretched on the driver's door of my car, every tendon on the back of my right hand standing out in sharp relief. Blood ran down my wrist onto the glossy white paintwork of the MINI, and between my index and middle fingers something gleamed silver in the half light.

I suddenly recognized the silver gleam for what it was, and shock slammed the breath from my lungs. I'd wanted a drink earlier. Now I needed one, if only to numb the horror of what I was seeing.

The object spiked through the web of skin between the fingers on my hand into the car's door…was a *nail*.

Chapter 3

"Damn." The low-voiced oath came from the direction of the idling car. I heard the sound of the vehicle's door being opened and the scrape of shoes on the pavement. After my first sickened glance at the nail through my hand I'd turned away, but now I made myself look at it again.

There's something about seeing yourself as a carpentry project that makes a girl want to throw up. I forced back the bile that rose in my throat and tried to pull the nail out with my free hand.

It wouldn't budge. I pulled harder, my grip slick with my own blood, but the nail was firmly lodged into the MINI's door panel. From the sound of his unhurried tread, the vamp wasn't in any ravenous rush but even so, I had only seconds to free myself.

I'd lived through Brazilian waxes. What I had to do next couldn't be more excruciating, could it? I closed my eyes, clenched my teeth and ripped my hand free of the nail.

I'd been right, the pain didn't beat out Brazilian waxes—not by much, anyway. But in my experience, the agony of a wax is always replaced by a delightfully sleek and sexy feeling after it's over. Seeing the torn and bloody web of skin between my fingers just made me feel like a rat that had gnawed off its own foot to escape a trap.

Not delightful. Not sexy. And definitely *not* as conflicted as I'd been a few minutes ago about staking the sadistic undead who'd done this to me. My Badgley slip dress looked like a rag that had been used to mop an abbatoir floor, and my hair was hanging around my face in damp hanks. As I scrabbled under the car for the fallen stake and my knees scraped painfully against the oil-stained pavement, a primal rage surged through me.

He wasn't playing fair. Vampires had the whole fang and super strength and flying thing going on, and all we humans had were wood and garlic and maybe a splash of holy water if we were lucky. For a vamp to add a nail gun to his arsenal was overkill—and where had he gotten it from, anyway?

Nausea rose up in me a second time. Of course. The son of a bitch had killed one of my carpenters and taken the tool from his dead body. I thought of the crew that had been working all day and into overtime this evening to get the club's stage rebuilt on schedule for me, and my anger grew. Nailing me through the hand had made it personal, but this made it war.

My fingers closed bloodily around the stake as the footsteps behind me came closer. I jumped to my feet and let my rage out in a scream as I raced toward the approaching vamp.

"Get ready to kiss your ass goodbye, you bastard! When I'm finished with you there won't be anything left but *dust!*"

I started to bring my stake up into position—wrist rigid, the power coming from the shoulder, if anyone's interested—and then I froze.

The man facing me was the carpenter who'd played havoc with my hangover today. On one of the few days when I'd pulled myself together early enough to show up at the club before the cocktail hour I'd seen him taking a break outside with some of the others in the crew as I'd hurried into the building, swathed in a silk scarf and wearing oversized Christian Dior sunglasses to keep the brilliance of the day from racheting up my pounding headache.

Which meant he wasn't a vamp. That fact wasn't as comforting as it might have been, because he was still trying to kill me.

"You're the one who's going to be dust in a second," he grunted, using both hands to steady the nail gun. "When you get to hell, tell your pals down there that Jack Rawls sends his regards."

As he finished speaking he depressed the trigger on the cordless nailer. I barely had time to leap out of the way before a deadly barrage of nails began flying at me.

"What do you think you're *doing?*" I yelled as I

turned my leap into a dive and slid across the hood of my MINI, losing my Manolos in the process. I fell rather than landed on the other side of my car and crouched there. A metallic pinging like hail on a tin roof told me Rawls was still firing.

"Gunning for a vamp," he said calmly over the pinging. His flat Midwest accent made his words seem matter-of-fact. "The nails are tipped with silver, and the gun's been modified to shoot up to twenty feet, so make it easy on yourself and stop trying to run."

My heart turned over. What did he mean, gunning for a vamp? There was no *way* he could know my most secret fear—no one did. How had he learned of it, and why was he so sure it wasn't just a fear, but the truth?

I could hear him walking around the front of the car. Still keeping low, I sprinted to the back of the MINI, ungratefully wishing Popsie had sprung for Hummers instead when he'd bought our birthday presents. "I'm not a vampire," I said tightly. "You were working only feet away from me most of the day, so there's no way you don't know who I am."

"No way at all," he agreed, his tone still unruffled. "You're Kat Crosse, and one of your sisters is the local Daughter of Lilith. I knew who you were before I hit town." I heard him exhale, and something in the raggedness of his breath made me realize his calmness was eroding. "I can't fault your sister for not being able to put you down, but I'm not going to lose any sleep tonight after I dust you, lady."

He stepped around the back of the MINI as he spoke and aimed the nail gun at where I'd been crouching. His head jerked up when he saw I wasn't there, but his reaction came too late.

I jumped off the car's roof and crashed into him, falling with him to the ground. Grandfather Darkheart's weeks of training might not have turned me into a vamp fighter like Megan, I thought grimly as I rammed the point of my stake to Jack Rawls's throat and glared down at him from my sitting position on his chest, but it definitely gave me an edge in a parking lot brawl like this.

His body went rigid. He stared up at me, and even in the poor light I could see implacable hatred in his eyes as blood traced a thin line from the point of my stake to his collar. "Do it," he said, his voice hoarsened by the pressure on his throat. "Go ahead and plunge it in. If you don't I'll do it myself."

He moved so fast I almost didn't have time to react. His head jerked sideways toward the stake, and even as I pulled back my weapon in shock I saw the trickle of blood deepen. I felt him brace himself to repeat the maneuver and I did the only thing I could think of to prevent him.

"Stop that!" The stake was instantaneously reversed in my hand—another move that Grandfather Darkheart's training had drilled into me—and as I shouted the command at Rawls I smashed the blunt end of the wood into his cheekbone. His head rocked sideways with the strength of my blow, and I sensed him gathering himself to break free of me. I hit him again, ignoring the blazing pain in my wounded hand, and then slammed the solid yew-wood stake against his temple a third time with all the strength I could muster. He went limp, the tension I'd felt in his body extinguished as instantly as a lightbulb being turned off.

"You've killed him," I told myself through numb lips. "That's what comes of going all altruistic and trying to save a man from himself, instead of sticking with what you know and being a ball-breaking bitch." I wiped my bloody hand on my hiked-up dress—the fact that I only felt the tiniest pang as I did so was proof of how distracted I was—and pressed my thumb to the side of his neck.

His pulse was slow but steady. Relief swept through me. I peered closer at his neck and saw that the small puncture mark from my stake was closer to his jawline than his jugular, and that the bleeding had already slowed.

"You're not dead," I told his unconscious form. "I like that in a man, but what I'd like even more is not having to worry about you trying to kill one or both of us. I guess I could keep knocking you out every time you show signs of coming round, except that would mean I couldn't ask you questions." I stood up and looked down at him. "And I've got questions, sweetie. Lots of them, starting with how you knew the one thing about me that I haven't dared tell anybody."

Stepping over him, I walked to the front of the MINI and reached inside to the console. I popped the trunk and hastened back again, flicking a wary glance at Rawls's prone body as I passed him. Ask me how long two coats of OPI polish plus a base and topcoat take to dry and I can tell you to the second, but predicting how long a man who's gone down for the count will remain down isn't my area of expertise.

However, I *did* have some handy gadgets relating to one of my areas of expertise in the small overnight case I always carried with me. Minutes later, having used them and a few other things on him, I surveyed the results of my handiwork with satisfaction.

"There's something about a man in handcuffs that always gets my motor revving a little," I murmured. "But just because a girl's got a wicked side doesn't mean she's a vamp, Jack—or at least, it doesn't mean she's turned into a vamp yet. If you'd known that much about me, we might have ended up using these hand-cuffs in a completely different scenario tonight." I'd straddled him as I'd cuffed him to the MINI's bumper and tied each of his legs with lengths of tough nylon rope to his own vehicle, which I'd moved up behind the MINI. Now I sat back on his chest and narrowed my gaze at him.

When I'd seen him earlier I'd been distracted, first by Terry and then by the confrontation with my sisters, and I certainly hadn't taken note of his physical attri-butes while he'd been trying to shoot nails in me. Jack Rawls wasn't a bad-looking man, I realized belatedly. He was in his late twenties, although by the leaned-down look of his jaw and the sun-squint lines interrupt-ing the tan at the corners of his eyes, they hadn't been twenty-eight or twenty-nine indulged years. His black hair was growing out from a close trim and I got the definite impression it would be ruthlessly cropped back again the minute it started to get in his way. Not drop-dead gorgeous like Jean-Paul, or all moody and wolfishly sexy like Megan's Mikhail, I decided, but definitely handcuffs-to-the-bedposts material. Somehow, though, I didn't think he was the type to go for that, even if we'd met under more conducive circumstances.

"Kansas farmer stock?" I hazarded as I waited for him to come to. "Idaho? From your accent, I'm guessing you're from one of those flat states where people do Norman Rockwell things like going to potluck suppers and having chores. It's not only the accent, it's the whole grim determination thing you've got going on, as if staking me is a duty you can't shirk. Such a shame, sweetie. As I say, these handcuffs could have been put to *much* better use."

"I don't sleep with vampires." As if he'd been conscious for some seconds and had simply been waiting for the right moment to startle me, Jack Rawls opened his eyes and stared emotionlessly at me. "I meant what I said. Kill me. I'm not interested in eternal life, vamp."

Without warning he jerked his arms powerfully toward his body and tried to do the same with his legs, like a mustang lunging desperately against restraints. I grabbed two handfuls of his T-shirt and tightened the grip of my bare thighs against his rib cage to avoid being bucked off as he tried to break free, expecting him to continue his fight for a few moments before realizing it was doing him no good. But he surprised me again. Just as suddenly as he'd exploded into movement he stopped—as if, I thought with sharp interest, he'd been in similar situations in the past and recognized when it was of more benefit to conserve his energy than to continue resisting uselessly.

I made a note to add his familiarity with restraints

to the list of subjects to explore with the mysterious Mr. Rawls, but my first question was a deliberately distracting one.

"Police issue cuffs, courtesy of a detective on the Maplesburg P.D. who liked playing good cop/bad girl with me," I told Rawls. "Or was it bad cop/bad girl? Anyway, they're not toys, Jack, and I got the rope I tied around your ankles from the trunk of your car, so you're not going anywhere until I say you can. I also ran over your damn nail gun, so don't bother trying to think of some way you can reach it and use it. Speaking of your car, I've got to ask—what's an upstanding, vampire-hating carpenter like you doing riding around in a vamp-mobile?"

"I got a deal," he said tonelessly. "Its last owner died in it."

When I'd moved his vehicle, I'd turned off the bright headlights, leaving on only its parking lights. My back was toward them but they shone full in Rawls's face, so I could see every flicker of expression that crossed his features, if there'd been one. But there wasn't. The only indication of his state of mind came from the cold hatred in his eyes as he stared up at me.

Now, cold hatred isn't the usual expression men have when they look at me. Unbridled lust, hopeless infatuation, puppy-dog pleading—those are some of the ways men look at me. Even when I'd dumped Terry this afternoon, I'd seen in his eyes that if I'd crooked my little finger as he'd stormed out, he would have turned right around and come back for the chance to spend another night with me. Rawls, on the other hand, had me sitting on his chest with the black lace of my pink panties peeking out under my hiked-up hem and, thanks to the ripped neckline of my ruined slip dress, my breasts practically spilling out of my push-up bra into his face—and still he was treating me as if I was something he'd scraped off his shoe.

I decided that Jack Rawls was beginning to piss me off just the *teensiest* bit.

"Its last owner being a vampire like you think I am, I suppose," I said, my patience at an end. "How can I put this so you understand? I'm not undead, I'm a real live female." A thought occurred to me. "You've seen me in the daytime," I reminded him, clinching the ridiculous argument. "What does the fact that I didn't burst into flames tell you, sweetie?"

"Fuck all." If anything, the hatred in his gaze intensified. "I've never seen you exposed to the sunlight. Far as I can tell, no one has in a while. Yeah, you've shown up here a couple of times in the late afternoon, looking as sick as a dog and wrapped up in scarves and wearing dark glasses. I've known a vamp or two in my time who can rise before dusk if they had to and if they take the kind of precautions you do. That hasn't stopped me from killing them."

"Then we'd better hope you never run into Tara Reid," I shot back, pissed by his "sick as a dog" observation, which didn't take much effort to translate into "skanky wreck." "News flash, Jack—when a girl's partied a little too enthusiastically the night before, sometimes she finds jumping out of bed at the crack of dawn and singing 'Oh, What a Wonderful Morning' a tad beyond her. She might even reach for the Ray-Bans and be a smidge tardy getting into work. Admittedly, most hangover cures I've choked down could better be classified as hangover punishments, but a stake through the heart is going too far, no?"

He didn't respond. I leaned closer to him, my arms braced on either side of his shoulders. "Okay. If I'm a vamp why haven't I bitten you by now? For that matter, why did I defend myself with a stake?"

Just as I decided he wasn't going to answer this time either, he spoke, his jaw clenched. "I don't pretend to know why you creatures do any of the things you do. My best guess is that you'll bite me when you're good and ready, but right now you're getting a charge out of this."

"A charge out of *what?*" I demanded. "Getting nailed to my car?"

His words ground past his teeth. "Out of sitting practically on my face and leaving nothing to the imagination while you're doing it. Out of seeing if you can make me hot for you by using your *glamyr.*" He exhaled tightly. "Out of knowing it's beginning to work."

I'd had enough. He'd used a nail gun on me. He'd shot my car, destroyed my dress and ruined my whole evening...but all of those were nothing compared to the fact that he'd somehow discovered my greatest fear and dragged it into the light. I still wanted answers from him, but what I wanted more right now was to do to him what he'd done to me.

It was obvious what his greatest fear was. It would be pure pleasure making him face it.

In one smooth movement I pulled my dress over my head and let it drop to the ground. I shook my hair out, looked at Rawls through my lashes and moistened my lips.

"Is it hot out here or is it just me, sweetie?" I purred. Arching my back and squirming my hips against him, I tipped my neck back and began to trail the fingers of my left hand down my body, giving loving attention to the curve of my breasts in my barely there bra. I let my fingers wander slowly toward the lace of my panties. "'Cause all of a sudden I just feel *so*—"

My throat closed and my words dried up. I pushed a sex-kitten strand of hair out of my eyes and looked across the parking lot at what had caught my attention.

I found my voice. "About running over your nail gun," I croaked, not taking my gaze from the pool of illumination shed by the farthest parking-lot light. "That might have been a *teensy* bit rash of me, Jack."

I heard the tremor in my tone, and all of a sudden I couldn't keep up the act anymore. I looked down at him. "We're fucked," I said flatly. "Three vamps just flew in and landed beside the club. They're heading our way, Rawls."

Chapter 4

"I should have known this was a setup," Jack muttered. "Your undead friends sent you out as bait to catch me off guard, and now the fun begins." I saw a muscle move at the side of his jaw. "Before the four of you start killing me inch by inch, tell me something, vamp— how long have your kind been tracking me? From the start, or was my trail picked up in Pennsylvania when that son of a bitch insurance salesman got away from me?"

I adore single-mindedness in a man at the appropriate time, but I consider the appropriate time for male single-mindedness to be when he's doing something exquisitely tantalizing and I can feel waves of shuddery ecstasy rising to a crescendo in me. Since the only thing rising in me right now was pure terror, Rawls's inability to move on struck me as a major drawback—one that I realized would take drastic action on my part to overcome.

All this went through my mind as I got off him and turned to his car. "I don't have the foggiest notion of what you're talking about, sweetie," I said tensely, not caring that I was giving him a Dita Von Teese-like view of my bottom as I bent over the front seat of his vampmobile. My fingers closed around the handcuff key I'd tossed there after securing him. "I'll probably hate myself in the morning for doing this, but two against three is better odds than one against three. Besides, if this doesn't convince you we're on the same side, I don't know what—" I turned to face him as I spoke, expecting to see him lying where I'd left him and found myself staring at the business end of the stake I'd dropped earlier.

"We'll never be on the same side, vamp," Rawls said with another of those cold smiles that looked like the grimace a Doberman would wear just before it lunged. "I told you, I'm not interested in playing for Team Dead. Maybe I won't be able to fight off all your pals, but I'm taking out as many as I can, starting with you."

He thrust the stake toward me with the speed of a striking snake, and I reacted with equal speed. My sideways leap wasn't as fast as a vamp's, but it took me out of the path of the pointy piece of wood aiming for me. I didn't have the opportunity to breathe a sigh of relief, however, since a split second later it was coming toward me again. Out of the corner of my eye I saw the trio of vampires walking across the parking lot, and I realized that doing the life and death tango with Rawls was using up time we didn't have.

I squeezed my eyes shut against the sight of the stake plunging toward me and held the handcuff key in front of my face, fully expecting to feel yew wood entering me before my heart could take another beat.

"I don't get it."

At Rawls's growled statement I cracked open one eyelid and peered cautiously through my lashes. He was staring grimly past the key to me, the tip of his stake frozen a hairsbreadth away from the skimpy pink satin cupping my left breast. Three thoughts occurred to me almost simultaneously. One: if I'd been a D cup instead of a nicely proportioned C, there wouldn't have been even a hairsbreadth of space between me and my confiscated stake. Two: the vamps—they were all female, I could see now—were only about thirty feet away from us. And three: Jack Rawls might be a total prick, but he had the sexiest eyes I'd ever seen.

Pure green, pure bedroom and fringed with thick, spiky lashes a covergirl would kill for. Not that any of that was relevant right at this moment.

"You don't have to get it," I told him. "You just have to decide whether you want to try fighting those bitches off all by yourself or whether you want my help. The fact that I was about to unlock your cuffs before I knew you didn't need a key to get free should win me some brownie points with you, no?" Approaching vamps or not, I was unable to hold back my next words. "Just how *did* you release yourself?"

He stared at me a moment longer and then lowered the stake with a quick, smooth movement, as if he'd come to a decision he wasn't thrilled about. "This fell out of your hair while you were giving me a free lap dance." I recognized the small object he tossed aside as one of the bobby pins that had held my now ruined chignon. "And this fell out of the heel of my workboot," he added without cracking a smile. One-handedly, he closed the gleaming steel of a switchblade and shoved it into his jeans' pocket. "I used it to cut the ropes around my ankles. Catch."

He tossed Megan's loaner stake to me as carelessly as he'd thrown down the bobby pin. I grabbed at it but missed, although that turned out to be a good thing because as I bent to retrieve it I saw one of my Manolos under the MINI. I slipped it on, spied the other lying on its side a few feet away, and speed-hobbled toward it.

I can hear some of you now—God, girl, why waste time over shoes, even if they are Manolos? All I can tell you is that as soon as my heels were elevated to their accustomed four inches above the ground I felt like Wonder Woman with her bulletproof bracelets on. I was even able to face the approaching vamps with something like resigned bravado.

My surface calm vanished as Rawls took his place at my side, cradling the nail gun like an M-16. Before I could ask him what the *merde* he thought he was doing, he aimed it at the ground.

Thunk-whap!

"It's not broken," I said unnecessarily.

"These things are built tough," he said without looking at me. "I'll take out the brunette and the blonde, you concentrate on the redhead."

I hadn't disabled his weapon. He'd managed to pick

the lock of the cuffs I'd secured him with and access a wicked-looking switchblade I hadn't even known about. Under the circumstances, the three vamps whose unexpected fly-in had interrupted Rawls's and my personal tussle might be the nearest thing I had to Flora, Fauna and Merryweather, Sleeping Beauty's fairy godmothers.

If Flora, Fauna and Merryweather had recently had an extreme makeover and now looked like Linda, Claudia and Naomi, that is.

All three were clad in leather. The redhead in the middle wore a bondage-tight pink leather catsuit with pink Christian Louboutin stilettos. The brunette had the whole decadent-schoolgirl thing going on, complete with teensy black leather kilt and thigh-high black stockings. But it was the blonde's outfit I immediately coveted. Her white leather dress was deliciously do-me, plunging outrageously in front to show off her creamy cleavage, and diamond-encrusted spaghetti straps glittered over the milky skin of her shoulders.

I was suddenly all too aware that my own look was less do-me than been-done, consisting as it did of blood-flecked undies, rat's-nest hair and a recently nailed right hand. With the I-don't-get-out-of-bed-for-less-than-$10,000-a-day arrogance of supermodels, the three of them came to a dead stop ten feet in front of Rawls and me just as Rawls aimed his nail gun at the blonde and pulled the trigger.

She *shimmered* sideways. That's what it looked like, anyway—as if her image faded and then took form again a few inches to the left of where she'd been. It wasn't the first time I'd seen a vampire move so fast that she seemed to blur, and I knew it was a bad sign. That ability only came with practice or by being turned by a powerful *vampyr,* and it meant Claudia and her girl-friends weren't going to be easy to dust.

"You missed, Chack." Her purr was thickly Teutonic. "You are losing your touch, *nein?*"

"Either that or we caught him at a bad time," the stunning redhead beside her said, flaring perfect nostrils. "Who's your Frederick's of Hollywood hottie, Jack?"

"Who bloody cares?" The English-accented brunette curled her top lip, her canines dazzlingly white against flawless mocha skin. "Let's fucking rip them apart and get this over—"

A stuttering stream of nails flew from Rawls's weapon, cross-stitching its deadly way across the three vamps at chest height—or at what would have been chest height if they'd still been standing in front of us. But they'd levitated upward before the first silver missile could reach them, and as I jerked my gaze up I got a momentary glimpse of their faces, no longer supermodel-perfect, but ugly with fury.

Although Rawls hadn't seemed to recognize them, from their expressions they obviously knew and hated him. I felt justified in taking that as a second bad sign.

They swooped down at the exact moment that the stuttering of the nail gun coughed and died. I saw Rawls trying to clear the jammed weapon before he was hidden from my view by three leather-clad bodies, and I stood there for a split second, paralysed with horror. Then I turned to run.

The memory of my turning from Rawls and the vamps swarming him has robbed me of more nights than I care to admit. All I can say in my own defence is that I only took two steps before I forced myself to turn back.

I saw leather and flying hair and yanked hard on a long black strand that whipped me across the face, pulling the Naomi clone off balance, but before I could shove my stake at her, the swatch of hair I was clutching parted from its owner. She glanced over her shoulder at me, her gaze a fiery red.

"Extensions, love," she hissed malevolently. "When we're finished with the fucking bounty hunter, I'll strangle you with one of them."

She turned her attention back to Rawls, who was on his knees now, the useless nail gun still in his hands. *Bounty hunter?* I thought, grabbing at the nearest piece of leather. It was pink and ended in a clawing hand that had just raked Rawls across his face. Blood dripped from the polished nails of the redhead as she whirled to face me.

"You picked the wrong man to go parking with tonight, honey," she snarled. "Now you're going to pay for it."

Her words were a definite cue to use the stake I was holding. I began to drive it toward her with all my strength and then the very thing I'd feared might happen, did happen.

My grip suddenly went weak and my arm felt nerveless, the way it had once when I'd been partnered with Tashya at doubles tennis and she'd whacked my elbow with her racket. As I saw the redhead's fangs rushing at me I tried desperately to hold onto the stake, but instead

I watched it detach from my hand, falling end over end to the pavement in what seemed to be dreamy slow motion. It bounced once and came to rest by the toe of one of my Manolos.

Time stopped. Or maybe just my heart did. Then it started up again, and as I snapped my gaze to the two razorlike canines slicing toward my neck, my numb-with-terror brain came up with the three words that saved my life.

"Galliano for Dior?"

As abruptly as if she'd run into an invisible wall, the redhead halted. Her glance flicked from me to her outfit and back again. "You know your designers," she said, surprise edging out the snarl in her tone.

"Oh, *please,* sweetie," I demurred, "the man's a master at cut and detail. He might as well scrawl his signature across everything he creates, no?"

I sounded calm. I even sounded languidly bored. Somewhere deep inside me the real Kat Crosse was gibbering with fear, but the primitive will to survive that exists in everyone had switched me onto fashionista autopilot.

I don't think I could have stayed on autopilot for long, but as it turned out, I didn't have to.

"That's exactly how I feel!" the redhead agreed. "Damn, I almost wish I didn't have to rip you from limb to limb. But after Jackie boy staked our divine Dr. M, the three of us swore we'd get our revenge. Like I said, honey, you just picked the wrong man to get naked with—"

Her sentence broke off in a sharp intake of breath, and she flung back her head so far that the cords in her neck stood out like garroting wire. I was still on auto-pilot enough to realize that with tendons as visible as that, Linda wasn't as young as I'd first thought, and when I noted the nearly invisible line under her jaw, everything fell into place.

I didn't have the luxury of dwelling on my discovery, however, because the next thing I noticed about the redhead was the silver tip of the nail punched through the pink leather of her catsuit.

And at that point I went off autopilot with a vengeance.

"Frederick's of *Hollywood?*" I exploded, thrusting my face close to hers. "Sweetie, I wouldn't be caught *dead* in—"

There's something basically unsatisfying about screaming at a pile of dust, even if said pile of dust is still vaguely recognizable as the bitch who insulted you. I choked off my defence of my lingerie just as the Linda vamp dissolved into nothingness in front of me, revealing the hate-filled expression of the blonde standing behind her.

"You staked my *friend!*" The Claudia clone didn't look much like the supermodel she'd been impersonating anymore. As her top lip lifted and her jaws flew open to accommodate her horrifically lengthening canines, I caught a glimpse of the same faint scarring on her milky skin that I'd seen on the redhead, but then she was upon me and I gave up noticing details in favor of fighting for my life.

Except fighting for my life was impossible, with my only weapon—a weapon I hadn't been able to bring myself to use, although Claudia didn't seem to know that—lying on the ground somewhere near my feet. Out of the corner of my eye I saw a flash of black leather launch itself at Rawls, and I gave up hoping that the Jack cavalry would save me a second time.

The blonde grabbed me by my bare shoulders and went for my jugular. I did the only thing I could and grabbed her by her arms in a vain effort to push her from me.

"No!" The denial rushed from each of us on identical smothered gasps. Eyes as blue as heaven met mine as Claudia and I froze into immobility.

Crimson world. Blood was everywhere…and it was *beautiful.* Gouts of it flew up from the man who'd abused the child she'd been long ago; fountains of it sprayed from a date-raping fraternity boy; a slow trickle of it ran from the eyes of the dead tycoon who'd married her and then discarded her for his next trophy wife. As a vamp she'd found the power she hadn't had as a human and even if the price was her eternal soul, she would never, *ever* give up that pow—

I threw back my head and screamed as white-hot agony seared its way through my flesh. I felt the pain, like a barb of fire, reach the wall of my heart and tear through it as easily as jagged glass slashing tissue paper. It sunk deep and began to tug me down into a blackness that wasn't really black at all, but the dark, jelled red of spilled blood.

My grip slid away from the blond vamp's arms. As I felt my backward fall halted by something I saw her screaming jaws turn to dust, but her blue eyes, wide with horror, were still fixed on me. Then they, too, disintegrated and there was nothing but a pile of ash by my feet.

I realized I was sagging against the door of Rawls's car. I also realized that the terrible pain in my heart had vanished. Shakily I pushed away from the car and looked down at myself, but there was no sign of the bloody nail I'd felt tearing through me.

Something cold and hard clamped around my wrist, sending a spike of panic through me as I belatedly remembered the third vamp. I spun around to face Rawls just as he racheted the other half of the handcuffs onto the door handle of his vehicle.

"Three down," he rasped. The gaze he leveled on me was partially obscured by the skein of blood running from a ragged gash above his smoky green eyes. "One to go, vamp."

Chapter 5

"Ever had a wet dream, sweetie?" From my uncomfortable sitting position on the asphalt by the car I looked at Rawls, ten feet away and hunkered over his disassembled nail gun. Giving no sign he'd heard my question, he picked up one of the metal components and began wiping it with an oily rag. I briefly debated with myself whether to make some pertinent comment about phallic symbols and weapons, but decided it wasn't worth the effort.

This was turning out to be the longest night I'd ever spent with a man, and not in a good way. When I'd first found myself cuffed to the car, I'd indulged in an impressive but ultimately futile display of outrage. After an hour I'd subsided into cold silence. When I'd realized my silence wasn't getting through to Rawls, I'd tried reasonable discourse, then shifted tactics and resorted to threats; later still, I'd descended to insults. For the past three hours I'd been mentally maxing out my credit cards at Bloomies, Saks and Neiman's, but now my fantasy shopping spree had come to an end.

I tried again. "How about a screaming orgasm?" I let the tip of my tongue trace my top lip. "Mmmm…I *love* those. Then again, I also adore a long, slow screw up against a cold, hard wall, but as a male, you're probably more partial to a blow job, *n'est ce pas?*"

Rawls set down the rag and began reassembling the nail gun. I sighed.

"A Long, Slow Screw being made with sloe gin, Galliano and Southern Comfort, of course; and a Blow Job being Kahlúa, Baileys and vodka in a shot glass topped with whipped cream and a maraschino cherry," I elaborated. "If the cherry stem's tied into a knot when you set down the empty glass, you get your next drink free. A talented girl can keep the cocktails flowing all night with that trick, as I know from personal experience."

Jack stood and turned away from me, bringing the gun into firing position and holding down the trigger. I clapped my free hand against my left ear, but even after he quit firing my right ear was still ringing. My earlier fury flared up again.

"Why do you have to be such a junkyard dog, Rawls?" I snapped. "I could have left you to those bitches, but instead I turned back to help you. Next thing I know, you're telling me we're going to wait here until dawn to see if I flash fry when the sun comes up because you still think I could be one of them. Aside from nearly getting my throat ripped open by Claudia, what more proof did you want that I was on your side?" I didn't expect an answer, but he surprised me.

"Seeing you stake one of them. And if you'd never met them, how do you know the blonde's name?"

I raised my eyebrows. "*Merde*, sweetie, don't tell me you didn't realize who they'd made themselves into, thanks to some expert nipping and tucking." At his scowl I sighed again, my anger dissipating into resignation. "Naturally you didn't. You're a hetero male, and from the Corn Belt to boot, I'm guessing. The only way you might have recognized who Claudia, Naomi and Linda were impersonating would be if they put supermodels on feed-store calendars. And if *you* never met *them,* how did they know your name?"

"A lot of vamps know the name of Jack Rawls," he answered briefly, lowering himself to the ground and extending his jeans-clad legs in front of him. He leaned back against the MINI, closing his eyes and folding his arms across his chest.

I ignored his none-too-subtle hint. "Vamps know of you because you're a bounty hunter, you mean?" I persisted. "Since the subject's come up, exactly how does that work? Who pays the bounty when you hunt down a vamp?"

"The families of victims." He didn't open his eyes. "They pay me what they can. Sometimes that's just gas money to make it to the next town."

"How deliciously Sir Lancelot of you, sweetie," I said, a trifle acerbically, "but I hope you got more than your mileage for this job. Forget the fact that I came close to being a vamp snack, since you're convinced I'm going to end up as a big pile of dust anyway, but if that slash over your eye had been any longer or the one on your bicep any deeper, Claudia and her posse would have ended your career tonight."

I wasn't totally convinced of what I'd just said. Being attacked by three vengeful vampires would put any other man down for the count, but except for a hiss of indrawn breath as he'd splashed holy water over his wounds from a plastic soda bottle he'd retrieved from his car, Rawls's demeanor had remained grimly stoic. His dark T-shirt was soaked even darker in places with his own blood, one knee of his jeans was ripped to show pavement-torn skin beneath, and there was a growing lump on the cheekbone under his left eye. True, I had a collection of assorted scrapes and bruises, too, the worst being my hand, although by now the pain had subsided into a dull throbbing. I hadn't rated holy water, but Rawls had supplied me with peroxide and some gauze to bind it with. The thing was, I had the feeling this was how Jack Rawls usually looked—like he'd just had the shit kicked out of him in a back-alley fight but had left the other guy looking worse.

He really was a junkyard dog—snarling, tough and way too dangerous to pat. A cautious woman would have heeded the conventional wisdom of letting sleeping canines lie, I suppose, but I've always found caution and conventionality *très* overrated qualities.

More important, I needed to keep talking. Talking meant I didn't have to think about the glimpse of Claudia's crimson world she'd shared with me just before she turned to ash.

"If the divine Dr. M was their cosmetic surgeon, I can understand why he inspired such fanatical devotion in his patients. Honestly, darling, staking a man with that kind of talent is like staking Mozart. Couldn't you have made an exception in his case and just put him under house arrest or—"

"Dr. M?" Rawls's eyes snapped open. "Dr. Middleton?"

I'd finally caught his attention. It was a trifle ego-shattering that my exposed curves hadn't been able to accomplish that feat, but at least I'd come up with *something* he found more interesting than sleep. "Linda simply called him the 'divine Dr. M.' Apparently, he was one of your past kills, which is why the three of them swore to hunt you down and take their revenge. As I say, I hope the good doctor was one bounty-hunting job that involved more than gas money—"

"Middleton wasn't a job, he was a link in a chain I was following. That chain started in Nebraska with a girl named Mary Lou Gilly," Rawls said, something smoldering behind the ice of his gaze. "The same chain led me straight here to you."

I reacted badly to his statement, I admit. Oh, pooh— I'd been reacting badly all day, whether it had been to Terry's dreary accusations or to Megan and Tash when they'd tried to pull their high-minded intervention in my social activities. But I was getting tired of being everyone's favorite whipping girl, especially when I was more than a little stressed out with my own private worries.

Not that I expected to spontaneously combust when the first streaks of dawn showed in the sky. As Rawls had noted, lately I'd been finding it harder to function in the daytime, but that was only to be expected with my party-till-the-wee-hours schedule. I'd yet to have the urge to sink my teeth into a handy neck and I'd felt no revulsion when I'd seen him splashing holy water on his wounds.

So maybe Tashya was right, and the Crosse triplet Zena had marked had gotten a Get-Out-Of-Vamphood-Free card when Megan had killed her. I wanted to believe that, but I couldn't, and neither could I believe there was a chance Tash had been marked instead of me. Even if I persuaded myself that my inability to stake vampires was due to paralyzing fear, I was still left with two inarguable points.

One was that I *knew* I was changing.

I'd first known it a few weeks ago, although I'd told myself I was imagining things. I'd also told myself that my decision to move out of the Crosse mansion and take an apartment on my own was totally unrelated to my fears. But during the past week, the feeling had become an almost daily occurrence—a strange sense of disloca-tion with my own psyche, my own thought patterns, that came and went instantly but left me feeling oddly invaded. I'd tried to chalk the feeling up to my higher-than-normal cocktail consumption, but when Claudia's crimson-soaked world had called to me tonight and something in me had wanted to answer its call, my fears became bleak certainty. Zena's twenty-one-year-old legacy was bearing its poisonous fruit. I was turning into what she'd been.

But I had absolutely no intention of thinking about *that* particular subject until I had a brimming glass of something numbingly alcoholic in my hand.

Thanks to Mr. Tall, Dark and Pissy, however, I wasn't going to be within hailing distance of a jigger of vodka for a while. To add insult to injury, he was apparently under the impression that I was linked to the late Linda's divine Dr. M, whose staking apparently had been a labor of love and not one of Rawls's bounty-hunting commissions; and to some Cornhusker State female with a name that sounded like it had been plucked straight out of a country and western hurtin' song.

I take back my mea culpa. Under the circumstances, I think I reacted with admirable control to Rawls's hostile declaration.

"That chain you followed must have had a broken link, Jack," I said in my most languid drawl. "All I know about Dr. M is what Linda told me before you dusted her, and as for a Mary Lou...Gilly, did you say?" I gave an exaggerated shudder. "Aside from the fact that I've never been within a hundred miles of Nebraska, she doesn't sound like someone I'd have a lot in common with, sweetie. I mean, the name simply *screams* big hair, a softer-side-of-Sears outfit and shoes with court heels, no?"

"I wouldn't know about that." Rawls got to his feet and looked down at me, his expression unreadable. "When I first knew her, she wore rolled-up jeans and Keds. When I ran into her years later, she'd graduated to crotch-high minis and see-through blouses. The last time I saw her she was naked and dead and covered in her own blood."

His tone was so uninflected that for a second the impact of his words didn't hit me. Then it did, and I drew in a quick breath. "I'm sorry," I said inadequately. "For talking like such a shallow bitch, as well as for what happened to her. How did she die?"

"Badly." His gaze on me was unwavering. "The vamp who killed her liked torturing the hookers he picked up before he finally finished them off, and as a former surgeon, his preferred method was a scalpel. He was a real Mozart with it."

I closed my eyes. "No wonder you made it your business to track down Middleton and stake him. You...you say he targeted hookers. Is that how—"

"I wasn't one of her johns, I was her half brother," Rawls said tightly. "When I was sixteen and big enough to stand up to the bastard who was my stepfather, I beat the crap out of him and walked out. The next time I saw Lou she wasn't a seven-year-old who hero-worshiped her big brother anymore. She was a fifteen-year-old who'd been selling herself on street corners for a year. She told me to go to hell and got into a Mercedes that pulled up to the curb. After searching all night for her and her john in one fleabag joint after another, the next morning I stood in a blood-spattered motel room and vowed to track down the bastard in the Mercedes who'd hacked her to pieces." His teeth flashed briefly white in one of his nongrins. "When I made that vow, I didn't know vampires existed, but since then I've become an expert on them. The most important thing I learned was that all trails lead back to an original infector."

"I can't imagine how you must have felt in that motel room," I said, still dwelling on the first part of his account. "If anything ever happened to one of my sisters—" I belatedly took in what he'd just said. "Original infector? Are you talking about *me?*" My laugh didn't sound as amused as I'd meant it to. "Sweetie, that's utterly ridiculous! If anyone around here was vamp zero, it was a bitch named Zena, and you arrived in Maplesburg about six weeks too late to—"

"I know," he cut in, "word travels. Your sister took care of her. I also know you aren't vamp zero."

"*Such* a relief, darling," I said with a carelessness I didn't quite feel. He was still cradling his damned nail gun, I noticed, and his finger was only inches from the trigger. "It must be a huge disappointment for you, finding out that Megan beat you to the punch. I'm sure if she'd known Zena was the vamp you'd been tracking for so long she would have let you do the honors," I commiserated.

"Zena wasn't the end of the chain, either," Rawls said flatly.

The man wasn't just a junkyard dog, he was a junkyard dog with a bone he wouldn't let go of, I thought in exasperation. "Of course she was. She was a queen and although she was superbly well-preserved for her age, she was definitely ancient. Whoever the *vampyr* was who turned her centuries ago, he's lost in the mists of time." I slanted my gaze up at him through my lashes. "Now that I've cleared up that little misunderstanding for you, would you mind terribly clearing up something for me?" I said carefully. "You said word travels. What exactly is the word on *me* in the vamp community?"

He narrowed his eyes at me. "That you received the

kiss of a *vampyr* when you were in the cradle. That as the daughter of a Daughter, when you come into your full strength you'll make Zena's powers look sick. Even if there hadn't been a connection between you and the vamp I was hunting, I would have taken the time to search you out and put an end to you. The only reason you're not dust already is because—"

He stopped abruptly and I narrowed my eyes at him in the same way he'd done to me. "Because I could have killed you when I had the chance. I could have left you to be ripped apart by Claudia and crew. I didn't do either, and now you're not so convinced that your information was correct." But his information *was* correct, I thought. Or at least, the part about me being marked by Zena was. And if the vamp underground knew that much about me, who was to say they weren't also right about the rest of it? *As the daughter of a Daughter, when you come into your full strength you'll make Zena's powers look sick...* I wouldn't think about it until I had that drink I'd promised myself in my hand, I told myself numbly. And instead of a single, it was going to be a double. Make that a triple.

But right now I had Rawls on the ropes, and I had to convince him he'd been wrong about me. The last thing I needed was a vamp hunter hanging around Maplesburg while I continued to go increasingly fang girl.

"Vamps lie like we breathe, Jack. Whoever your informant was, he fed you a line of *merde* about me and you know it. If you thought otherwise you'd have used that nailer on me by now, so why don't you give up this wait-until-dawn farce?"

"Because the waiting's over," he replied matter-of-factly, looking past me and over the top of his car. "The sun's coming up over the horizon right now."

I stared at him in disconcertion. Then I wrenched my gaze away and glanced around, seeing dark gray where a moment ago all had been black. For no good reason my heart seemed to squeeze in my chest, and I scrambled unsteadily to my feet, barely feeling the metal bite around my wrist as I pulled too far from the cuff holding me. As soon as I looked over the roof of Rawls's vampmobile, I saw he was right.

I'd been sitting in the shadow of the car. Beyond it, the parking lot's few lights had begun to look sickly and washed-out and beyond that, the dark horizon was rimmed with a pale line. Looking at it, I was suddenly filled with dread.

In a moment that pale line would brim over and spill forth. In a moment it would become the day's first ray of sunlight, shooting from the edge of the world straight toward me. And judging from my response to Claudia before Jack had staked her, wasn't there a chance I'd progressed far enough along the path to full vamphood tonight that I might just flash fry as soon as that first ray of sun hit me?

My initial reaction was to duck back down behind the car in panic. I forced myself not to give in to it and went with my second reaction, which was to toss back my hair, moisten my lips and stand up straight. If I was going to die in the next few seconds, I damn well wasn't going to die cringing in the shadows like a vamp, I decided, I was going to die like the fabulous Kat Crosse.

I just hoped I could pull it off.

"Goodness, I feel all butterflies inside, Rawls." My hands were shaking, the left one so badly that the gauze I'd wound around it had unravelled and the right one clattering its cuff in a catchy bongo beat against the car door. I gripped the vampmobile's handle to muffle the noise. "I mean, sweetie, could it *be* more Romeo and Juliet? Here we are, just you and me and the dawn. Is this what they call sparking out in Nebras—"

"Just you and me and that maniac in the pickup with the smoked windows driving hell-for-leather into the parking lot," Rawls said, bringing the nail gun into firing position and aiming it at me. "You almost had me fooled the past few minutes, but I might have guessed there was a reason why you weren't too worried about sunrise. Too bad for you the vamp rescue squad left it so late, though."

"Vamp rescue squad?" With an effort I shifted my gaze from the sight of the glowing line on the horizon and saw twin headlights cutting through the rapidly dissipating predawn gloom. The red pickup jounced over a bump in the parking lot as it sped toward us and a dark shape flew from the bed of the truck. The shape rolled once when it hit the ground, but instead of continuing to roll it seemed to gather itself and then race alongside the pickup that had just ejected it. As I watched I saw the shape begin to outstrip the vehicle.

"As if I didn't have enough to worry about right now," I exhaled. "Rawls, lower your weapon! If he doesn't think you're a threat he won't attack—"

The rest of my warning was drowned out by the

stacatto coughing of the nail gun as he opened fire. The gray shape abruptly swerved, but it didn't change course and when it got to within leaping distance of Jack it launched itself into the air.

"*No,* Mikhail!" I screamed out the command but like my warning, it was ignored. The huge wolf crashed into Jack and the two of them went down. The pickup truck screeched to a halt. Its door burst open and Megan flew out, dressed in de rigueur Daughter of Lilith black. All that was needed to complete this French farce of a scene was a scantily clad blonde, I thought before remembering that I was playing that particular role.

"Megan, call off Mikhail—" I began, but like everything else I'd said in the past minute my words had no effect. Megan shot one appalled look at me and then brought her stake into throwing position. "*Don't!*" I yelled.

She froze. I felt a moment's gratified relief that someone had finally listened to me before I realized that my command hadn't been what had stopped her.

Mikhail, still in wolf form, stood over Rawls, his bared teeth inches from his neck. Rawls, his face a grim mask, held his finger on the trigger of the nail gun that was jammed into Mikhail's thick ruff. It was the classic standoff, but how long it would remain that way I didn't want to guess.

A pale shaft of light had fallen upon Rawls's upturned face, intensifying the green of his eyes so they looked like blazing emeralds. Megan drew in a harsh breath and slowly lowered her stake.

"Stand down, Mikey baby," she said hoarsely. The

wolf immediately went to her side. Just as swiftly, Rawls got to his feet and Megan spoke again, her voice cold and hard. "You've got five seconds to explain why my sister's cuffed to your car and why you were holding a weapon on her when we drove in. Make it good, because this stake works just as well on human creeps as it does on its usual customers."

I was beginning to feel invisible. I opened my mouth to tell Megan I was perfectly capable of telling her myself what had happened to me, but the words died in my throat. Slowly I raised my uncuffed right hand and stared at it, horror rising in me like bile.

Where the morning light fell across it my skin was smoking. Even as I watched, a couple of heat blisters bubbled and popped…and the gory rip that had been between my fingers only moments ago was now perfectly healed.

I raised my eyes and saw Jack Rawls looking past Megan at me. "If you need an explanation, just look at your sister, slayer," he said thinly. "Your *vamp* sister."

Chapter 6

"My vamp sister?" Megan sounded taken aback, but I thought I also heard a trace of apprehensive fear behind her confusion. "What are you talking about?"

All of a sudden I was grateful to Jack Rawls. He'd saved her from having to stake me, I thought as I felt more sunlight pour over me. He'd saved me from having to die by my own sister's hand. I looked down at my arms, sure they were starting to burn now, and for a moment I couldn't breathe.

A final wisp of smoke drifted and died in the air. The heat bubbles on my skin collapsed without bursting. Even as I watched, my skin became once again smooth, as if I'd imagined everything I'd seen. No, not quite, I realized a second later. The torn web of skin between the fingers of my right hand remained healed, only a few runnels of dried blood remaining to show where the wound had been.

Megan hadn't glanced at me in time to see what Jack had seen, I realized. Breath rushed into my lungs and I spoke before he could answer her. "*Too* embarrassing, sweetie, but you've caught us out. The glowering hunk of male standing beside you is Jack Rawls, one of the deliciously sweaty carpenters you might have seen yesterday. Jack, my sister Megan, who's *very* disapproving of my extracurricular activities." I paused delicately. "We were playing vamp and slayer, Meg. It's a variation I've thought up on the serving wench/lord of the manor, dancing girl/sheik scenarios. See, Jack's the slayer with the big, dangerous weapon and I'm the naughty vamp who's trying to seduce him into letting me—"

"I get the picture." Megan's cool gaze flicked over my messed-up hair, my chewed-off lipstick, my scanty attire. "Next time you turn the great outdoors into your bedroom, Kat, give us a heads-up not to worry when you don't answer your cell phone." I glanced down at the pieces of my Nokia, smashed during my initial fight with Rawls and now hidden from Megan's view under the car as she went on. "You're lucky. Darkheart was all for coming with Mikhail and me to see if you were okay, but I persuaded him not to. However, I wouldn't put it past him to change his mind, so you'd better use this."

"*Grandfather* almost came with you?" I was so rattled I almost didn't catch the small key she picked up from the pavement where Jack and Mikhail had been tussling and tossed my way. I fumbled it into the cuff's lock. "*Merde,* why?"

Megan flicked a glance at Jack. He didn't seem to be paying any attention to us. He opened the passenger door of his vehicle and laid his nail gun on the front seat but she lowered her voice nonetheless. "Oh, I don't know, Kat—maybe because not all the vamps in Maplesburg are bored club owners looking to add some kinkiness to their sex lives, do you think? Because some of them are real and he was worried about you?" she said in a furious undertone. "And he was worried for another reason, too. Tash spilled the beans about your theory that this town could have been vamp-infected while Dad lived here. Darkheart seems to think it's important we set your mind at ease on that score, so he's decided that tracing your AC/DC vamp should be the agency's first case." Her gaze hardened. "He and Tash are both of the opinion that your recent *excesses,* to put it politely, have something to do with Zena's slam against Dad. I don't agree. You made it clear when you bought the Hot Box and took your own apartment that you didn't want to get involved with Darkheart & Crosse, and you're just making sure we leave you alone."

"That's ridiculous—" I began, but she wasn't finished.

"Don't you think *I've* wanted to go back to living a normal life, Kat? Don't you think I'd like to turn my back on responsibility and duty and just have fun? But I don't get to, because I'm the damn Daughter! So forgive me if I'm not too sympathetic to your attempts to weasel out of the Darkheart legacy, okay?"

She might have gone on, but the thunk of the

vampmobile's door closing brought a soft growl from the throat of the wolf standing beside her, and at Mikhail's muted warning she looked toward Rawls.

"God, talk about rough trade," she muttered as Jack, his battered body and face more visible than they had been moments ago in the early-morning grayness, walked around the front of his car. "You should choose your boy toys more carefully."

Coming as it did on the heels of her comment about my trying to escape my legacy—how *dare* she say that, I thought in cold fury—her advice on men was the final straw. "And you should butt out of my business, sister dear. Tell Tash the same goes for her," I said, dredging up my most languid drawl with difficulty. The effort was worth it. Megan's mouth tightened. "Although I really should thank her for her words of wisdom earlier today when she scolded me for using men like Kleenex," I continued. "I took her advice to heart, so get used to seeing me with my rough trade carpenter, sweetie. Jack and I just might become an item, like you and your main squeeze."

I didn't mean any of what I was saying, of course; sisters always know how to get under each other's skin and that's what I was doing. But I'd made the fatal mistake of forgetting that my audience didn't consist of Megan alone. I felt a heavy arm drop carelessly over my shoulders, and swung around to see Rawls giving my sister a feral grin before turning it on me.

"We're gonna be an item, all right," he said, snugging me close enough that I could see the banked murder in his green eyes. "I've been looking for someone like you for one hell of a long time, and now I've found you I'm not letting you get away." He pulled me closer and put his mouth to my hair. From Megan's stony expression I realized that to her it probably looked as if he was tonguing my ear, but I knew differently even before his whisper, hoarse and edged, reached me. "I don't kill humans, and the only reason I can think of for you not burning is that you've still got some human in you. But you and I both know you're turning, and when you do I intend to finish what I started tonight. That's a promise, vamp."

I don't know what got into me at that point. Well, maybe I do. Over the past ten hours I'd been nailed to a car, attacked by vamps and handcuffed. I'd had Jack snarling at me, three supermodel clones hissing at me and my sister reaming me out, and I was tired of taking all the *merde* being thrown at me without fighting back.

And maybe I also wanted to see how far I could push my junkyard dog. I think I've mentioned that caution's never been my strong suit, no?

Rawls began to move away from me. I pulled him back, wrapped my arms around his neck, and gave him the deepest ten-second French kiss any man's ever had. Even as I felt him tense with fury I broke it off. "You'll never keep that promise, Jack," I breathed against his lips. Our faces were so close I could see a fleck of hazel marring the green of his right iris. "I've left better men than you begging for mercy, sweetie, and you don't stand a chance against me."

"Get a room, sis," Megan snapped. "On second thought, don't bother. Come on, Mikhail, let's go." She headed for the pickup, but my gaze remained on Jack, gauging his reaction.

Except I couldn't gauge it. Men are usually an open book to me—admittedly, a book I more often than not skim and then lose interest in halfway through—and it was beginning to irritate me that I couldn't read Rawls at all. The only thing I was sure of was that having my tongue doing deliciously erotic swirls in his mouth and then teasingly retreating hadn't affected him one iota. His features were expressionless. His voice was, too, when he spoke.

"It's not me who doesn't stand a chance against you, it's your sister. Even if she suspects what you are, when it comes down to a face-off between you and her, she's going to hesitate. Maybe only for a fraction of a second, but that'll be enough." His gaze glittered coldly. "There's a rumor going around that your old man went over to the dark side and a Daughter died as a result. Looks like history's about to repeat itself, vamp."

His words hit me like a punch to the heart and I reacted without thinking. The palm of my hand made contact with his jaw so hard that I felt the jarring impact all the way down to my elbow, and Rawls's head snapped sideways. "You fucking bastard!" I spat.

"I take it you two aren't an item anymore?" Megan asked. Rawls's comments had been too low-pitched for her to hear, but at the gunshot loudness of my slap she'd halted by the door of the pickup. Despite her sarcasm, she was watching me intently. "Maybe we'd better stick around until your newest ex leaves," she said, leveling a hard stare at Rawls. "You can take that as a hint, asshole," she added. "Whatever you said to my sister, it must have been pretty offensive for her to slap you. I'd advise you to get the hell out of here now."

Her warning was unnecessary. Rawls was already walking unhurriedly to the driver's side door of his sedan. He started to get in, then paused and looked at Megan. "Watch your back," he said in a flat tone. "I know I'm going to watch mine."

And *that,* sweeties, is how my long night with Jack Rawls came to an end. With violence. With threats. With tears—mine, not his, of course, and if you think I let the ridiculous things slip past my lashes where anyone could see them, you still don't know the first thing about me. No, by the time my very own junkyard dog exited the parking lot in the car he'd taken from a dead vamp, I was totally in control of myself again. As soon as the black sedan was out of sight, Mikhail shape-shifted into human form, which for him meant gorgeous, six-foot-two male—I have to admit, there are times when I understand what Megan sees in him—and I airily waved off his offer of an escort back to town. I didn't have to airily wave off any offers from Meg, because she apparently remembered that she was almost as mad at me as she was at Rawls and ignored me. Mikhail was barely in the passenger seat of the truck before she tromped on the gas and shot out of the parking lot, following the dust cloud Jack's vehicle had stirred up.

Which left me in a pair of panties, a bra and Manolos, standing in the Hot Box lot all alone with my thoughts.

Fifteen minutes later, however, I was ensconced in

my office with a fortifying concoction from the bar and wearing a crinkled voile wraparound top with ruffled sleeves over a distressed pair of Antik Denim jeans, both of which I'd grabbed from my office closet. I drained my glass, set it down on the desk in front of me and took a deep breath.

My long night with Rawls had also concluded with me being terrified he was right. Sitting in my office with the alcohol I'd just downed not numbing any of my terror, I reached for the phone.

And punched in a number I hadn't called since the last time I'd been at the end of my rope.

"The last time I did this, I wasn't lying down," I said, turning my head in an attempt to see the man I was speaking to. He was too far out of my sight line for me to catch more than a glimpse of a brogue-shod foot and an inch of brown sock. "I used to like doing it in a chair. Sometimes I'd even get up halfway through and walk around."

"If lying down makes you truly uncomfortable, Katherine, certainly you may sit in a chair. But try it this way first. In my experience, when the body is relaxed one can go deeper."

"That's been my experience, too, sweetie," I said before I could stop myself. I bit my lip. "Sorry, Doctor, I guess I'm just nervous." That last was the understatement of the century, I thought, tightly closing my eyes and feeling the leather of Dr. Leibnitz's couch under my curled-up fingers.

"That's understandable. After all, when you went

looking for a lifeline this morning, I wasn't the one you hoped would throw it to you." Leibnitz's voice held a trace of mild humor, and I allowed my fingers to uncurl slightly.

"No offence, Doctor, but I suppose I thought talking to Dr. Hawes would be easier simply because I was his patient seven years ago when he helped me get over my supposed eating disorder," I said with a small laugh. "Too silly, really. I mean, what teenage girl *doesn't* occasionally crash diet? Grammie's a darling, but a tad mother-henish, if you—"

"Ah, yes." I heard a page being flipped over behind me. "Anorexia interspersed with bouts of gorging and forced vomiting—bulimia, to be precise," Liebnitz murmured, turning another page. "Dr. Hawes kindly faxed over your case notes."

I repressed the urge to say bully for Dr. Hawes. I also repressed the urge to say that if Hawes really had wanted to be kind, he could have bumped one of his other appointments to make room for the former patient who'd rung his emergency number this morning, instead of telling me he had a months-long waiting list and giving me the names of three of his colleagues, two of whom were female and out of the running as far as I was concerned.

If I'd been looking for a father confessor to bare all to, I wouldn't have cared about that part. But I had no intention of baring all, and in my experience, female father confessors are *much* harder to manipulate than men.

Although Liebnitz wasn't exactly playing ball with

the easy-to-manipulate thing right now, either. Suddenly the story I'd planned to tell him seemed less seamless than it had when I'd come up with it on my way to his elegant brownstone office.

"Yes, well, the anorexia's behind me now," I said. "Ditto the bulimia, Doctor. What I really need is to talk to someone about the dreams I've been having."

Maybe manipulating Dr. L wasn't going to be as hard as I'd feared. I could almost feel him quiver to attention at the magic word. "Dreams?" He took the bait like a trout rising for a fly. "Can you describe these dreams for me, Katherine?"

I cast my line with an even more irresistible bait. "They're about my father. But he and my mother died when I was a baby, as I assume you know from Dr. Hawes's notes. Probably they don't mean a thing."

"No, no!" He caught himself and continued in a calmer voice. "Dreams can be symbolic signposts pointing the way to deeper problems."

You've got that right, sweetie, I thought. *Deeper problems like am I following the same path dear old Dad did when he betrayed Mom, and if so, what the hell do I do about it?* My nails were digging into the couch again and I forced myself to unclench my fingers. "I hope they're just symbols," I said with a little laugh whose shakiness wasn't totally assumed. "I mean, in them Father's a *vampire.*"

"A vampire?" Liebnitz sounded nonplussed.

I nodded. "Like Dracula or Tom Cruise. Tom in that movie, naturally," I added, "where he sucks the life out of every woman he meets and takes away their free will. A vampire. In my dreams that's what my father is, and he ends up betraying my mother and causing her death."

"Leaving you and your sisters orphans," Liebnitz mused as I heard the sound of his pen scratching across paper, "which signifies a betrayal of you, as well. Very interesting."

I nodded again, this time slowly, as if he'd illuminated something for me. "I never thought of it like that. That makes the rest so much worse, because in them *I'm* turning into a vampire, too, and I keep getting closer to betraying the people I love, just as he did. Or as he does in my dreams, I mean," I hastily corrected.

"Mmm…" Dr. Liebnitz fell silent, although his pen kept up its steady scritch-scratching across his notepad. Impatiently I waited for him to finish writing, feeling like I was teetering on a knife edge. I wanted him to tell me there was nothing to worry about. I wanted to hear that my fears were unfounded, that just because there were some similarities between David Crosse and his daughter didn't mean his history would replay itself in me.

Liebnitz's pen stopped scratching. "Go on."

It was my turn to feel nonplussed. "That's all there is. So what does it mean, Doctor? Am I fated to follow in my father's footsteps? In the dreams, of course," I amended.

His cough was dry. "The answer to that question can only come from you. It may take months, possibly years. Dreams are often only the tip of the iceberg of our subcon—"

I shot bolt upright, swinging my legs off the couch

and turning to face him. "Months? *Years?* I need to know today!"

The man was a professional, I'll give him that. Faced with a wild-eyed patient who looked as if she was about to leap up and grab him by the lapels of his understated English-tailored suit, his gray eyes didn't so much as flicker. I had the feeling that even if I did wrench him from his chair and begin shaking him, his neatly groomed salt-and-pepper hair would remain in place and his calm smile wouldn't falter. Despair swept through me. Then he gave a light sigh, and I felt a flicker of hope.

"Therapy is a voyage of self-discovery, not a guided tour. The most I can do is help you clarify the most pressing points of the issue bothering you, starting with the vampire symbolism of your dreams." He smiled faintly. "Assuming you don't really think your father was Count Dracula."

My answering smile felt sick. "That old symbolism just keeps popping its nasty head up all over the place, doesn't it? I mean, look how the cigar industry's fallen off since Freud's day, for example."

"But in this case, the cigar's not a cigar..." Liebnitz said decisively "...and your father's vampirism stands for something you fear in yourself. Since you never had the chance to know anything of him but his absence in your life, do you think it's possible that you fear you're absenting yourself?"

No, Doctor, I think it's a whole lot simpler than that. In fact, in this case I think the cigar's no more compli- cated than a great big mother of a Cuban Monte Cristo that's already got a lighter flame to its tip. I shrugged. "How could I be absent from myself? I mean, there've been mornings when I might want to put some distance between me and the wrung-out disaster staring back at me from my mirror, but unfortunately that's just not possible, is it? Not unless you're talking about multiple personalities, and whatever other problems I have I've never felt the slightest impulse to put on a one-woman show of *The Three Faces of Eve.*"

"Not distance from yourself," he said with unruffled firmness. "Distance from others. Your dreams depict you as carrying on your father's legacy, and as with any parent who dies too soon, his most obvious legacy is the gulf that death created between him and those who loved him. From what you've told me, I surmise that you subconsciously fear you're creating a gulf between yourself and those close to you."

For one paranoid moment I wondered if he'd been talking to his esteemed pop-psychologist colleagues, Drs. Megan and Tashya Crosse. Then I got hold of myself. "Believe me, Doctor, I'm not the type who has trouble with close relationships. Quite the opposite, in fact." I looked at him through my lashes. "Let's just say that from the moment I discovered both boys and naptime in kindergarten, my report cards always included the comment, *Plays well with others.* Except for the games being infinitely more interesting now that I'm all grown up, nothing's changed, if you catch my meaning."

"You're saying you have an active sex life?" Liebnitz made it sound as exciting as knitting. His pen was once more scritch-scratching across his pad. "How long have you been in your current relationship?"

I felt my smile slip a little. "Right now it's more a case of so many men, so little time, Doctor."

"So you're between relationships." *Scritch-scratch.* "How long did the most recent one last?"

I stopped smiling and glared at the top of his head as he kept writing. "Three days," I said shortly. "But I don't—"

"And the one before that?"

"A night." My tone should have frozen the ice in his pen, but the damned thing kept scratching across the page.

"Before that?"

I had to think. "A weekend," I said finally. "Very well, I'll admit it sounds a trifle tawdry when one lays it out on the table like this, but I adore each and every one of my beaux while I'm with them."

"And when they break off the relationship with you? How do you feel then?"

I widened my eyes at him. Then I shook my head, amusement edging out my irritation. "Nobody, but *nobody* dumps Kat Crosse, Dr. Liebnitz. Handing out the walking papers is my job." I recalled Terry and added emphatically, "Not that I'm a ball-breaking bitch or anything, despite what some of my more disgruntled ex-suitors might say."

Liebnitz gave one of his dry coughs and his pen stopped moving across his notepad. "It seems I've merely proved my point, Katherine—therapy isn't about snap diagnoses. You seem to have healthy, if varied, relationships with men, and from Dr. Hawes's notes, I see that you're also very close to your two sisters. That's still the case?"

"We squabble occasionally, like all sisters do," I said uncomfortably, "but yes, we're very close."

"Then your dreams of following in your father's footsteps seem to be unfounded," he said, laying down his pen and smiling faintly at me. "At least, inasmuch as my inaccurate reading of their being symbolic of a fear of withdrawing from the human race. If you'd confessed to be a ball-breaking bitch—" his smile grew wry "—as you so eloquently put it, or to a recent and serious rift in your relationship with your sisters, then I might wonder if your dreams held some truth. If I also learned that your father really had betrayed his family before his death, that, too, might be an element worth exploring. But as it is, I'm afraid I can only repeat my earlier advice to you—it may take months of therapy to—"

His words turned into a droning buzz that I barely heard. Liebnitz was wrong, I thought numbly. I didn't need months of therapy to confirm what Jack Rawls had accused me of this morning. I *was* following in David Crosse's footsteps. Not that I could blame Tashya and Megan for dismissing Zena's dying assertion that our father had renounced his soul and betrayed his slayer wife. I might have dismissed it, too, except for one thing—I had proof that Daddy dearest had been a vampire. When Zena had consigned me to hell, I'd seen him there with the rest of the damned.

Confession time, sweeties: I fibbed when I said earlier that I'd blanked out on the little vacation in the toasty place Zena had sent me to during our final showdown with her. Don't take it personally, I also told Megan and Tashya and Darkheart I couldn't remember anything about it. But although I'd tried to bury the memory in the deepest part of my mind, it had all rushed back when I'd seen my skin sizzle.

And Liebnitz had just confirmed the other half of my fears by forcing me to be honest with myself, if not with him. Tashya and Megan had written me off. I'd been avoiding Darkheart. By running through almost all of the eligible men in Maplesburg I'd made my isolation complete, and now I was free to rocket along the same primrose path David Crosse had taken...the path to betrayal. Quite a legacy to receive from a man I'd never known, I thought, my nails once more digging into the couch. I had a few photographs and Grammie and Popsie's stories to make up a picture of who he'd been, but that picture didn't do anything to explain Zena's final revelation or my one glimpse of the damned man who'd met my eyes across the flames during my brief sojourn in hell.

"...will dredge up feelings of pain, of course." Dr. Liebnitz's quiet voice broke through my thoughts. I looked up to see him extending a box of tissues. "I can see that even this initial session has made a break in your emotional barriers."

My lashes were wet, I realized. I plucked a tissue from the proferred box and blotted them, aware that my hand was shaking. Liebnitz could take that as a further sign of the pain he assumed I was feeling, I thought, just as he assumed my tears were. But pain had nothing to do with it.

I was shaking with anger. My tears were tears of fury. And the man I was angry with was a ghost who'd disappeared from my life before I could confront him.

"Your quest for the truth behind your dreams will be worth it, however," Liebnitz went on, "if only to bring closure to issues that have been haunting you for years. I can fit you in next Tuesday at this time, but before you agree to further sessions, are you sure you're ready to commit to this?" As he spoke he rose from his chair. I began to make an excuse and then stopped.

Forty-five minutes ago, I'd walked into this office like a woman lost in a thick fog. The fog hadn't completely dissipated, but now I could see a pinprick of light through it. "Closure would be good," I said slowly. His back to me, Liebnitz had crossed the room to his desk where an appointment book lay closed, but it didn't matter that he couldn't hear me. I was speaking to myself, not to him. "Even though finding out the truth won't change anything, at least I'll know why the bastard betrayed Angelica and let Zena mark me. Learning that might make what I'll eventually have to do easier."

What I'll eventually have to do... Put that way, it sounded innocuous enough, but the reality would be a replay of this morning, with one important difference. When the time came that I could no longer trust myself, I would walk out into the dawn. This time the sun's rays on my skin wouldn't merely sizzle slightly and then drift away in smoke, they would burn me alive. I thrust the vision away and stood up from the couch as Liebnitz turned from his desk.

"Next Tuesday's just fine. As for whether I'm ready to commit to my search for the truth, don't worry, Doctor—I'm committed," I said. I gave him a smile I was pretty sure looked a lot like Jack Rawls's junkyard-dog grin. "In fact, you might say I'm committed right to the bitter end."

Chapter 7

"...and at last night's dance we won first prize, girls! The purser got a photo of Popsie dipping me with a rose clenched between his teeth—the tango is such a thrillingly hot-blooded *dance, don't you agree? I'll send the picture with my next letter, but toodles for now! Love, Grammie."*

"I know." Tashya's china-blue gaze took on a momentary sympathy as she saw the shudder I couldn't quite repress. "Popsie with a rose between his teeth, Grammie feeling hot-blooded. I'm glad they're having a good time on their cruise, but yuck."

She reached across the reception desk for Grammie's letter, and I gave it back to her. As she opened a drawer and dropped the brightly postmarked envelope back into her purse, I took a curious look around at my surroundings.

It was the first time I'd seen the second-floor office in the slightly run-down area of Maplesburg's downtown that Grandfather Darkheart had rented a few weeks ago, after Tashya's brainwave about starting a vampire investigation agency, and although my walk from Dr. Liebnitz's brownstone had only taken ten minutes, the two places were worlds apart in ambience and elegance. In fact, *office* was too kind a term, I thought, surreptitiously glancing at the frayed rug that covered the scarred wooden floor and the battered oak desk Tashya was sitting behind. The place looked like its last tenant had been Humphrey Bogart as Sam Spade. Tash, wearing a tangerine-print Escada halter dress with a perky matching bow holding back her red gold curls, looked totally out of place.

But that wasn't my concern. I was here for one reason only, and that reason had nothing to do with Tashya's wardrobe. It did, however, have everything to do with the Darkheart & Crosse agency's computer, and I saw with relief that the sleek Mac sitting on the oak desk looked light-years more cutting-edge than its surroundings.

"So why the unexpected visit?" Both Grammie's letter and the temporary sisterhood it had kindled in Tash had vanished. She looked at me suspiciously. "And don't give me any caca about just dropping by on a whim, because I hear your whims run more along the lines of carpenters and outdoor sex these days."

I arched an eyebrow. "Jealous, sweetie? If you want, I'll toss the disreputable Mr. Rawls your way when true love's run its course."

I saw a thoughtful glint in her eyes before she shook her head. "He sounds bad-boy delish and just the fact that Megan disliked him on sight means that I'd probably go for him, but no thanks. I prefer the type of man I can kiss on the doorstep at the end of a date over the kind you have to slap across the face." Her gaze narrowed once more. "But you haven't answered my question. Why are you here, Kat?"

I shrugged. "After our little dustup yesterday, I got to thinking about what you'd said, and I realized you were right. To make up for my recent appalling bitchiness, I thought I'd whisk you and Megan away from your Darkheart & Crosse grindstone to spend an hour or so window shopping downtown before finishing up at that sinful Italian gelato place by Colette's Shoes."

Tash isn't a poker player. That's just as well, because she'd make an awful one. Her face signaled her fleeting emotions with all the subtlety of a Times Square billboard: instant interest, belated remembrance, sulky disappointment. "I can't. Meg spent the last four nights patrolling until dawn, and she's exhausted. When she went home an hour ago to get some sleep she made me promise to stay here and hold down the fort, just in case a client shows up." Her tone was disgruntled. "Like that's going to happen. We've been open for business for two weeks, and so far we haven't had a single paying customer. If I'd known vamp investigation didn't get any more exciting than visiting an old lady in a retirement home, I'd have kept my big mouth shut about starting this stupid agency."

I was momentarily diverted. "What old lady?"

She gave me an annoyed look. "Edith Hazlitt. Thanks to you and your story yesterday about that teen vamp who attacked you, Darkheart wants to know who he was and when he was turned. I'm almost as good as you are on computers and this one's loaded with some amazing and probably illegal software, courtesy of a furtive Russian guy from Queens who set it up for us. But there's only so much information you can get from a computer before you actually have to get off your butt and do some legwork. I found out that Old Man Hazlitt died last year, and his wife moved into Whispering Pines Retirement Home shortly after, but that doesn't help us with our inquiry into a Hazlitt's Drugstore employee from a couple of decades ago who might have dated your Mr. AC/DC Pizza face. For that, I'll have to question Edith Hazlitt personally." Tash sighed dramatically. "Gawd, it must be awful to be old. For all I know, she won't be able to remember what she had for lunch. When you think about it, there's something to be said for the whole vamp staying-young-and-hot-forever thing."

"Too bad it also comes with the whole vamp losing-your-soul-and-being-damned-forever thing," I said, more sharply than I'd intended. I forced my lips into a stiff smile. "And too bad about our little shopping date, sweetie. I guess I'll have to go to Colette's sale all by my lonesome." I blew Tash an air kiss and turned to go, but she reacted as I'd expected.

"Colette's has a *sale?*" she squawked, leaping up from her chair so quickly she almost overturned it.

"Up to fifty percent off everything," I said, shading the truth a bit. Actually it was ten percent off selected stock, but I needed Tashya's motor revving. "Weren't you drooling over some sizzling Christian Lacroix red satin evening sandals earlier this week?"

"And an adorable pair of Gucci wedges," she replied, yanking the desk drawer open and grabbing her handbag. "Omigod, now I can get them *both!*" She gave me a pleading look. "The old Megan would have understood that a shoe sale this good takes precedence over work, but since she became the Daughter of Lilith she's changed, Kat."

"I've noticed, sweetie," I commiserated.

"If she finds out I hung a Closed sign on the door to dash down to Colette's, she'll go ballistic," Tash continued desperately. "If you really want to make up for being so horrible, stay here for half an hour and cover for me?"

I feigned disappointment. "It would have been more fun to have a girls' afternoon out like we used to, sweetie, but I *do* owe you… Okay, I'll cover your butt in case Megan phones. We'll go together some other time."

"You're an *angel.*" Tash blew me a kiss. I felt a twinge of compunction for my fib, but it passed as soon as it came.

"I know, but don't let it get around. It's taken me years to build up this bitch-goddess reputation."

My witticism went unheard by her. She was out the door while I was still speaking, and then I heard her clattering down the old-fashioned oak stairs at the end of the hall instead of waiting for the equally old-fashioned elevator.

I hadn't been completely joking when I'd told her I preferred to keep my slightly bitchy reputation rather than have my softer side revealed, and there's another side of me I don't exactly advertise, either. Truth be told, sweeties, I'm one hell of a hardheaded businesswoman. The Hot Box had been an impulse buy, but I hadn't gone into the deal without tumbling the numbers. Of course, I hadn't let on to the creditors who held the paper on the late Zena Uzhasnoye's business that I knew it was worth more than they were asking. No, I'd gone into my meetings with them to tell them in my breathiest dumb-blonde voice that I thought it would be such a kick to own my own club, didn't they agree? They did everything but nudge each other in the ribs, and when my offer was accepted they barely seemed to notice they'd sold the club to me at ten thousand less than their original asking price.

All of which is to illustrate that I'm not just a pretty face, sweeties, no matter what impression it suits me to give. And while I'm good with numbers, I'm practically a *whiz* with computers. I'll spare you the details of how I accessed the programs I needed on the Mac, but suffice it to say that twenty minutes later when I printed a hard copy of the information I'd found, I was *très* impressed with the snoop software Darkheart's Russian contact had installed.

In fact, I was so pleased with the results of my clandestine labors that I almost got caught red-handed. I was just cramming the sheaf of papers into my Hogan bucket bag when the door to the office opened and Grandfather Darkheart entered.

He looked like a wreck of his usual self, and I saw that not only hadn't he noticed what I was doing but he barely registered my presence at all. His thick steel-gray hair looked as if he'd been running a hand through it, and his normally eagle-sharp gaze was preoccupied and clouded.

Also, it was red. I took in the rest of him—the flipped-up pocket flap of his unbuttoned jacket, the creases in his shirt, the silvery stubble on his cheeks—and I realized with shocked amusement that Anton Darkheart was hungover.

I beamed cheerily at him and spoke in a louder tone than I needed to. "I finally decided to drop by and check out Maplesburg's newest commercial enterprise, Grandfather. I must say, I expected more of a hive-of-activity thing going on, but I guess it'll take time for word to spread about the agency." I took pity on him and lowered my voice slightly. "A Red Eye," I said sagely. "That's what you need."

He squinted painfully at me. "Katherine." His voice was hollow, a far cry from his usual deep rumble. "Where is Natashya?"

"Out." I glanced at my watch. I still had a few minutes before I needed to leave to put the second part of my plan into effect. "Whiskey, coffee, Tabasco sauce, a raw egg and orange juice all blended together. It sounds vile and it is, but I prefer it over the old sauerkraut juice remedy."

Darkheart closed his eyes. "Remedy?" he said weakly.

"To muffle the sound of that orchestra playing the 'Anvil Chorus' in your head and the one playing the 'Volga Boat Song' in your stomach," I informed him.

"A hangover remedy. You really must have tied one on last night for the effects to be still lingering this afternoon. Were you and Liz on a pub crawl?"

Elizabeth Dixon was the local art gallery owner whom he'd started seeing after the final battle at the Hot Box with Zena—Elizabeth being one of the Maplesburg women who had been involved in the fight. Mikhail, whose talents don't merely include shape-shifting, had wiped the memory of that evening from the minds of the rest of the non-Darkheart or Crosse participants, but his mass hypnosis hadn't worked on Liz—mainly, I suspected, because he'd seen her interest in Anton and realized that if they were going to be an item she'd eventually need to be in the loop about Grandfather's antivamp activities anyway.

"*Nyet*," Darkheart said shortly. "I had a date with Liz but I cancelled it."

"Because of me," I said, feeling suddenly guilty as I remembered what Megan had said about his worrying about me. "I'm sorry about that—"

"Cancelling date had nothing to do with your situation," he interrupted with a trace of his usual Carpathian rumble. "I tried to reach you on *sotovyj telefon* only to ask your advice about something. Is not important now, however."

"You sure?" I looked at my watch again and realized I really had to get going. "Because if you've got any questions about Maplesburg's business bylaws, maybe we could do lunch this week and I'll try to answer them. Believe me, I've run into my share of bureaucratic snarls since buying the Hot Box, but there's usually a way to bypass the red tape. That was what you needed to ask my advice about, wasn't it?" I added as I made my way to the door.

"As I say, not necessary now," Darkheart said, pressing his fingers to his temples in a gesture I sympathized with, since I'd made it myself once or twice in the past.

"Okay." I paused in the doorway. "Tashya should be back soon, but I've got to dash, Grandfather. Remember, throw the raw egg in, no matter how gross it tastes. Gives the whole mixture some protein."

"Da," he said queasily, sinking into the chair. "Protein."

I wanted to stay and commiserate, I really did. After all, I'd been there and done that myself, no? Instead I simply waggled my fingers at him and breezed out... and by the time it occurred to me that by racing off from my grandfather I'd taken yet another step along the path of isolation from my family, it was too late to go back and change things.

Although maybe it was too late right from the start.

"Boss, I only got three questions for you—why me, why here at a bar called the Sledgehammer, for God's sake, and what the hell you up to, *chica?*"

Ramon punctuated this speech with a suspicious brown-eyed gaze at me. Unfortunately it lost some of its punch, being directed as it was over the open paper frill of a cocktail umbrella. His expression lost more punch as he pursed his lips together over his cocktail's straw and noisily sucked up the last of his Singapore Sling.

I caught the bartender's attention—not hard, since

he'd been undressing me with his eyes since I'd walked in—and twirled my finger in a "hit us again, barkeep" gesture that encompassed Ramon's Sling and my empty martini glass. Then I gave Ramon a reproachful look. "I'm truly wounded, sweetie," I began, but he didn't let me finish.

"I'm wounded, too, girlfriend. It hurts me just to look at all these studly construction workers and know I can't hit on any of them," he retorted, glancing furtively at a trio of brawny men sitting at the bar a few feet away. "Even if one of them felt inclined to take me up on an advance, he'd have to stomp the *mierda* out of me just to prove to his buddies he's not gay. So answer my questions."

"In the order you asked them, because I want to get to know my club's manager better, I thought we'd have a better opportunity to talk in a place where we wouldn't run into anyone we know, and I'm not up to anything at all, sweetie." I sat back in my chair as the waitress who'd previously served us banged my martini and Ramon's lurid cocktail onto the sticky tabletop. I handed her a bill and turned back to Ramon. "Now, isn't this fun?" I asked brightly. "Tell me, have you discovered any hot new restaurants in the area lately? I've heard there's an outrageously expensive raw food place that's opened on the other side of town, or are you more of a *bifteck* and *pommes frites* kind of guy? See, I hardly know anything about you! I ask you, what kind of a relationship is that for two people who're going to be working together?"

"A working relationship, where you're the boss and

I'm your employee," Ramon said, narrowing his gaze at me. "*Chica,* you either spill the beans about why you really phoned me at the Hot Box and told me to meet you here, or I'm hustling my gay ass out of here. You've got dozens of friends, plus your sisters, so why invite me out for drinkies?"

I opened my mouth to protest further, but one look at his pudgily resolute face convinced me it was a waste of time. I met his eyes defiantly. "Because you were the only person I could think of who'd come." I shrugged. "Dozens of friends? Dozens of acquaintances, I suppose, people who show up when I throw a bash or have front-row tickets to fall fashion week. But in case you haven't noticed, sweetie, when it comes to bosom buddies, I'm the Kat who walks by herself. Not a problem most of the time, but right now a smidge inconvenient. I need a witness, sweetie."

"A witness to what?" At five foot ten and with his round face, limpid brown eyes and beginning-to-thin hair, usually Ramon looked like a dissolute and slightly aging cherub. Now he looked like a cherub who suspected he was being rooked by a shady used-car dealer. I realized I had to come clean with him—up to a point.

"To my not getting murdered," I sighed. "Look, I'm trying to carry out what the British call a spot of blackmail, okay? Not very laudable of *moi,* I admit, but it's the only way I can get the blackmail-ee to do what I need him to do. Said blackmail-ee being one of the carpenters you might have noticed working at the Hot Box lately," I added, "the one who looks like a junkyard dog with a nail gun. His name's Jack Rawls."

"*Chica,* you been holding out on me." Ramon's expression was hard to identify—a mixture of reluctant admiration, disbelief and apprehension. "You got *cojones.* Big brass ones, but they don't make up for the fact that you got no brain. If you're talking about the guy I think you are, one look at him should have told you he's not the type you can mess with. Take my advice, girl, and stick with your usual milk-and-water conquests. That one's out of your league."

"No man's out of my league," I assured him, "and I'm not trying to get him into my bed, I'm trying to persuade him to do a job for me that no one else can do, so I can't fall back on my usual milk-and-water conquests. Is that really what you think about my stable of studs?" I asked with a touch of pique.

His wry gaze was more eloquent than words. I held out against it for a moment, and then found myself giving him an even wryer smile in return. "Oh, pooh, I suppose they *are* a trifle easy to manipulate, but that's the way I like my men."

"There's easy to manipulate and then there's shooting fish in a barrel," Ramon observed before sucking back half of his Singapore Sling. He removed its paper umbrella and pointed it at me as if he were trying out for the part of Yum-Yum in *The Mikado.* "The carpenter isn't easy and he isn't a fish. Neither am I. Well, under the right circumstances I guess I can be easy," he added honestly, "but as delectably sexy as you are, *chica,* you're not part of those right circumstances for me. So put away your girlish wiles and tell me the whole story straight. Why are you blackmailing the carpenter, what do you have on him and how come you've been losing your looks lately?"

"Losing my *looks?*" Ignoring everything else he'd said, I focused on the unforgivable barb. He shrugged, unperturbed.

"Don't wet your panties, girlfriend, you're still gorgeous. But you've been looking a little haggard lately, and you know it as well as I do. So dish, or I walk out of here and leave you to face Mr. Nail Gun alone."

His gaze on me was unwavering, and all of a sudden I realized I'd misjudged him. Under his amusingly catty exterior and flamboyantly gay manner, Ramon was nobody's fool, least of all mine. He was right—I *had* hoped to manipulate him into sticking by my side while I presented the contents of the manilla envelope to Rawls and told him what my terms were. At most I'd expected to spin some spur-of-the-moment story to explain my actions, but now I knew Ramon would see through me immediately.

I was going to have to tell him the truth. He wouldn't believe it, of course, but I didn't have any other option. I tossed my martini back in a bracing gulp and set my glass down on the tabletop. "I'm turning into a vampire," I said flatly. "Rawls knows and he intends to kill me when the change is complete. That wouldn't be a problem, except I want him to do a job for me before I go totally vamp, and somehow I think this isn't a situation where batting my lashes at him and saying pretty please is going to do the trick. Hence the blackmail." I sighed and waved a hand at him. "You don't have to give me two weeks' notice, Ramon. I'll pay you what you've got coming with a month's extra on top, and I'll write a glowing reference to the next person lucky enough to hire you. Rawls should be here any minute now, so you might want to finish your drink and leave before he arrives."

"You're firing me?" He raised an eyebrow. "Because if you are, *chica,* I want two month's severance pay. If you're not, then you must think I'm quitting."

"Well, aren't you?" I smiled tiredly. "Now you've found out you're working for a crazy woman, that is."

"Crazy don't bother me," Ramon answered, raising and lowering the paper umbrella. "Vampires do, but since you aren't one yet, I guess I'm safe enough for now. Besides, I always wear this." He parted the collar of his retro-trendy Nat Nast bowling shirt. Nestled in a veritable Brillo pad—his chest hair certainly wasn't thinning, I thought distractedly—was a gold crucifix on a gold chain. "My mother's," he said, hiding it from view again. "And not the only thing I got from her, *chica.* She believed in everything—werewolves, *el chupacabra* and of course, *vampiros.* She told me that when she was a little girl, one of her uncles became one. The villagers found his daytime resting place and staked him."

I goggled at him—not an expression I usually indulge in, but I made an exception this time. "I must have heard you wrong. Did you just say you *believe* me?"

He shook his head. "I said I believe in *vampiros.* That doesn't mean I believe you're turning into one, it just means I don't think you're crazy for thinking you might be. What happened, did one of your stable of studs get excited and love-bite your neck while the two of you were doing the dirty? Because going one step further than a hickey don't mean nothing, *chica*. If you really were infected you'd be noticing symptoms like not being able to go out in the daytime and cringing away from my *crucifijo* when I showed it to you just now." He looked suddenly worried. "*Did* you cringe a little?"

"Yes, but only at your chest hair," I assured him distractedly. "You really should bite the bullet and go for a wax job, sweetie. But although I still can look at a cross, the sunlight thing kicked in this morning. My skin…" I swallowed. "My skin *smoked,* Ramon."

"*Madre de Dios,*" he breathed. He swallowed, too. "You sure, girlfriend?"

"I'm sure," I said drearily. "And I didn't get infected from a love-bite, I got infected by a queen vamp when I was a baby. I'm turning into a *vampiro,* all right, just like your great-uncle did, and Rawls wants to do to me what the men of your mother's village did to—*ohhh!*"

My sentence ended in a gasp as a cascading stream of beer flowed over Ramon and splashed onto the tabletop, spattering me. I shoved my chair back and jumped to my feet, but it was too late. The tan silk of my designer dress was dappled with amber drops of Old Milwaukee, and instead of wafting the delectable scent of the designer perfume with which I'd sprayed myself earlier, I now smelled as if I'd taken a bath in hops and barley. But my condition was nothing compared to Ramon's. Beer plastered his hair to his skull. Beer soaked his no-longer-natty shirt. Beer dripped in a little rivulet from the tip of his nose to the table.

Standing over him was a beefy construction type, the glass he was holding still tipped downward above Ramon's head. I gave him a look guaranteed to turn him to stone if he met it, but he was smirking at a trio of his buddies at the bar, so I stepped forward and tapped him on the forearm. It was like tapping concrete. He turned.

"I've got a teensy question I wonder if you could answer for me," I said conversationally.

"Shoot, sexy," he grinned.

I grabbed him by the collar of his plaid shirt. "Just for interest's sake, *why,* jerk?" I ground out between my teeth.

"*Chica,* let it go." Ramon stood up and reached for my arm. "He's a gay basher, okay? And I don't think he's the only one here. Let's leave."

"Let's," I agreed tersely. "I'll just have a last one for the road." As I spoke I picked up the half-consumed Singapore Sling. I plucked the tiny pink parasol out of it, tossed what remained of the sticky pink drink into Beef Boy's face and tucked the open parasol behind one of his ears like a hibiscus blossom worn by a hula dancer. "*Now* I'm ready to go, sweetie," I informed Ramon in satisfaction.

"Oh, shit," he gulped, giving an appalled glance at Beef Boy's purpling face. "Not a smart move, *chica.*" A corner of his mouth began to twitch. "Although fuchsia *does* seem to be his color, don't you think?"

His eyes met mine. For a moment we held on to our composure, but then I made the mistake of darting a look toward the ruffle of parasol peeking coyly out from behind Beef Boy's ear and I cracked. As soon as the first snort of amusement escaped me, Ramon lost it, too. In a second we were both seized with an insane fit of the giggles.

"He gon' kill us, Kat, you know?" Ramon gasped through howls of laughter.

"Mop the floor with us," I affirmed, doubling over as a fresh gust of hilarity hit me. "You think it might look more flirty behind his left ear?"

"You fuckin' bitch." The parasol flew to the floor by my feet, and a massive workboot ground it into oblivion. "When I'm finished with the fag, I'm workin' you over but good!"

"Exit stage left?" A final snort of laughter escaped Ramon as his eyes flicked to the door.

"Sounds like a plan," I agreed, sobering up.

But we'd left it too late. Even as we began to make a run for it, I saw Beef Boy's massive left hand clamp onto Ramon's beer-sodden shoulder as his equally massive right paw balled into a fist. And for the second time in twenty-four hours my training with Darkheart kicked in.

"Trahnite vas, zadnij prohod!" I yelled in a close approximation of Anton at his most Russian as I grabbed the plastic and metal chair I'd leaped out of when Ramon's beer shower had spilled onto me. I wasn't positive what the oath meant, but since I'd heard Darkheart mutter it a few weeks ago at a driver who'd passed him and given him the finger, I was pretty sure it had a *fuck you* in it somewhere. I lifted the chair high and

brought it crashing down on Beef Boy's head before his fist could make contact with Ramon's chin. He let go of Ramon with a roar and turned to me. "*And* the horse you rode in on," I continued, this time borrowing a favorite phrase from Popsie's lexicon as I shoved the chair's legs into his gut, driving him backward so quickly that he lost his balance. He crashed heavily onto the floor.

At which point the bar exploded into a redneck version of a Wild West saloon brawl.

Up until now, Beef Boy's buddies had been content to watch the proceedings without interfering, but seeing their fearless leader downed by a girl galvanized them into action. They poured off their bar stools and rushed us, the meanest-looking one making a beeline for me.

"This is about showing queers they're not welcome in the Sledgehammer, blondie," he growled. "You need to learn not to interfere."

I backed up, meaning to skip sideways out of his trajectory, but I'd forgotten the table behind me. Meaty hands reached for me, and then Ramon was between us. "It's me you want, so leave my friend out of it, you big lug," he said fiercely, aiming a kick at my would-be assailant's knee. His kick connected—from where I stood it looked as if that connection had more to do with luck than unerring aim on Ramon's part—and a bellow of surprise and pain came from the lug's mouth. But although it slowed him down, it didn't stop him, and by now the rest of his and Beef Boy's crew were pouring toward us. I glimpsed the bartender hastily grabbing up the phone and punching in a number, but I had the sinking feeling that even if the Maplesburg boys in blue raced straight over here, they wouldn't be in time to save Ramon's and my derrieres from a serious smack down. For now we were on our own. Then I saw a burly type in a hard hat loom up behind the jerk Ramon had kicked. He clamped a hand on his shoulder, spun him around and landed a punch on his jaw.

It really *had* turned into a brawl, I realized. Half of the bar's patrons might be on Beef Boy's side, but the other half just wanted to rumble. Within seconds the focus had shifted from Ramon and me to a free-for-all, with chairs crashing down on heads and fists flying. Ramon caught my eye and the two of us began heading for the exit, weaving our cautious way between the brawlers like two cats slinking through a dogfight.

As if thinking about dogfights had conjured him up, at that moment Rawls entered the room. He paused for a moment and then began pushing his way through the melee toward the bar.

"Jack! Over here!" I yelled, ducking as a chair leg whistled through the air above my head. Rawls glanced my way and one of the brawlers attempted to grab him. Barely breaking stride, he rammed an elbow deep into the man's ribs, stiff-armed another who lunged toward him and drove his fist into the face of a third who swung at him. Then he was at the bar, shoving a bill across its surface to the rattled bartender.

A man after my own heart, I mused, and obviously one who had his priorities straight. My appraisal was interrupted as another man who also knew what his priorities were tugged on my arm. "We've got a clear path to the door right now," Ramon shouted over the commotion. "Move your tush before we—"

His words cut off as he followed my glance. The harried bartender had plunked a glass in front of Rawls. Floating on top of one ice cube was a red cherry. Rawls removed it and downed his drink—bourbon on the rocks from the look of it, although why any bartender in his right mind would garnish Jim Beam with fruit was beyond me. Tossing the cherry, stem and all, into his mouth, he turned from the bar and shoved through the crowd toward Ramon and me.

"I take it back—you *are* crazy if you think you can blackmail that one," Ramon said, raising his eyebrows. "Even when he's eating a cherry he looks like he should be chewing nails."

"The tougher they are, the harder they fall," I said in an undertone, "and besides, with you as a witness to my little transaction I hardly think he's going to try anything." I raised my voice as Rawls approached. "Sorry for the pandemonium, Jack. Why don't we find a quieter place—"

My words dried up as he gave me what looked like a briefly humorless grin and I saw the cherry stem clamped firmly between his teeth. He released it and for a moment twirled it between his fingers, his gaze green and watchful on me.

"You seem to have a habit of causing trouble wherever you go, vamp," he said. His voice was a low rasp, but even with the uproar all around us I heard him just fine. "One of these days you're going to start a situation you won't be able to control. Let's get out of here."

He didn't wait for a reply but began clearing a path through the free-for-all. As he did he tossed the cherry stem away, but not before I got one final look at it.

The stem wasn't just tied in a knot, it had been twisted into a tiny, perfect bow. It arced through the air and fell to the floor before being lost to sight under a brawler's boot.

I swallowed dryly. Beside me I was aware of Ramon doing the same. "I think I'm in love, *chica*," he croaked.

I looked past him to Rawls, now several feet away. "I don't blame you, sweetie," I said huskily. "I think I am, too."

Chapter 8

"Excuse the mess, darlings," I said as I stepped inside my apartment and reached for the light switch. "I may be in awe of the Suzie Homemakers of this world, but that doesn't mean I'm one of them. I do manage the basics, however...corralling dust bunnies, changing bed sheets and, of course, *never* running out of the essentials." I threw open the doors of the massive armoire standing against the far wall, revealing a built-in wet bar complete with a minifridge. "To misquote the fabulous La Dietrich, what'll the boys in the back room have?"

I was prattling, I knew, but I couldn't help it. After slipping out of the Sledgehammer seconds before Maplesburg's finest had begun pouring in, I'd taken one look at Ramon's beer-soaked state and suggested my apartment as a venue for the business I needed to conduct with Rawls while my drenched manager showered Old Milwaukee off himself. I'd expected Jack to insist I tell him what this was all about, but he'd merely nodded and agreed to follow my MINI in his car. He should have been full of questions, I thought uneasily as I drove the short distance to the shabby but sadly unchic six-plex I now called home, Rawls's vampmobile visible in my rear-view mirror. After my session with Liebnitz, I'd consulted my BlackBerry for Jack's pager number—I told you I was a hardheaded businesswoman, sweeties, and I make a point of having contact numbers for everyone who works for me. To be honest, I know a situation like the one with Terry might arise at any time, and I have no intention of being left in the lurch without vital information just because one of my temporary flings has ended badly.

Oh, God, I'm prattling again, aren't I?

The message I left on Rawls's pager was cryptic: I merely advised him it would be in his best interests to meet me at the Sledgehammer, since I had an envelope I would be dropping into the nearest mailbox if he didn't show. With what I'd learned about him in my search on the Darkheart & Crosse computer, I'd guessed his survival instinct would prompt him to comply, and I'd been right. He *had* shown up. He'd even agreed to come with Ramon and me to my apartment. But he hadn't asked a single question, and that struck me as just a smidge ominous.

Hence the prattling. Hence my desire to be holding a glass of something bracing when I got down to brass tacks with the dangerous Mr. Rawls. The inconvenient surge of raw lust that slammed through me when I'd realized what a talented tongue the man had was irrelevent to my state of nerves, I thought as I retrieved a bottle of Grey Goose from the bar fridge.

"I'm having a vodka martini, but how about one of my fabulous Long Slow Screws for you, Jack?" As soon as the words were out of my mouth I had a vision of the bow-tied cherry stem. Quickly I tried to cover my Freudian come-on. "Sloe gin and Southern Comfort, remember?"

In his jeans and dark T-shirt, and with assorted scratches and bruises, Rawls looked exactly as Megan had described him: rough trade. I felt another frisson of heat run through me, followed by a cold dose of reality. The man wanted me staked. I was about to blackmail him. Either of those factors ruled out any chance of an erotic dalliance between us, and the two of them together made it a definite nonevent.

My return to reality, however, lasted only until Jack spoke.

"I don't like sloe gin." His gaze held mine. "And to me, a long slow screw isn't a drink."

Hundreds of red-hot needles seemed to be prickling my cheeks. For one fearful moment I was sure I was about to burst into flames, but then I realized how impossible that was. I was inside my own apartment. Even if I hadn't been, the sun had set. A second later, I understood the unfamiliar sensation for what it had to be, and the realization was almost worse than my imaginings.

I was blushing. Katherine Crosse, aka the Kat, aka *moi*, who had last blushed in first grade when little Tommy Briggs had offered to show me his if I showed him mine, was *blushing*. I'd turned Tommy down, but in recent years I'd taken more than one delectable male up on similar offers and if anyone had blushed during those torrid encounters, it definitely hadn't been me.

"Right now I'd rather have that shower you offered than a cocktail," Ramon said, gazing at Jack with lustful adoration, "and I'd better make it a cold one. Where's the bathroom?"

"Second door off the hall," I informed him, glad of the opportunity to gather my scrambled composure, "and check the Lost and Found closet beside it for something to wear. Not that any of the males who've left oddments of clothing behind were *quite* your build, sweetie," I added tactfully, "but you should find something that'll do."

With one last smitten look, he left the room. I turned back to the minibar, poured myself a slug of chilled Goose and downed half of it in one gulp. "Here's to business," I said brightly, turning to Jack. "I suppose you're wondering why—"

I saw with a jolt that he'd crossed the room and was standing only inches from me. The next moment the glass I was holding was plucked from my hand. "Here's to extortion, you mean," he said flatly. He tossed back the other half of the vodka and reached past me to set the glass on the bar's counter. I tried to step back, but there was nowhere to go.

"Extortion?" I widened my eyes. "What gave you—"

"You never stop playing games, do you?" Jack's tone was dangerously soft, and I suddenly knew that sending Ramon off to the showers had been a major mistake.

"Sweetie, why should I?" I widened my eyes further, determined not to let him see he was rattling me. "I mean, isn't that what makes the whole male/female thing so deliciously fun? And despite the fact that we've got business together, Jack, I *am* a woman and you're a man," I added in my best purr, the one designed to bring strong men to their knees.

Except this time it didn't work. Not only wasn't he on his knees, there was an expression in those ice-green eyes that looked an awful lot like…like…

The universe, or at least the part of it that contained me, slipped sideways a little. The look in his eyes was *boredom*.

"Get one thing straight," he said. "Even if you weren't a vamp, shallow and high-maintenance isn't my type, so stop wasting your time trying to manipulate me and just go for the blackmail angle. Hell, I'll even make it easy for you," he added. "You found out I escaped from Tecumseh State. Instead of turning me in you arranged this meeting, so you must want something from me. What's my batting average so far, Crosse?"

"Not bad." My voice wasn't as cool as I'd have liked, but it wasn't a total giveaway to my state of mind. "You just got one thing wrong, Jack. I'm every man's type— well, maybe not Ramon's, but every straight man's. Even yours." I tipped my head to one side, letting my hair brush my shoulder. "Haven't the dreams you've been having about me over the past week while you've been watching me made that clear to you?"

He was good, but not good enough. An instant before

his expression closed down I saw something flicker behind the ice of his eyes, and my universe righted itself again. "I don't dream about you, vamp," he said harshly.

"Now you're playing games, Jack. An escaped con I can handle, but a man who won't keep to his own rules…" I shook my head. His jaw tightened, but before he could react further I changed tactics. "How did you guess I'd found out about your murky past, by the way?"

For a moment longer, his gaze held mine. Just as I was beginning to feel uncomfortable under it he broke off eye contact. "I'll have that drink now," he said, turning away.

Our little tussle of wills hadn't left me in the mood to play gracious hostess. I scooped an ice cube from the tray in the bar's freezer, plopped it into a glass and drowned it with Beam. "How did you guess?" I repeated.

He took the drink from me without a word of thanks. "I told you I'd been watching you for some time. It didn't take long to realize that whatever else you are, you're too smart an opponent for me to underestimate. When you asked me to meet you today I knew you'd done some digging." He swallowed a third of the Beam. "I didn't kill her," he said, liquor giving a roughness to his words. "It happened like I told you."

"Except you left out the part where the cops burst in on you while you were standing over Mary Lou's body," I noted. "Also the part where you were convicted of her murder. It made for some fascinating reading, sweetie, but what really interested me was the size of the reward leading to your recapture. The state of Nebraska wants you back pretty badly. Not surprising, seeing as how witnesses report seeing you use a homemade wooden stake to stab two guards during your breakout." I nodded at the manilla envelope sitting on the sofa where I'd tossed it. "According to the information I accessed today, the bodies of those guards were never found. They were vamps?"

He raised his glass to his lips. "They didn't leave bodies behind for the authorities to find, but I somehow doubt I'll be able to use that as a defence if I ever go on trial for their murders. So what's your price for not buying me a ticket to ride Old Sparky?"

"Oh, come *on*, sweetie," I protested. "Do you have to make this sound so drearily *sordid?* I'm merely proposing a mutually advantageous deal. When you hear what I have in mind, you might even find it fun to—"

"No," he interrupted, "you don't get to turn this one into a game. This isn't a deal, it's a threat, and unless you want me to kill someone for you I'll probably go along with it. But working with you isn't my idea of fun. Being sent back to face the death penalty isn't, either. What's your price?"

I opened my mouth to protest further. Then I closed it. Ramon had been right, I thought, unsettled. Rawls was immune to me. I could bite my lip, bat my lashes, inject pure sex into my drawl, and instead of allowing himself to be wrapped around my little finger like every other male I'd ever met, he would just keep staring at me with those cold green eyes. Which presented a *teensy* problem.

I didn't know any other way to deal with a man.

Anger surged through me. If he wanted raw honesty, I'd give it to him—ugly, unvarnished and unpalatable. And I hoped he'd choke on it. "I intend to dig up some old bones," I said flatly. "You're going to help me."

"I don't get it, *chica*." Ramon, no longer reeking of beer, had rejoined us shortly after I'd begun outlining my plan to Jack. Now, half an hour later, his comment filled the silence as I finally finished speaking. "You say you want to find out if David Crosse turned *vampiro* while he was still living in Maplesburg?"

"Or whether it happened years later," I said, less interested in Ramon's reaction than Jack's. Jack didn't seem to have a reaction, however. He'd missed his calling, I thought in irritation: if he'd chosen the pro poker circuit over vamp hunting, he'd be driving a Mercedes now instead of a thirty-year-old clunker with painted-over windows. "It's not rocket science, sweetie, so what don't you get?" I asked Ramon a trifle impatiently.

Wearing an oversized, Hawaiian-print shirt and holding a margarita, he looked like he should be leaning back in a lounge chair on a Key West beach instead of against the pillows of my pewter velvet couch. "Why it matters," he said with raised eyebrows. "You don't seem to think there's any question your father went over to the dark side at some time in his life, so what difference does it make when it happened?"

"It changes the level of betrayal." For the first time Jack spoke, his words directed at Ramon but his hard gaze on me. "Vamps don't fall in love. If Crosse turned before he met the Daughter, his marriage was part of a plan to bring her down."

"Part of Zena's plan," I muttered, moving toward the uncapped bottle of Grey Goose on the bar. "I told you, the bitch's last words before my sister sent her to hell were that David Crosse had given himself to her."

"Must be convenient for a vamp to have a Daughter of Lilith for a wife," Jack said as I reached for the vodka, "but if you're counting on your slayer sister to turn the same blind eye to what you're becoming as Angelica did for David, you could be making a big mistake. From what I saw of her this morning, I'd say this generation's Daughter takes her hereditary role a lot more seriously than your mother did."

I turned to face him, forgetting my need for a drink. "What the hell are you implying, sweetie?" I asked with brittle calm. "That Angelica knew all along that she was married to a vamp—knew and didn't do anything about it?"

If he heard the undercurrent of fury in my voice he didn't seem bothered by it. "She was a Daughter. If she didn't sense what he was the first time she laid eyes on him, she must have figured it out damn soon."

"That's true." Ramon nodded over his margarita, and as I turned a grim glance on him I decided he looked less like a Key West habitué than Benedict Arnold in a loud shirt. "Face it, girlfriend—the lady had to have noticed her new hubby wasn't big on daytime activities. Not to mention the no-reflection-in-mirrors thing, or how his incisors were *waaay* too sharp sometimes," he added blithely. His glance met mine and his casual air slipped. "Love does crazy things, *chica,*" he protested weakly. "Maybe she knew but she didn't let herself know, you know?"

"*Glamyr* does crazy things," I said, feeling my hands curl into fists the way they'd done on Liebnitz's couch. "Angelica's worst crime was in trying to turn aside from her heritage and live a normal life. That made her as susceptible to vamp *glamyr* as any normal woman would have been, but it didn't make her a traitor to what she believed in." I swung back to Jack. "I told you—when Mikhail did that creepy mind-meld thing on my sisters and me the night he and Darkheart were trying to convince us that one of us was destined to take up the fight against vamps, he made me see Angelica's final battle against Zena." I shook my head. "No, he made me *relive* it. I was there. I saw her plunge her stake into that red-haired bitch. I saw her turn away to her three babies in their cribs, to make sure we were safe, and then I saw Zena fall upon her. My mother's aim might have failed her but her courage didn't," I said tightly, "because after Zena bit her and left, I also saw Angelica choose death rather than the horror of turning vamp from Zena's bite. So your insane theory about her being as bad as my father is total *crap,* Rawls!"

My last sentence came out in a near shout. I reached for the bottle with a shaking hand, hoping he'd make the fatal error of saying one more word about my mother so I could justify braining him with it.

He didn't. He made another fatal error, instead.

"If you want my help in backtracking your father's

possible vamp contacts in Maplesburg, you better lay off the sauce, lady. I don't work for boozehounds."

My hand tightened on the neck of the bottle as I struggled against temptation—and I'm talking about the temptation of flinging it at him, sweeties, not of pouring myself a nip. In the end, my better nature won out by a sliver.

"I. Am. Not. A. Boozehound," I said with icy clarity. "Now we've got that straight, am I right in assuming that you just offered to help me?"

"I just buckled under to your threat of exposing my whereabouts to the authorities," Jack corrected, glancing sideways at Ramon. "Were you in on this, pal?"

"No, he wasn't," I said before Ramon could answer. "Ramon, the surly Mr. Rawls is talking about the fact that he's an escaped con, but don't worry, he didn't commit any of the murders he's wanted for. Well, he staked two guards, but they were vampires so they don't count." I saw the puppy-dog adoration return to Ramon's expression as he gazed at Jack, and I sighed. "If I'd known you had such a thing for bad boys, darling, I'd have thought twice before dragging you to this meeting. As it is, now that we're past the negotiation stage, there's no reason to involve you any further in my unsavory affairs." I gave him a quick smile. "Call a taxi, sweetie. Tell the driver to charge it to my account and don't worry about coming into the club tomorrow morning. In fact, take the whole day off as a little thank-you for helping me out tonight," I added with distracted magnanimity before turning my attention back to Jack. "Since they seem to feel the need to verify his story I've decided to leave the AC/DC Pizza face angle to my sisters and Darkheart. I'd rather concentrate on the hunt for Maplesburg's vamp zero—and whatever else Mr. Acne-and-Heavy-Metal was, he certainly wasn't that. Zena would have been my first guess, but for the fact that her recent visit here was the only time she ever came to America," I mused out loud.

"Hey, *chica,* I got an idea—why don' you snap your fingers while you're getting rid of me?" My stream of consciousness rambling was broken by Ramon's antagonistic words. He was fixing me with a lopsided smile that seemed out of place on his cherubic features. "Funny, for a while tonight I started thinking of myself as your friend. I guess it's a good thing you reminded me I'm just an employee." He drew himself up to his full height. Since his full height wasn't exactly impressive and half of it was clad in a loud and too-large Hawaiian print, his maneuver should have looked ridiculous. Somehow it didn't.

"Of course you're my friend, sweetie." I blinked in confusion. "I don't understand what—"

"You never understand, Kat," he went on in a slightly unsteady voice. "That's what makes it sad. You couldn't understand why you had to call on your club manager tonight instead of one of your dozens of acquaintances. You don't understand how you've gotten the nickname, Queen of the B's. You won't understand—"

"Queen of the B's?" I interjected. "Who calls me that? And what does it mean?"

"It means Queen of the Ball Breakers, and everyone calls you it behind your back," he snapped. "Like I'm saying, you wouldn't understand…just like you won't understand why my resignation's gonna be on your desk tomorrow."

I stared at him in shock. "You're quitting? But sweetie, we open in a week! You can't do this to me!"

"If I was a friend, I wouldn't," he said with the same aloof dignity he'd shown a moment earlier. "As someone you just use and dismiss when it suits you, I don't got no problem with it. I'll stay until the new Hot Box opens, but then you're on your own. Get used to that feeling, girlfriend, 'cause I think it's going to be a familiar one."

He deposited his empty margarita glass on the bar. In stunned silence I watched as he turned away and headed for the apartment door, but instead of seeing him, I was seeing myself.

Myself on Liebnitz's couch today, facing the unpalatable truth that my sisters had just about written me off…realizing I'd been avoiding Darkheart…admitting I was well on my way to making my isolation complete.

"Sweetie, wait!" He grasped the doorknob and I tried again. "Ramon, don't go. I—I think I'm going to need a friend over the next little while." Slowly he let his hand fall from the door and turned to face me as I went on, the words easier to say than I'd thought they would be. "And you're the only one I have," I said huskily.

For a long moment our gazes held—his steady, as if he was assessing my sincerity, mine a trifle blurred because of the ridiculous moisture that had sprung up behind my eyes. At last a faint smile quirked up the side of his mouth.

"Whose fault is that, girlfriend?" he said with a shrug.

"Some days it's like you're permanently stuck in PMS mode, know what I'm saying? The only reason I can take it is because I'm kind of a bitch, too, *chica*. This one here, now—" he jerked his head at Jack, who was watching the two of us expressionlessly "—he seems tough, but he don't know what he's getting himself into."

"Are you sure you do?" I asked worriedly. "This could be dangerous, Ramon. We're hunting Maplesburg's original big bad, and I've got the feeling that when we find him he's going to make Zena look like a pushover."

"I got this, remember?" He parted the collar of his shirt to reveal the crucifix he wore. "And the faith to go with it," he added more somberly. "But what I don't understand is why you think the big bad *vampiro* who turned AC/DC and maybe your father over twenty years ago is still hanging around town, like he's got nowhere else to go."

"I don't think he's been in Maplesburg all this time," I said, looking at Jack. "I think he paid my hometown a flying visit way back when to prepare the ground for his protégé's arrival this year. I'd guess that part of his preparation included turning a few vamps so that Zena would have a base army to work with when she came here, but the one thing I'm sure of is that he's back in town...and he wants me." I heard Ramon drag in a sharp breath, but my attention was on Jack. "You knew. That's why you were so sure that your hunt for the original infector would end here."

"I told you, word travels," he said, his eyes narrowing on me. "Vamps talk, especially when they think talking might save them. But how did you figure it out?"

I met his stare coolly. "I didn't have to—not in any conscious way, at least. From the moment Darkheart came into my sisters' and my lives, I've had the feeling that everything that's happening to us is somehow preordained. Maybe even before he showed up," I amended, "since it was by my action that the last protection guarding us from Zena was removed." I saw Ramon's uncomprehending look and realized I hadn't told him about the silver crosses my sisters and I had worn from childhood right up until six weeks ago, when we'd rashly removed them just in time for all hell to break loose. "I'll spare you the tedious details, sweetie, but what's important is that even though I knew I was exposing us to danger, I couldn't stop myself. It was as if I was playing a part that had been written for me before I was born—and yes, I do realize it sounds like I've gone totally *fou*," I added hollowly. "But as crazy as these glimmers of intuition seem, I think they're the only sane things in my world right now."

"Sane or not, they bear out the rumors I've heard that Maplesburg's vamp zero is the ancient who turned Zena centuries ago," Jack said curtly. "I'd also heard the part about him creating a sleeper cell of undead, which is where you think I come in."

"Who better, darling?" I inquired. "You *do* have a certain knack for coaxing information out of those who've gone over to the dark side, no? And you're equally adept at tracking your quarry down, so my plan is for you to find another AC/DC and learn all you can from him about the master vamp who turned him— including where said master spends his daytime hours.

Then all that's left is for us to pay him a social visit, during which I'll politely ask the son of a bitch whether he sucked Daddy dearest's soul out of him the previous time he was in Maplesburg. It's a perfect plan, if I do say so my—"

"It's a shit plan," Jack interrupted brusquely. "I'm good at tracking vamps down because I stay below the radar, but I've already blown my cover in this town. Vamps aren't stupid. They're not going to attack a trained enemy when they could have their pick of naive citizens, and if I can't draw them out I can't question them. We need a stalking horse."

I smiled sweetly at him. "And I'm sure that if we were in Nebraska we'd have no trouble finding live-stock, but—"

"A stalking horse is bait," Jack said, interrupting me again. "In this case, human bait—someone who looks like an easy kill, who gives the impression of vulnera-bilty."

"Like in those nature shows on television." Ramon nodded sagely. "The bad-ass lion following a herd of antelope, he don' go for the big ones with horns, he waits until he sees one who's kinda small and conspicu-ous. That's not a bad idea, but who you got in mind for the antelope?"

His gaze resting on Ramon's short figure clad in the loud print shirt, Jack didn't bother replying. Even as I saw Ramon swallow in sudden comprehension, I exploded.

"Oh, no you don't!" I strode across the few feet that separated us and without thinking, grabbed a handful of Jack's T-shirt, yanking it away from his chest.

"Ramon's off-limits! If you want a stalking horse or a wounded antelope or whatever the hell your name is for a patsy, *I'll* take the job, not him!"

"You're halfway to full vamphood yourself, and getting closer every day," Jack ground out. "Even if you still retained enough humanity to tempt other vamps, don't forget the other rumor going around about you." He knocked my hand away, his breath coming hard. "As the dark-sided daughter of a Daughter, you're their future Queen of the Night, sweetheart, and even the most blood-hungry vamp in this town knows you're under the protection of the master. They won't touch you, so either Ramon volunteers to draw them out or we forget the whole thing."

"He's right, girlfriend." Ramon's face was pale but resolute. "I don't like the idea, but I don't see any other way. Just promise me that you guys'll be covering this gay antelope's ass the whole time, okay?"

"*Not* okay," I retorted. "I won't let you do this for me, sweetie. There's got to be some other—" The shrill ringing of the phone on the table beside the couch cut across my words, and I let out an oath as I saw the caller ID. "*Merde,* it's Megan. If I don't pick up, she'll mount a search party for me like she did last night," I muttered as I snatched up the phone. "This better be good, Meg," I warned into the receiver.

"It's not Meg, it's me," Tash's voice quavered over the line. "Get over here, Kat, and fast. Liz Dixon had a date with Grandfather Darkheart tonight, but before he could pick her up she phoned with a message. She's been snatched by a master vamp and if he doesn't give himself up in her place…" Tash gulped audibly before she went on. "If he doesn't give himself up she'll be *killed*, Kat."

Chapter 9

After slamming down the phone on Tash it took me ten minutes to race across town to the Crosse mansion with Ramon riding shotgun beside me, if *riding shotgun* is the right phrase to describe a man clutching a cocktail shaker and sipping the remains of a margarita. I shot the MINI through two amber traffic lights and barely tapped the brakes at a third intersection where the light was red, Jack's vampmobile right behind me. When I turned into the familiar curving drive, I admitted to myself that my edginess wasn't completely due to Liz's situation.

"Moment of truth time," I said under my breath as I approached the mansion's front door. "Here's where we separate the wheat from the chaff, the goat from the lambs, the made-in-Taiwan knockoff Fendi baguette bag from the real—"

"Don't be surprised if you can't cross the threshold without an invitation," Jack growled from behind me as I grasped the door's knob. "It all depends on how far you've turned vamp."

"It appears I'm still a made-in-Milan original," I said in relief as I stepped into the foyer without incident. "By the way, are you just happy to see me or is that the muzzle of a nail gun I can feel sticking into my spine? Because if it's the latter, you can lower it now."

I heard Ramon stifle a margarita-fueled snort of amusement as we walked into the living room, but I immediately forgot all about him and Jack as my gaze fell on Megan and a distraught-looking Darkheart. My triumph over the door seemed suddenly negligible in light of the cold stare my darling sister was giving me. "I thought I told Tash not to call you," she said, bypassing the niceties in her new Daughter-of-Lilith way. "The situation's under control, so why don't you—" Her gaze went past me to Jack and she sucked in a breath. "What the hell is *he* doing here?"

"This situation sure don't look like it's under control," Ramon offered, apparently unfazed by Meg's less-than-warm welcome. "Usually when a situation's under control there isn't an old guy standing around with his hair sticking up like he put his finger in a light socket, know what I'm saying? And excuse me for mentioning it, girlfriend, but that divine Chanel demisweater you're wearing is buttoned up wrong. Coco must be spinning in her grave."

Megan's glance snapped downward. As Ramon had noted, the gleaming gold buttons embossed with interlocking *C*s that marched down the gossamer-fine black wool of her sleeveless top didn't match up with their buttonholes, betraying the careless haste with which she'd dressed. Her fingers fumbled with the offending fastenings, setting them right as her already tight lips tightened further.

"I'm warning you, Kat, get your 'What Not to Wear' buddy and your rough-trade boyfriend out of here," she said thinly. "If you haven't noticed, we're in crisis mode, and for once the crisis isn't all about—*hold it right there, Rawls!*"

Her hand shot out as Jack moved toward Darkheart, her fingers wrapping around his shoulder like a steel clamp. Jack spun to face her, his eyes chips of pack ice in the tan of his face. "You're not the first Daughter of Lilith I've run up against," he said with soft menace, "and I don't like you any more than the others I've met. You all seem to think your hereditary roles mean you're the only ones licensed to kill vamps, but I've got news for you, sister—the occupation's not limited to your little sorority. Maybe us male vamp bounty hunters don't have secret handshakes or designer weapons—" his glance dismissed the leather-wrapped stake holstered at Meg's left shoulder "—but we dust our share of undead, so stow the attitude. You need my help. If you're going on the assumption that the Dixon woman's been snatched by a master vamp, you've already made a mistake that could get someone killed."

"*Da,* is right." Darkheart raised his head from his hands and shock ran through me as I saw his haggard expression. His keen gaze and strong features had always reminded me of an eagle, but now he looked like an eagle with its wings broken. He went on in a hoarse echo of his normal voice. "I am thinking like stupid old man, or I also would have seen. The *truslivyj ubl'udok* who took Liz could not be master *vampyr.*"

"Why not?" Tashya's voice, almost drowned out by a sharp clattering, floated from the stairs leading from the upstairs bedrooms to the main hall that opened onto the living room. As she entered I saw that the clattering had come from the thigh-high stiletto boots she was wearing. They were topped by a butt-skimming cro-cheted mini, which in turn was almost concealed by a body-caressing silk tunic. As the pièce de résistance, an enormous goth-styled cross on a leather thong dipped in and out of her revealing neckline.

Megan's pained glance met mine and for a moment it was like old times as we united in silent exaspera-tion over Tash. Then her gaze hardened into Daughter-like determination again. "You'll break your ankle if you have to fight in those things," she curtly informed Tashya before turning back to Dark-heart. "What do you mean, the bastard who snatched Liz isn't a master? She said he was in her message, didn't she?"

Without waiting for his reply, she strode across the living room to where a telephone sat on a small table. Another B.D.—before Darkheart—memory flashed through me, this time a recollection of Grammie sitting at this very table crossing names off lists as she indulged in marathon phone sessions to raise money for one charity or another, but as Megan punched the replay button on the answering machine all thoughts of Grammie and more innocent times were shattered.

"Anton, if you're there, pick up!" The voice on the answering machine's tape was Liz Dixon's, but the chic gallery owner's usually light tone was thick with terror. "I thought it was you at the door, Anton! I was getting dressed and I called out to come in, the door was unlocked. God help me, I invited a *master* into my—"

A male voice overrode her. "I'll take it from here, pet. Just sit there and gibber with fear like a good girl, will you, while I leave the rest of the message for your rather over-the-hill boyfriend and his scrumptious trio of granddaughters—the delectably stern Megan, the adorable Tashya—" he paused for the space of a heart-beat "—and the *very* intriguing Kat."

There was a Kennedy drawl to some of his words and a hint of laughter in his…oh, who am I kidding, sweeties? I didn't give a *fig* about his accent, and as for monitoring his tone, I was suddenly way too busy feeling my internal temperature shoot upward past Normal, screech past Mildly Turned On, to come to a panting halt at Excuse Me While I Orgasm Right Here And Now.

His voice was the aural equivalent of oral sex. It was an is-it-hot-in-here-or-is-it-just-me confirmation of everything the Pointer Sisters sing about in their timeless make out classic, "Slow Hand." It was melted Godiva chocolate on my breasts, it was the soft stroke of a feather down my spine, it was silky velvet sliding up my inner thighs, it was—

Well, you get the picture. And from the glazed look in Megan's and Tashya's eyes as they listened, they got the picture, too. With an effort, I forced myself to concentrate on our caller's words instead of his voice.

"I'm holding your lady-love hostage, Anton. If you value her life you'll give yourself up in her place by midnight tonight. She's made it clear to me that she'd rather be dead than undead and as I'm not one to force a lady against her will, if you don't find us in time I'm afraid I'll have to kill her." His laugh was softly regretful. "I'm sure you're eager to commence the hunt, so I'll ring off now. Tash, if you're the one who stumbles upon my hidey-hole, don't let my charm fool you, I'm rather tricky. Megan, gorgeous as you are, I'd prefer not to meet you when you're in your Daughter of Lilith mode. And fascinating Kat…I hear you're the one who most takes after David." His sigh almost undid me. "Ah, happy days on the Charles," he murmured. "Some day you and I must meet for cocktails, lover. Oh, dear, someone wants to say goodbye."

"Anton, don't do it!" Liz's scream ripped through the langorous afterglow I was basking in. *"Don't give yourself up for—"* Her words were cut off, this time by the click of the connection being ended. The answering machine tape stopped. For a moment no one said anything, then Tash broke the silence.

"Wow," she breathed. "I mean, 'Love Potion No. 9' or what. Have you ever heard a sexier—"

"Are you *insane?*" Megan whirled on her. "A fucking master vamp's threatening to kill a woman we both know and all you can think of is how *hot* he sounds?"

Her fury would have been more convincing if her cheeks hadn't still been flushed and her bottom lip hadn't swollen slightly from where she'd been biting it while Mr. Dreamy Voice had been speaking. I was debating whether to point this out to her in the interests of sisterly helpfulness when Jack spoke.

"Master vamps don't make deals," he said, his tone a hard contrast to the one I'd just been listening to. "He might want us to believe he's one, but he's not."

"Makes no difference," Darkheart said hoarsely. "Important thing is find where he is holding Liz so I can take her place."

"I can't let you do that," Megan said automatically. "When Mikhail reports in on whether he was able to track a scent from Liz's apartment, I'll—"

"Nyet!" thundered Darkheart, slamming his fist down on the telephone table. The sick-eagle look had gone and his determination was back at full strength. "I am responsible and I must make right! From start I knew could be dangerous for her, but I let myself forget terrible lesson I learned so long ago! And now death will come to her, just as it did to—"

His mouth clamped shut and he shook his head. Megan frowned. "Just as it did to Angelica? Tragic as it was, Mother's death wasn't your—"

But he was shaking his head again. "No more talk," he muttered. "Is time for action."

Megan seemed about to say more, but she must have seen the implacability in Darkheart's expression. She released a tight breath. "All right, you win, Grandfather," she said grudgingly. "But you're not going off alone. In fact, since I'm still not convinced this vamp isn't a master, no one hunts solo tonight." Her glance swept over us. "Darkheart and I will meet up with Mikhail. Tash, you and Kat pair up."

"And what about us, girlfriend, we just sit here and play gin rummy till you get back?" Ramon planted himself in front of Megan. "Maybe I'm not real experienced in this vamp-killing business, but Jack here is. Why leave us out?"

"Because she's a Daughter, and Daughters have a problem with people they can't order around," Jack stated, hoisting his nail gun. "That's fine by me. I'll hunt alone."

"And while you're hunting alone, I'll watch your back," Ramon said promptly. He met Jack's flinty stare. "You don't want the gay guy along, just say. Maybe I'll hunt alone, too."

Frustration crossed Jack's features. "Not a good idea," he said shortly. "If you're so hell-bent on being part of this, you'd better have a partner. Come on, let's move."

"You can borrow a spare stake from me," Tash offered, attaching herself to Ramon and Jack. She shot me an unrepentant look. "You don't mind, do you, Kat? I mean, thanks for showing up tonight to give moral support and everything, but I've seen how you fold when you go up against vamps. I'd really rather tag along with the guys."

"Dammit, Tash!" Megan began, but I cut her off.

"Sweetie, don't explode at the brat on my account. She's right, my batting average against vamps is abysmal—which is why I don't see any reason for me to offer my less-than-impressive services to this mission." Delicately I covered a yawn with my fist. "I think I'll head home, pour myself a teensy nightcap and then make up for the beauty sleep I missed last night. I'm sure the rest of you will do just fine without me."

Megan's disbelieving look iced over with contempt. "I'm sure we will, too." Pointedly she turned from me to Jack. "Tash has a cell phone and so do I, so stay in touch." She paused. "I may have misjudged you, Rawls. That seems to have become an occupational hazard with me lately."

It was as close to an apology as she was likely to make, and it didn't escape my notice that Jack, not me, had been the one she'd directed it to. My Daughter of Lilith sister didn't see me as an ally anymore, I thought as I watched everyone pile into their respective vehicles and drive away. From there it was a short step to seeing me as an enemy.

But there was nothing I could do about that. Master or not, somewhere out there was a vamp who was just *dying* to meet little ol' *moi*...and ball-breaking bitch or not, I had no intention of standing him up.

I'm a veritable *stickler* for dating etiquette, sweeties.

Megan's weapon of choice is her stake. Jack's is his nail gun. I, on the other hand, don't feel properly girded for battle unless I'm freshly showered, delectably spritzed with Caron's *Coup De Fouet*—my inner dominatrix simply can't resist a perfume whose name translates as "Crack of the Whip"—and wearing something utterly devastating. So as I coasted the MINI to a stop by the iron gates of Forest Lawn Cemetery and stepped out into the night, I felt that my ten-minute stop at my apartment before coming here had been more than justified.

I smelled divine. My hair was twisted into a sexily undone chignon and the midnight-blue Manolos on my feet were a perfect match for the midnight-blue Alexander McQueen dress I'd impulsively bought last week. All in all, I was as girded for battle as I would ever be, but as I pushed open the gates that should have been locked at this time of night and weren't, I felt suddenly as naked as a jaybird.

Make that a terror-stricken jaybird. A few minutes later, after aerating a swath of manicured lawn with the heels of my Manolos, I made my way to one of the small landscaped rises dotting the cemetery grounds, the last resting place of Maplesburg's more financially comfortable citizens spread out below me in the velvety darkness. Here and there throughout the parklike vista, stately oaks stood sentinel by gravestones, and the dark silhouettes of weeping willows arched mournfully over granite markers. To my left, a small fountain tinkled softly, its falling water illuminated by a few stray beams of starlight. Straight ahead, two stone angels lifted frozen wings in a perennially futile attempt to fly away from the mausoleum they flanked.

Which is where the terror-stricken part came in. Because if the angels had been put there to stand guard over the templelike structure, they'd obviously screwed up big time.

Candles blazed on every available surface, from the shallow steps leading to the hammered bronze doors of the mausoleum to the squat marble columns lining the steps. A polished block of black granite bearing the name of the family interred inside shone in the candle-light like a dark mirror. On top of the block was arrayed an assortment of bottles, and beside it, looking like the world's dishiest bartender, stood a man with a silver cocktail shaker in his hands.

I tried to take a step forward, but my feet seemed glued to the ground. I tried to swallow, but my mouth was too dry—which was ironic, since my palms were suddenly too damp.

His voice had been pure sex. The man himself was a walking wet dream. He gave no sign that he knew he was being watched but continued shaking up his batch of cocktails while I stood looking down on the incongruous scene, unable to do anything except let my gaze drink him in.

Gawd, sweeties, how can I describe his impact? I mean, I could say that Brad Pitt at his peak looked like his much less attractive brother. I could tell you how the wavering candles that illuminated the area in front of the mausoleum turned his blond hair to molten gold and made his perfectly cut white dinner jacket almost gleam with shimmering light. I might go on and on about the way his quick smile as he set down the shaker and glanced up to where I stood on my little hill had the same dazzling impact as if someone had suddenly flicked on the power at Shea Stadium; I might describe in loving detail how his slightest movement gave a pantherlike impression of strength and masculine grace; I might natter interminably about the incredible navy-blue shade of his eyes. I might do all of those things, but I won't, because even if I did I couldn't come within miles of describing how devastatingly, swooningly *sexy* he was.

Suffice it to say, sweeties, that the man was a Greek god, but presumably without all the inconvenient broken-off bits. He even came with his own soundtrack, because somewhere in the back of my mind I could hear the Pointer Sisters singing "Slow Hand" again….

"…interest you in a drink, lover?"

If there's anything guaranteed to elicit a Pavlovian response in yours truly, it's the sight of two cocktail glasses being held by an attractive male. His query penetrated the erotic fog surrounding me, and I realized I hadn't been hearing the Pointer Sisters but his voice, and from his rueful expression—God, couldn't you just *die* when a gorgeous man does the rueful thing?—he'd been forced to repeat himself while I'd been off in my own little X-rated fantasy world.

I made a valiant effort to pull myself together. Letting my lips curve into a cool smile, I forced my feet to begin moving again. "I'd simply *adore* one, sweetie," I answered as I strolled across the grass, trying to inject a note of negligence into my croaking reply and at the same time hoping I wouldn't stumble over any sunken gravestones. "What are we drinking to?"

"To quote *Casablanca*, the beginning of a beautiful friendship?" he suggested, the corners of those incredible navy-blue eyes crinkling up a little at the corners. As I reached the marble apron that fronted the mausoleum, he handed me a champagne glass brimming with something pale green and delicious-looking.

I took it but shook my head, desperately holding on to my cool. "Just a *teensy* bit premature, with you being a vamp and all, not to mention the naughty way you set up this meeting. I think I'll reserve judgment on the friendship possibilities between us for now, darling. Pick another toast."

"Wise Kat." He nodded solemnly, his eyes still dancing. "And you're absolutely right, the kidnap scenario was utterly unworthy of me." He touched his glass to mine. "You must be bored with men drinking to your beauty, so I'll drink to your intelligence. What tipped you so quickly that this was all a ploy to lure you into my clutches?"

He raised his glass to his lips but I didn't follow his example. "As flattered as I am by your proposed toast, I've got a question of my own before I'll drink with you," I said, my tone no longer as light as it had been. "Is Liz okay?"

He lowered his glass. As his eyes met mine I saw that all trace of amusement had left them and when he spoke, the mock solemnity was suddenly real. "Untouched and unharmed. You have my word on it." The rueful quirk reappeared at the corner of his mouth. "That used to mean something, once," he said in an undertone before lifting his glass again and downing his drink in one quick motion.

Curiouser and curiouser, I thought, feeling as though I'd dropped into the copy of *Alice's Adventures in Wonderland* Grammie used to read to me before I received my first subscription to *Vogue* and promptly ditched the works of the queasily child-adoring Mr. Carroll in favor of the more wholesome world of twelve-page color spreads. But I didn't let his odd comment distract me. "She didn't sound untouched and unharmed when she left that message," I disputed, depositing my Miu Miu clutch on the marble block and casually snapping it open. "In fact, she sounded rather *distrait,* as the French might say."

The amusement was back in his gaze. "Only because I *glamyred* the lady into the misapprehension that she was trying out for a leading role in a horror flick. I might even have persuaded her to take a little drive out of town for a few hours, but have no fear." He shot an immaculate cuff and glanced at the platinum Rolex on his wrist before pouring himself another drink from the shaker. "The *glamyr* should be wearing off just about now. After wondering why in the world she decided to go for a drive at this time of night, your grandfather's charming ladyfriend will turn around and head home."

I stared for a long moment into the unwavering navy of his eyes and came to a decision. "You know, I think I believe you," I said with a rueful smile of my own as I released my grasp on the object in my bag and reached for my still-brimming cocktail. "There's every chance you could be *glamyring* the hell out of me this very minute, but somehow I don't think you are. Let's go with your original toast, darling—to the beginning of a beautiful friendship." I touched my glass to his and took a sip of my drink. "Although a friendship usually starts with introductions, I assume we can dispense with them in this case, since you obviously know my name and I've got a good idea what yours is." I read aloud the name carved into the black granite. "*St. John.* One of Maplesburg's more illustrious families, but sadly all deceased now, as I seem to recall from what Grammie's told me. Even the St. Johns' only son and heir, who had a tragic encounter with an avalanche years ago while skiing in Gstaad." I shook my head in commiseration. "Too terrible, never having your body found, sweetie, not to mention missing out on the brandy those valiant St. Bernard dogs carry in little casks on their collars to revive survivors. You *are* Jude St. John?"

"At your service, lover," he said without missing a beat. "Now, satisfy my raging curiosity and tell me how you guessed that the kidnapping was a smokescreen."

The white flash of smile he directed my way made me feel as dazed and languid as if I'd been basking in the sun. I set down my cocktail glass before it could drop from my suddenly weak fingers. "A girl just knows when a man's interested," I said huskily, swaying infinitesimally toward him and looking up at him through my lashes. "And, besides, you did rather let the cat out of the bag."

"How inept of me," he murmured, his actions anything but as he smoothly closed the space between us even further and traced my lips with one finger. A shiver ran down my spine. "Hair the color of cream…eyes like sapphires…skin like silk… How did I let the cat out of the bag, dear heart?"

His last words were breathed against my mouth. "You mentioned David Crosse," I breathed back against his lips. "That might have been a *teensy* mistake, sweetie."

The navy eyes inches from mine blinked. Then they widened and I felt him stiffen—although not in the way men usually do when they're in a clinch with me. Which wasn't surprising, actually, since we're not talking about the kind of localized stiffening that comes with lust, but the full-body freeze that comes when a vamp realizes he's one false move away from being dusted…which was a *very* real possibility in the delectable Mr. St. John's current circumstances.

"Or maybe a big mistake," I said, the languidness falling from my tone and every word coming out with cold clarity. I tightened my grip on the stake I'd surreptitiously retrieved from my Miu Miu clutch and jammed its tip more assertively into the immaculate dinner jacket he was wearing. "You made an even worse one when you made that reference to the Charles River. You were on the Harvard rowing team with my father, weren't you? Don't bother denying it, because ever since I can remember, Popsie's had a photo of the team on the wall of his study—not a very clear one, but the names of all the rowers are listed and yours is among them. So I've just got one question for you before I send you to hell, handsome—did you turn him while you were at school together or later, after he got married?"

"Neither." The broad shoulders beneath the dinner jacket began a shrug but immediately stopped as my hand tensed on my stake. St. John gave his patented rueful smile. "I can see you don't believe me, but somehow that's not as important as I thought it would be. Eternal life lost what little thrill it had for me when I realized that the one person I could ever see sharing it with was dead. I arranged our little meeting tonight because I had some notion that vengeance might be a substitute for what I'd lost, but now that I've met you I've changed my mind. You're too much like her for me to drag you into a vendetta that could end with you dying like she did. Go ahead, lover, and do what you came here to do."

"I came here to find out the *truth*," I exploded, "and so far all you've given me is *merde!* Who am I supposed to be too much like? What do you mean, a vendetta? And if you didn't turn David Crosse, who did?"

"A master vamp named Cyrus Kane. He turned your father, and then David turned me. But not before I knew that the woman I loved was doomed…and not before I swore to cut down the evil that had changed my friend into a heartless monster. I held on to that resolve even after I became a vampire myself." Jude's smile now seemed more like a grimace of unbearable pain. "Who'd have guessed this shallow heart of mine could have been capable of holding on to a love that transcended her death and my undeath?"

"Who are you talking about?" I demanded. When he didn't answer, I jerked him closer and saw a thread of red run down the white of his jacket. *"Who was the woman?"*

I knew what his answer was going to be before he spoke, but hearing it still froze the blood in my veins. "Angelica Dzarchertzyn," Jude St. John said in a voice hoarse with feeling. "I blame Cyrus Kane for what happened to both of your parents, Kat."

I hesitated for a fraction of a second, searching his face.

And realized with a sense of shock that it was like looking into a mirror. His eyes held the same hopeless pain I'd glimpsed in my own lately. Behind the pain was a burning hatred and behind that was despair. Then a shutter seemed to fall over his gaze, and once more Jude St. John's expression was that of a man who indulged in the more frivolous pleasures in life and who didn't care who approved or disapproved of the choices he made. I recognized that look all too well, too.

There was only one thing I could do. Stepping back from him, I picked up my cocktail and drained it in one gulp. Purposefully I handed him the empty shaker. "Mix us up another batch of these and then you and I can start figuring out how to bring down Cyrus Kane."

I set my stake on the bar and met his gaze with a brittle smile. "Since we're on the same side, sweetie, we might as well take down the bastard together."

Chapter 10

"...And then David told old Hathaway, 'I don't know, sir, the donkey was in the lecture hall when we arrived!'" Jude threw back his head and roared with laughter before tipping the silver cocktail shaker toward my glass. *"Sláinte,"* he said. "Or have we already drunk an Irish toast, dear heart?"

"Think so," I said with the enunciation of a dental patient who still has a needleful of Novocain numbing her lips. "I know—here's to eggs, milk and cimmamon! That's French toast, sweetie," I added with a giggle as I tossed back my cocktail.

The two of us were sitting on the mausoleum's steps, our backs against the massive bronze doors and an assortment of candles stuck in empty bottles flickering around us like tiny campfires. The sitting-around-the-campfire theme had extended to our conversation, too, because Jude had diverted me with a seemingly endless supply of anecdotes about my father and their time in college together. Kane hung between us like the last and scariest ghost story that couldn't be told until the fire was nearly out, but as my giggles subsided I knew I couldn't put it off any longer.

I set down my glass, my alcohol-fueled euphoria suddenly draining away. "You've told me a lot about the pre-Cyrus David Crosse, sweetie, but that man died after Kane turned him. I need to know how and when it happened."

"Because of your own situation?" Jude met my quick glance. "It's no secret among the vamp community, lover. Everyone knows Zena marked one of Angelica's babies. Zena had a habit of indulging in pillow talk, and believe me, she laid her head on a lot of pillows."

"Yours being one of them?" I arched an eyebrow. "Not that it's any of my business, but I wouldn't have said she was your type. Aside from the fact that she was centuries old, her style sense was a tad tacky, no? I kept expecting to find her propositioning johns on Maplesburg's four corners, what with her thigh-high boots and fishnet stockings and the way she was constantly in danger of spilling out of her tops."

"Your claws are showing, kitten." Jude's grin flashed white in the shadows. "Of course I slept with her. She was a queen vamp, with all the irresistible *glamyr* that entails. But I never swore allegiance to her, the way—" He stopped abruptly, but I knew what he'd left unsaid.

"The way David did," I said with a smile that felt plastic. "Don't worry, Zena blabbed about that, too, before Megan staked her. How did she put it? Something about my mother being lucky she died before she learned that the man she loved had given his soul to a queen vamp. That's when I suspected that the father I'd idolized all my life had been a total *merde*." I stilled the tremor in my voice. "Too amusing, really. I mean Kat Crosse, of all people, hanging on to some tattered illusion for all these years that her daddy was a knight in shining armor? How pathetically starry-eyed of—"

"It wasn't like that," Jude said sharply. "By the time David met Zena, he didn't have a soul to give her. Kane had cut it out." His mouth drew into a line, his debonair man-about-town facade falling away. "Is that what you came here to know? If it is, take my advice—forget what I've told you and keep those illusions you used to have about him. He was everything you've ever been told he was—a great guy, a loyal friend, a loving son and husband and father, right up until the moment Cyrus Kane turned him. As you say, David Crosse died that night. Let him rest in peace."

His choice of words touched a nerve in me. "Rest in peace? That's rich, sweetie." I scrambled to my feet, my unsteadiness only partially the result of the cocktails I'd imbibed. "David Crosse isn't resting in peace, he's burning in hell—and I should know because I saw him there!"

Jude got to his feet, too, and although his movements were more graceful than mine, I could see from his expression that my statement had jolted him. "What do you mean, you saw him there? How could you glimpse hell, if you haven't yet—"

"Turned into a full-blown vamp?" I finished for him. "It hardly seems fair, does it? I'm getting all the inconvenient symptoms, like smoking when the sun touches me and having a mini–Club Dead vacation in the underworld with Daddy dearest, but the *glamyr* and living-forever parts haven't kicked in yet. Although to be strictly honest, my little sojourn in hell was courtesy of Zena, not a result of my turning vamp," I added with a tight shrug. "She sent me there during her final battle with Megan."

"And you saw David?" Jude's voice still sounded strained. "You're sure about that, dear heart?"

"His photograph's held pride of place on my dresser since I was a baby. Of course I'm sure."

His gaze on me was probing. "That must have been devastating for you," he said quietly. "And when you came here tonight, you assumed I was responsible for what happened to him. No wonder my *glamyr* was useless against you."

"Not completely useless. I'll confess my heart gave an extra pitty-pat or two when I laid eyes on you, sweetie." I met his gaze, struck anew by how totally gorgeous he was. He had none of Rawls's junkyard dog roughness, but his suavely elegant blond good looks only made his essential maleness more intriguing. "It's just that vamp *glamyr* doesn't have the same effect on me that it does on most vulnerable humans. I used to wonder why, but now I know."

"Because you're turning into one of us?" Jude was still

watching me closely. "You said something about your skin smoking in the sunlight. Tell me how that happened."

His sympathetic tone was almost my undoing. I turned away to reach for the cocktail shaker, gleaming silver in the light of the guttering candles on the marble steps leading to the mausoleum, only to set it back down as I realized it was empty.

"I'll make a new batch," Jude offered, but I shook my head.

"I'm tempted, darling, but no. My sisters seem to think I may be overindulging just a teensy bit lately and although I don't agree, I suppose I might try to cut down a little." I turned abruptly back to face him. "It happened for the first time this morning. I thought for a moment that I was going to end up the same way as the three vamps we'd just killed."

Jude held up a hand. "You've lost me, beautiful. What three vamps? And who's *we?*"

There was a familiar note in his voice that I couldn't place at first. Then I realized his tone of detached interest reminded me of Dr. Liebnitz's professional prodding, and suddenly unburdening myself to him felt easier. "The three vamps weren't locals. And by *we* I mean myself and a surly vamp-slaying bounty hunter by the name of Jack Rawls. Actually, Rawls did all the killing. I tried to help but when it came down to it I found I couldn't go through with the deed, which I took as another ominous sign of my approaching vamp- hood." I looked down at my hands and found I was clenching them. "I...I identified so strongly with them that when Jack killed the second one, for a few seconds

I was convinced it was *me* he'd gotten. And when the sun came up I was sure I was a goner."

"But you weren't, which means we still have time to change your destiny, sweet Kat." His somber mood falling away like a cloak, Jude flashed me a devastating smile. "We find Kane. We kill him. Since he's the master who turned Zena centuries before she turned you, with his death the final bonds that tie you to vamphood are destroyed. Unless you taste blood before then, of course," he added with a raised eyebrow. "You haven't felt the urge yet, have you?"

I thought of the attraction I'd felt toward Claudia's crimson-soaked world and thrust the memory away. "Of course not," I said quickly. "What you say about Kane turning Zena—would that make him vamp zero in this particular line of undead?"

He'd turned to the collection of bottles and the crystal bowl of ice arrayed along the flat top of the memorial plinth of the mausoleum. "Let's see," he frowned, "Vodka, *crème de pêche*, orange juice and…"

"And amaretto," I prompted. "Is Kane vamp zero, Jude?"

"You've tried a *Baiser de Vampire* already? Damn, and here I was hoping I'd be the one to initiate you into its seductive delights." Broad shoulders shrugged under the white dinner jacket. "If vamp zero means do we all trace back to Kane, yes. Is that what your tame bounty hunter calls him?"

"Jack's not my bounty hunter and he's certainly not tame," I said, throwing my earlier attempt at abstinence to the wind and accepting the frothy drink he held. "In fact, he came close to killing me when he learned what I was."

"He may have come close, but he didn't carry through with the deed, adorable Kat. Obviously the man's smitten with you." Jude's tanned lips curved into a grin. "Not surprisingly, I hasten to add."

Only one day into knowing the taciturn Jack Rawls, I thought, and already I was losing the ability to banter with an attractive man. Jude's deft compliments weren't what I wanted to hear right now. "Take it from me, sweetie, he's not smitten. Granted, he may have the hots for yours truly, but so far he's had no problem keeping his baser instincts under control. Let's concentrate on Cyrus, shall we? You still haven't told me how and when he turned my father."

Jude took a judicious sip of his drink and set it down. "If you must know all the grim details, dear heart, it happened in Paris a month or so before Angelica's fatal encounter with Zena. David was in Europe to get signatures on a contract or some such boring legal errand for his firm, and his stay there was supposed to be a flying visit, no more. I'd been skiing at my family's chalet in Gstaad, but I'd had enough of yodels and ei-delweiss and fondue, and in my usual impulsive way decided that a few days in decadent Par-ee might cure my boredom. When I ran into him, he'd been in town for a week."

"Kane had already turned him?" My mouth felt dry and the hefty swallow I took of my *Baiser de Vampire* did nothing to relieve it.

"So I later learned." There was no amusement in

Jude's short laugh. "At the time, David spun me some story about having trouble getting one of the signatures he needed to complete the contract. Truth to tell, I was so delighted to meet up with him that I didn't need an explanation. I mean, he'd been my best friend when we were in college and when the two of us were articling in New York, but I hadn't seen much of him since he'd gotten married. Which was understandable," he said with a wry smile. "If I'd been the one Angelica had been attracted to when your father and I first met her, I would have thrown over my old friendships, too, just to concentrate on her. But right from the start she only had eyes for David."

I was momentarily diverted. "Grammie and Popsie saw her as the perfect daughter-in-law and Anton's memories of her are bound up in grief and conflict," I said slowly, "but you knew Angelica as a person, Jude, not as a woman with a tragic destiny. What was she like? Besides being a Daughter of Lilith, who *was* Angelica Darkheart?"

"The one that got away." He shot me a crooked smile, but then relented. "For a start, she was the most desirable woman I'd ever seen. I'm not exactly a stranger to beautiful women, but when she looked right through a man with those ice-blue eyes of hers that always reminded me of a Siberian wolf's and gave him a go-to-hell stare, every other female in the room seemed to fade into the wallpaper. The only man she never looked at that way was David." Jude downed his drink in one quick swallow. "He was the only one she let down her defences for. In the end, that was her mistake."

"What happened in Paris?" My voice sounded harsh.

Jude's gaze darkened. "From what I learned afterward, your father had a late meeting with one of the clients in a Latin Quarter restaurant. The Quarter's a maze of badly lit alleyways, and he got lost on the way back to his hotel. He stopped Kane to ask for directions."

"And Kane obligingly showed him the way to damnation," I said, not making it a question. "When you showed up, David did you the same favor."

"By then he'd been introduced to Zena by Kane, and David was enthralled with her," Jude said. "I was to be his offering to her—a blood offering. Luckily for me she wanted me in another way, so she ordered him to turn me. A few nights later when the change came completely over me, I went to her bed." For the first time, a trace of anger edged his voice. "I never blamed David for what he did to me. Hell, life as a vamp isn't all that different from life as an aimless playboy—up all night, sleep all day, taking my amoral pleasures wherever I can find them. But for what he did to Angelica, I hope he rots in hell forever."

The trace of anger in his voice turned to white-hot savagery on his last sentence. I felt an echoing hatred of the man who'd fathered me, but I tamped it down to ask the question that was foremost in my mind. "Lapsed or not, Angelica was a Daughter. Identifying and killing vamps was in her blood, the same way it's in Megan's. As soon as he returned home, she would have known he'd gone over to the dark side, no?"

"As you say, she'd turned her back on her heritage," Jude said, his glance not meeting mine.

"That's *merde* and you know it, sweetie. Don't tell me Angelica lived in the same house and slept in the same bed as one of her sworn enemies and didn't notice, or that she made love to the father of her children and never realized what he'd become. She *had* to have known!"

He didn't reply to my protest, but merely held my frowning gaze with a noncommittal navy-blue look. A heavy weight seemed to settle in the pit of my stomach. "You think she didn't let herself know, don't you?" I said through stiff lips. "She didn't dare, because if she acknowledged the truth about the man she loved, she'd have had to kill him. And Angelica couldn't bring herself to do that."

"I told you, from the moment they met she only had eyes for him," Jude said tightly. "Yes, I think she lied to herself. There's no other explanation that fits."

I clutched at a straw. "But what about other people? His coworkers? Their friends? Grammie and Popsie, when he visited them?" Even as I came up with the questions, my mind supplied ready answers for each of them. "We lived in New York City then, not Maplesburg. I suppose it's easy to pass as human in a metropolis where no one makes eye contact, and he wouldn't exactly have been the first ambitious young lawyer to get into the office before dawn and leave after dark. As for Grammie and Popsie, he probably *glamyred* them into seeing what he wanted them to see. But there's one flaw in all of this that maneuvering and *glamyr* can't explain away—why didn't he turn Angelica?"

"I don't know." Jude reached out and cupped my chin in his hand. "I wish I had all the answers you need, but I don't. The only one who might is Cyrus Kane."

I narrowed my gaze at him. "You're a good liar, sweetie. Just not good enough to fool Kat Crosse. I'm sure Cyrus knows why my father didn't try to turn my mother, but I think you know why, too." I drew back from his touch. "If you're afraid of shattering any last illusions I might have about him, forget it. I don't have any left."

Jude's hand dropped to his side. "I should have known you'd see through me, dear heart." He looked at me with pity in his eyes. "He didn't turn her because Zena ordered him not to. She wanted the thrill of taking down a Daughter and of infecting the daughters of a Daughter…and he set up Angelica so that his vampire mistress's hungers could be satisfied."

"He betrayed us to her." Hearing my fears confirmed wasn't as bad as I'd anticipated it would be, I thought with detached calm. David Crosse had arranged the death of the woman he'd loved. He'd delivered his daughter into the hands of a vampire queen. Granted, it was a smidge worse than having a father who missed your first ballet recital or gave your prospective boy-friends the third degree when they came to take you to the prom, but now that I knew the truth I could handle it. "Angelica never wanted to return to the old country, but he persuaded her she had a duty to introduce Anton to his granddaughters. Arranging things that way allowed Zena to destroy three generations of Darkhearts in one fell swoo—"

I whirled around and took four swift steps into the darkness past the perimeter of the candlelight. Jackknifing suddenly, I vomited the alcoholic contents of my stomach behind a handy bush. For a moment I stood there in a doubled-over position, too weak and shaky to move.

"The last thing I ever wanted was to hurt you." Jude's words came from a few feet behind me, and although it was some relief to know he'd remained on the mausoleum steps to give me my privacy—no girl wants a handsome man witnessing her tossing her cookies into the bushes—I still found myself resenting the intrusion of his voice. "I shouldn't have told—"

"Sweetie. Shut. Up," I said, my jaw tight with the effort to hold back the ridiculous sob that was trying to rise from my throat. For one insane second I wished it were Jack here with me instead of Jude. Then sanity reasserted itself. Right now I might see Rawls's taciturnity as a virtue, but it was more than outweighed by his desire to see something sharp and pointy sticking out of my heart. I took a deep breath and straightened up from my bent-over position.

I'd thought I'd come to terms with the possibility that David Crosse had betrayed his family. Obviously I'd been wrong about that. The pain of hearing the truth from Jude was as bad as having one of Rawls's silver nails rip through me, but with one important difference. I could survive this. And not only could I survive the pain, I could use it.

"Be a darling and toss me the bottle of crème de

menthe I saw in your stockpile of booze, would you?"
I requested of Jude in a more even tone than the one I'd
used a moment ago. I turned and caught the squat
missile that arced through the shadows in my direction.
Uncapping it, I took a hefty swig, swished the minty
liquor over my palate a few times, and daintily spat it
out. Then I took a second and smaller sip, letting the
mouthwash-y taste trickle down my throat.

Feeling prepared to join the human race again—
although since I was rejoining Jude, I suppose I should
say the vampire race—I walked back to where he stood
by the mausoleum steps. "Sorry for the interruption.
Where were we? Oh, yes, you'd just told me about
Daddy dearest delivering his family into the hands of
his undead bitch of a mistress. I'm a little shaky on one
detail, though—when Megan's shapeshifting lover
Mikhail did his nifty mind-control thing on my sisters
and me the night Anton showed up in our lives, we
relived the scene in the Carpathian cottage as Grandfather Darkheart had experienced it. I saw Zena trick
Angelica into lowering her guard and at the end I saw
Anton stake Angelica to prevent her from turning vamp
and losing her soul. But before all that I saw David
Crosse's body lying across the cottage threshold." I
raised my eyebrows. "Which doesn't fit with him being
a vamp. I mean, if Angelica staked him when she
realized he'd invited a *vampyr* queen in to kill her, he
would have dusted, no?"

"That's the traditional manner in which we vamps
shuffle off this mortal coil," Jude agreed drily, "not that
it's my favorite image to dwell on. But David wasn't

staked. As Zena told you, Angelica went to her death never knowing for sure that the man she loved had betrayed her. You have to understand," he added, "I wasn't there at the time. And when I found out what had happened, I broke with Zena." He shrugged. "I wish I could say my estrangement from her stemmed from revulsion at her actions, but I'd be giving myself too much credit. I wanted Angelica for myself. I'd lost her to David in life, but I hoped she would choose me over him once she was undead."

"Too much information, sweetie," I said firmly. "As unusual as the situation is, we *are* talking about my mother here. And if there's anything more uncomfortable than discussing one's parents' tangled love life, I don't know what it is, so let's get back to David Crosse. I know vamps can't be knocked unconscious, so I have to assume he was feigning death. Why didn't he simply attack Anton when my grandfather turned his back on him?"

"Because he *had* been knocked out," Jude said with a thin smile, "by Cyrus. You're right, vamps don't go down for the count in a fight with humans, but Kane's an ancient and powerful immortal. Your father wouldn't have stood a chance against him. As for why Kane found it necessary to remove David from the battle against your mother, maybe he worried that a remnant of the man David had once been might surface at an inconvenient moment."

"Like when he saw his wife or his children in peril? Somehow I doubt that was ever a possibility," I said coldly. "Obviously when Daddy dearest turned vamp his humanity was extinguished completely."

"No prizes for guessing how it went for him after that," Jude mused. "He must have come to after your grandfather left with you and your sisters, realized his queen had no more use for him and staggered into the dark a broken man. Being discarded by Zena would have been damnation enough, but presumably he made it official by taking a stake in the heart at some point, according to what you witnessed."

I heard the overlay of doubt in his voice. "You still think I might have been mistaken? How's this for a clincher, sweetie—I not only saw him, he spoke to me. He—" Bile rose again in my throat. "He asked my forgiveness," I said bitterly. "The man betrays his whole family, saddles me with the legacy of turning vamp someday and then thinks he can wipe all that away with a 'Daddy's sorry, honey, I didn't mean for things to turn out like this.' If Megan hadn't killed Zena and released me right at that moment—" I pressed my lips tightly together, pushing down the fragile feeling surging up in me. "Want a good laugh? Despite everything, until tonight I kept hoping there was some other explanation for seeing him in that place. But now I know the facts, I can get on with what I have to do— which is staking the master vamp who set all this in motion. Where does Kane go to ground in the daytime?"

"I wish I knew, dear heart." With another of his charmingly rueful smiles, Jude took a sip of his drink. "Too much *crème de pêche*," he decided out loud. "Given its name, you'd think I'd be able to mix the damned thing perfectly, but I just—"

"Cut the *merde,* sweetie, of course you know," I said a trifle impatiently. "That's what this alliance is all about—you tell me where Kane is and I pay a welcome-to-Maplesburg visit on him with a goodie basket of stakes, garlic and holy water. Unless—" I stopped, suddenly aware that he was standing between me and the granite block and even more aware that my Miu Miu clutch with my stake in it was sitting on said block. Then my glance fell on a chunk of ice beside the silver bucket by the liquor bottles…the chunk of ice, and what was sticking out of it. I took a quick step toward it. "Unless this isn't an alliance," I said coolly. "Unless this whole meeting was for the purpose of setting me up. If that was your plan, sweetie, you shouldn't have brought along a spare weapon for me to use against you."

My hand flashed forward and pulled the lethal-looking silver ice pick from its frozen sheath. I held it in front of me, its wickedly glittering spiked end facing toward him.

Jude lifted an eyebrow at me over the rim of his glass. "You've been hanging around your slayer sister and your bounty-hunting boyfriend too long, Kat. I told you I broke with Zena. Although I've taken care not to let Cyrus Kane know I hate him even more than I did her, he's had his suspicions of me since. Oh, I've worked my way up through the ranks to become one of his closest aides, but I know he doesn't fully trust me—not with information as dangerous as the location of his daytime lair, at least."

"So why did you let me believe you could help?" I exploded. "I mean, under normal circumstances I'm not one to say no to drinkies with an attractive man, but these aren't normal circumstances! I'm about to lose my soul! There's a damn time line here! Thanks to you, I've just wasted hours I don't have only to hear you tell me you don't have a clue—"

"He'd never be caught undead in a place like this," Jude said, cutting through my outburst with unruffled suavity. "You won't find him in a cave or an abandoned well or the cellar of a deserted house, either." He glanced at the marble and granite mausoleum with a deprecating shrug. "I like to think I have my standards, but when it comes to daytime lairs, Cyrus makes my not-so-humble abode look like a squatter's refuge. Look for a deconsecrated church. In a pinch he'll even take up residence in a ruined monastery or a convent, but as far as I know, Maplesburg's history doesn't encompass any former religious communities."

"Would the old fairgrounds on the edge of town count?" I asked weakly. "I think the Baptists used to hold a yearly tent revival there."

"Kane's an ancient. Do you really see him laying low in the fossilized remains of candy corn and Red Hots? No, delectable Kat, the fairgrounds don't count," Jude rejoined drily. "Now, am I back in your good books again? Because if I am, don't you think you should put down that gruesome weapon before someone gets hurt?"

I was still holding the ice pick, I realized in consternation. I let it drop, feeling almost dizzy with gratitude and relief. "You're more than in my good books, sweetie, you're my hero! There can't be that many disused churches in Maplesburg. Why, by this time tomorrow night I might even have staked Kane and lifted the curse, you wonderful, *wonderful* man!"

Words didn't seem adequate thanks. I rushed toward him, my arms flung open to wrap themselves around his neck in a hug, but even as I threw myself against his white dinner jacket I saw Jude's wryly suave expression disappear.

I barely had time to register the look of absolute horror on his face before he shoved me violently away from him.

Chapter 11

My confidence was certainly taking a beating recently. First I'd been treated like Typhoid Mary by the zit-ridden AC/DC, then Jack had failed to be melted by my feminine wiles. Now Jude St. John, by his own admission one of the most dedicated, if undead, playboys of the western world, had thrust me from him as if he were a Puritan elder and I was wearing a big scarlet A on the front of my dress.

As I fell back against our impromptu bar with its crystal bowl of ice and collection of bottles, I had a split second in which to wonder whether I'd missed a memo telling me that the whole male sex had suddenly gone gay overnight. Then I saw something blur through the air in front of me and come to a quivering halt in the old iron-hinged oak door of the mausoleum a few feet away.

It was a stake. And if Jude hadn't pushed me from him as he'd moved with vampiric speed out of its trajectory, the chances were that it would have come to a quivering halt in *moi* instead of the mausoleum's door.

My already shaky legs gave way, and I sat down suddenly on the granite block. The next moment I was on my feet again, feeling like my derriere had just been stung by a dozen furious wasps.

"Enter the bounty-hunting boyfriend." Coming from the edge of the mausoleum's plot, Jude's low tones sounded amused. I turned swiftly to see him melting into the darkness, his dinner jacket and pale blond hair mere glimmers in the guttering candlelight. "Good luck hunting Kane, dear heart. I'll be in touch."

He disappeared into the shadow of a weeping pine tree—and none too soon, at that. I saw a second blur whiz past me, and an instant later the pine's trunk was pierced by the harder wood of a stake.

"Hell."

Even if Jude hadn't already given me a heads-up on the identity of the stake thrower, the toneless expletive could have come from only one person. I whirled around to see Jack about to let fly a third stake.

"Rawls, it's me!" My hands flew up in surrender, but as my skin-tight sheath tugged upward, the pinpricks of agony in my tush intensified. I lowered my hands, had second thoughts on the wisdom of that, and ended up with one hand facing palm out at shoulder height and the other somewhere around waist level. Then I took a deep breath and forced myself to say the most humiliating words I'd ever spoken to a man in my life.

"I appear to have had a little accident involving broken glass, Jack. How good are you with a pair of tweezers and a bottle of antiseptic?"

"One of my exes told me an unofficial vote at the Maplesburg Country Club last summer proclaimed this the most luscious rump ever to be partially covered by a bikini bottom," I said between gritted teeth half an hour later. "Do you know how many men would die to be in your shoes right—*ow!*" I heard a *clink!* as another sliver of crystal dropped into the stainless steel bowl by my averted head, and gasped at the burning sting that followed. When I caught my breath I turned my head to glare at the grim face above me. "Anyone ever tell you your bedside manner sucks, sweetie?"

We were at my apartment, and at first glance an observer could have mistaken the scene for one of the titillating games I adore indulging in as a kind of yummy hors d'oeuvre before getting down to the main course with a man. From my position across Rawls's lap, this game, if it had been a game, would have looked like the "naughty Kat's getting a spanking" variation.

Unfortunately, it wasn't a game. Yes, I was lying face down across Jack as he sat on my sofa, and yes, my dress was hiked up and the back of my panties hiked down, displaying my booty, but even I was having a hard time finding anything yummy about having shards of broken cocktail glass removed from my butt before having disinfectant splashed on the punctures. And I couldn't fool myself that Jack was getting the least bit turned on by his task, either. Sprawled across him as I was, I'd have been the first to notice any sign of interest, and so far the man had shown all the reaction of an Easter Island statue.

"I don't have a bedside manner when it comes to you, Crosse." As if to confirm my assessment of his non-raised pulse, eyes as green and cold as pack-ice flicked with no interest to my face before returning with even less interest to that part of my anatomy he was picking glass from. "You might not be on my official hit list yet, but from what I saw at the mausoleum you've got no problem fraternizing with the enemy. I'm still not convinced you weren't involved with that fake abduction tonight."

I hissed in a breath as he extracted another piece of glass. "I've told you, I only learned Jude had *glamyred* Liz when he told me. Before this evening I'd never even met the man."

"That doesn't fit with the scenario I interrupted," Jack said tersely. "The two of you had been having one hell of a time together, judging from the candles and the booze and the way you were about to throw yourself at him when I showed up. Add in the fact that this outfit isn't what you were wearing earlier, which means you must have gone home to dress up for your date with the bastard, and I'd say your whole damn story's a lie. Hand me another bandage, this cut's still bleeding."

I resisted the impulse to hurl the box of bandages at him. "I've told you the truth, Jack," I said, conveniently not mentioning that I hadn't told him the *whole* truth. "Jude's reference to the Charles River made it clear he'd been on the Harvard rowing team with my father.

When I put that together with the sad story Grammie's often mentioned about the St. John family dying out after their son and heir was killed while skiing in Europe, I decided to pay a visit to the cemetery. I mean, even though his body was never found, I figured the mausoleum was the nearest thing to home he had in Maplesburg, no? As for being charming to him, surely you've heard the one about catching more flies with honey than vinegar....or maybe you haven't. Sorry, for a minute I forgot who I was talking to. But, anyway, I wanted information from him about my father—information I might have gotten if you hadn't barged in and started throwing stakes when you did. Which reminds me," I added, "why weren't you using your nail gun?"

"Because your nonslayer sister took it upon herself to use it without asking me and she jammed it. Then your cocktail-swilling sidekick tried to fix it and spilled his drink on the belt mechanism," he replied, tossing a shard of glass into the steel bowl with so much force it almost ricocheted out again. "Lucky for them your other sister phoned to call off the hunt and tell us the Dixon woman had shown up safe and sound, because I was a heartbeat away from leaving Ramon and Tashya to get home by themselves." Roughly he affixed the adhesive bandage on my left butt cheek. I was about to renew my protests against his none-too-gentle treatment when all of a sudden I felt an intriguingly different sensation from the manhandling I'd been receiving so far.

The tips of Jack's fingers drifted over my skin, sending an immediate rush of heat tingling through me. A moment later I felt his palms lightly skimming the curves presenting themselves to him above the ruched-down strip of chartreuse silk panties I was barely wearing. At the feel of his hard carpenter's hands I felt my control slipping deliciously away.

"Mmm…" I purred in pleased surprise. "S'nice, sweetie. I feel like a pampered Persian cat getting stroked in all the right places. I always suspected that despite your big act about not being attracted to me, sooner or later you just wouldn't be able to hold out against my particular brand of sizzling appeal—" His hand halted. The next second the cold steel of the tweezers painfully pinched my derriere, and I gave a startled squawk. "Ouch! What the hell, Jack!"

His palm passed briskly over me one last time. "I can't feel any more glass," he informed me with all the enthusiasm of a horse dealer allowing that the nag he was inspecting might be acceptable for the glue factory. "Get up. We need to talk."

Okay, darlings, here's the not-so-sweet and lowdown on the fabulous Kat Crosse: occasionally I can feel just a *smidge* insecure. Oh, I know my reputation as a heartbreaker who just has to crook her little finger to get men to fall all over themselves, and for the most part it's all true. Which is good for me. Because without that constant validation, I might find myself remembering what it felt like to be little Katherine Crosse, who used to wonder why all the other children she knew had parents while mine had loved me so little that they'd disappeared from my life.

Eventually, of course, Katherine grew up to be Kat and learned she could get all the love and adoration she wanted just by turning on the charm and turning up the heat when she was with a man. And eventually that feeling of insecurity went away…or if not completely, at least I managed to forget it most of the time.

But lately it had begun to come back. Lately I'd been feeling more and more like unlovable little Katherine and less like fabulous Kat. Mostly that was due to the dismal fact that with every passing day I was getting closer to becoming one of the scourge of the earth, shunned and feared by the whole human race, but Jack's attitude was the final straw.

He *couldn't* be impervious to sex-goddess Kat, I thought as a cold feeling I tried to tell myself was anger trickled down my spine. Because if he rejected her, all that was left was Katherine…and Katherine didn't have anything *any*body wanted—

Before the terrifying thought could be completed I ruthlessly blotted it out with my most languid drawl. "Of course, sweetie, but before we talk I think there's one last sliver on my upper right thigh." I felt his hand slide up my leg and raised my tush a little. "Not there, higher…and more to the inside."

He paused. Then his palm skimmed to where the swell of my derriere met the top of my thigh before stopping again. I glanced over my shoulder to see his eyes narrow on me, and I gave him my best wide-eyed look. "It's driving me *crazy*," I breathed huskily. "Be my hero and do your best to relieve it, would you, Jack?"

The Kat was back. Even before Rawls broke off eye contact with me and I felt his hand move slowly up my inner thigh, I knew I had him. He'd put up a tough fight.

He'd even made me begin to doubt myself, a feat no other male had ever come close to accomplishing, but my doubts had been ridiculous. Sliding into vamphood I might well be, but the fabulous Kat Crosse had made another conquest.

The fears that had been pressing in on me a moment ago subsided and I gave myself over to the absolutely dreamy sensations Jack's touch was starting to arouse in me.

"Silk." The single word came from him in a taut mutter. A small smile curved my lips and I let my legs accidentally-on-purpose move slightly apart as I turned my head and peered at him through a strand of my hair.

"Wazzat, sweetie?" Before he could answer I went on in a steamy sigh, "Mmm-hmm, that's close to where it must be. Just a smidgen higher, darling."

"Your skin. It's like silk." His growl hoarsened as his fingers slid upward between my parted thighs. Through my hair I saw a muscle jump in his jaw. "I don't feel any glass slivers, Crosse. I don't feel anything except…" His voice came to a gravelly stop but his hand kept moving.

"Except what?" Interesting things were happening to me. My breath had a hitch in it, someone seemed to be lightly trailing a feather duster up and down my spine and my toes kept wanting to curl. Something interesting was happening to Jack, too, I noted from my vantage point across his lap. "You don't feel anything except what, sweetie?" I breathed.

"Except you." The words sounded dragged from him. "Anyone ever tell you that when your hair's falling down over your shoulders like that it looks liked spilled cream, Crosse?"

His breath had a noticeable hitch in it to match the one in mine, but I barely registered that fact. My status as an impartial observer was rapidly eroding as Jack's palm slid fully between my legs and his thumb began moving in a slow circular motion—although I wasn't so over the edge as to tell him that every man I'd ever flirted with had come up with the platinum-blond hair/spilled cream comparison. "Not that I recall." My lie came out on a shuddering sigh. "I *adore* the way you play doctor, sweetie. Maybe not the tweezers and anti-septic part, but what you're doing now is...is..."

A wave of pleasure crested in me, cutting off my sentence with a gasp. The next moment I felt myself being deftly flipped over onto my back and Jack was straddling me, his palm still between my thighs while a series of tingling tremors ran through me. He lowered his mouth to mine. I had a split-second glimpse of sexily smoldering green behind dark spiky lashes, another split second to wonder how I ever could have thought his gaze was cold, and then he was kissing me.

Nice girls don't kiss and tell. I, on the other hand, firmly believe that one of the many perks of a hot and heavy makeout session is the female's inalienable right to dish all the down and dirty details to other females afterward. And believe me, sweeties, Rawls knew how to get down and deliciously dirty.

For starters, his tongue was as sinfully talented as his demonstration with the cherry stem had promised. Now, I love a superb kiss as much as the next girl, but normally I see it as part of the tantalizing preliminaries before one moves on to the truly earthshaking stages of a romp between the sheets. Less than a minute into Jack's kiss, however, I found myself hoping it would last all night.

His mouth took mine like a Viking raider pillaging a village. Or maybe it was more like a pirate seizing a galleon. Whichever it was, I felt immediately and deliciously *ravished,* and briefly wished I had a bodice so he could rip it. Then I stopped thinking altogether in order to give myself over to the heat-lightning sensations Jack's wickedly adept tongue and his hard and busy hand were coaxing from me.

One moment his mouth was completely covering mine and his tongue was going deep, while his hand did the same in its own chosen area of my anatomy. The next minute he would catch me off balance by withdrawing. Even as I arched upward to keep his fingers and mouth where they were, his tongue would begin tracing the inner curve of my lips and his hand would unerringly find the spot I fondly think of as my speed-release button—you know, the one that too many men don't seem to know how to locate on a girl, let alone manipulate properly.

Jack knew how to manipulate every inch of me. He knew how to bring me to the edge of quivering ecstasy and how to retreat, leaving me sinking my teeth into my bottom lip in a vain attempt to hang on to some shred of control. At a point I realized that the sinking-my-teeth-into-my-lip thing wasn't working, and the next time he left me shuddering and gasping on the tantalizing rim of nirvana I blindly bit down on his shoulder to relieve my frustrations.

If I'd thought about it I might have held back. The man bounty hunted vamps, so one might assume he had a phobia about being bitten no matter how swept up in the moment he was. But from his harshly indrawn breath and the sudden flush that heated his granite cheekbones, my tiny nip was doing for him what he'd been doing for me. Psychologists can use labels like "the pleasure/pain principle," but what it really comes down to is that a teensy bit of sexual antagonism can be *trés* titillating. That's why makeup sex is so good.

But Jack and I weren't having makeup sex, we were having adversary sex. Even as our tongues teased each other and we wrestled off articles of our clothing while still groping each other, I knew our basic relationship hadn't changed. When I kicked him out in an hour or two we'd still be Kat and her junkyard dog, hissing and growling whenever we met. I wanted to prove to him that I could bring him to his knees whenever I set my mind to it. He was trying to prove to himself that he could bed the notorious Kat Crosse and still remain in control of the situation. What we both forgot was that sex is an elemental force, like fire…and like fire, when you use it against someone else, you're both liable to end up getting burned.

Which was exactly what happened.

There we were, Rawls and *moi,* pushing each other closer and closer to the point of spontaneous combustion. He'd pulled my dress over my head and had flung it halfway across the room, leaving me clad only in panties and bra and a particularly spicy garter belt, its exquisite embroidery trim depicting some of the more eyebrow-raising poses from the *Kama Sutra*. I'd shoved his khaki-colored tee upward past his washboard abs and rock-hard pecs and was doing something interesting with the tip of my tongue against the fine line of dark hair that led from the top of his rib cage to where it was obscured by his Levi's. Deciding that I was ready to unobscure that line of hair and everything else the Levi's were hiding, I lifted my mouth from his stomach for a moment while my fingers deftly worked the zipper of his jeans. Giving him my most sultry under-the-lashes look, I spoke the fatal words that blew straight to hell both Jack's and my chances for getting some that night.

"After all you've said about not sleeping with vamps I was beginning to think we were never going to do the dire deed together, sweetie," I purred as I slid his zipper halfway down. It stuck, not through any fault in its manufacture but because it was under a certain amount of strain, which I took as a promise of things to come. I went on, tugging the zip downward. "I'm thrilled you've changed your attitude. Even on our first date when you were busy nailing me to my car door and I was busy knocking you unconscious I had the feeling that a one-night stand with you could be a truly special—"

"I haven't changed my attitude about sleeping with vamps, Crosse." Spoken as they were against the skin of my neck, Jack's words were muffled and I wondered if I'd heard him right.

"Of course you have, sweetie," I informed him, giving his zipper an impatient jerk and feeling it slide free. "I mean, in a minute or two we're going to be rocking each other's world, no? Maybe you stalwart Nebraskans have another term for it, but here in Maplesburg that constitutes sleeping with each other. And since nothing's happened to convince you I'm not turning into a vampire, you've obviously set aside your prejudices against me."

His hands slid down my shoulders and his thumbs slipped under the lace of my bra to my nipples. "I'm still prejudiced against sex with vamps. The only thing that's changed is my opinion about whether or not you're turning into one. I think I was wrong about that."

Okay, pop quiz time, sweeties. Can any of you tell me the words that every red-blooded female desperately yearns to hear from a man? No, not, "I love you." Not, "That outfit makes you look way too slim, honey." Not even, "Take these away, doesn't Tiffany's have any higher carat diamonds?" although that runs a pretty close second in my personal estimation. But the phrase we all long to hear from the male sex and hardly ever do has to be, "I was wrong." Those words had just come out of Rawls's mouth. And at the risk of being drummed out of the sisterhood, sweeties, I have to confess that I almost didn't notice.

In my own defence, I was a smidge preoccupied, what with feeling all melty and shaken by the whirlpools of pleasure Jack's circling thumbs were creating on my peaked nipples. When he flicked the tip of his tongue under the frill of Chantilly lace edging my bra, miniorgasms exploded like tiny depth charges along all my synapses. But some part of my female radar must have remained vigilant despite the champagnelike static fizzing through my brain, because in the brief moment that he raised his head from the left side of my cleavage to pay equal attention to my right, I managed to rouse myself enough to utter a faint, "Whazzat, sweetie?"

"Wrong about...*ahh!*...you being vamp..."

Jack's words were even more disjointed than mine, being partially obliterated as they were by his indrawn breath as my hand slid under the waistband of his briefs to resume my determined exploration of the arrow of hair I'd traced down his abdomen. As my fingertips sunk into the crisp triangle of curls on his groin I felt as dizzy with triumph as de Soto must have when he discovered the Mississippi Delta, and for a moment Jack's reply went right over my head. Or perhaps it went over my head because I was in the process of lowering my mouth to that part of Jack that had been so naughtily responsible for putting a strain on his jeans until I'd released it. The fingers of my right hand curled delicately but securely around him—the right amount of firmness in a girl's grip can be the difference between a marathon of ecstasy and an embarrassingly speedy end to the festivities, I've found—my lips closed over velvet-wrapped rigidity, and my lashes fluttered shut in anticipation as I began to sink down on him.

Wrong about me being a vamp?

My eyes snapped open and I jerked my head up. My grip tightened convulsively, I heard Jack give another indrawn hiss of breath but this time with no pleasure behind it, and I let go of him. I stared at him. *"What* did you say?"

A moment ago his gaze had been the same smoky-green as the core of a flaring match flame. Even as our eyes held I saw his take on their usual hard look. "Hell," he said without emphasis, breaking off his gaze to glance downward as he yanked up the fly of his Levi's more recklessly than I'd unzipped it. A quick wince crossed his shuttered features. "Why couldn't I have kept my mouth shut until afterward," he said as he took a thin breath. He gave me one of those streetfighter grins of his that held no humor. "I said I don't think you're a vamp, Crosse. You want an apology for me nearly nailing you the first time we met, fine, I apologize."

His offhand tone had the same effect on me as if he'd just rolled a live grenade toward my feet. The last wisps of erotic fogginess dissipated from my brain and I exploded. "How about an apology for nearly nailing me now, Rawls," I demanded in tight fury. "If you've learned something, your first priority should have been letting me in on the secret, not taking time out for a quickie! How was this supposed to play out, anyway—wham, bam, thank you ma'am, and oh, by the way, you might not be losing your immortal soul in the forseeable future?"

"Just as an aside, lady, a quickie isn't what I had in mind," Jack said, his jaw tight. "And the way I remember it, you were the one doing the bare-assed lap dance that started everything, anyway."

If any men are reading this, here's a newsflash,

sweeties: there's a time and place for cold, hard reason, and the middle of an argument isn't it. That Jack was right and I'd gone to some lengths to seduce him was totally irrelevant in the grand scheme of things. The fact that I would have been almost as furious if he *had* done the noble thing and resisted my overtures was equally irrelevant. It was a lose/lose situation for him, and he was going to have to take it like a man.

Too bad for him that I had no intention of dishing it out like a girl.

I hauled off and socked him a good one in the jaw. Or at least that was my intention, but just before my fist made contact Jack jerked his head backward. It was enough so that my punch didn't land with the round-house strength I'd learned in my vamp-fighting sessions with Darkheart, but it wasn't enough to save him completely. My knuckles made awkward contact with his jawbone, his head snapped farther back, and I felt a white-hot bolt shoot up my arm as the nerve I'd hit in my hand sent its message of zinging pain all the way to my elbow.

"Dammit, Jack, why'd you move!" I realized how ridiculous my question was as soon as I asked it, but I didn't care. I cradled my forearm and wondered how long it would keep zinging. "What kind of ungallant jerk ducks a girl's punch, anyway?"

"A smart one," he growled, massaging his jaw. The laser-green of his glare could have melted plutonium. "Thanks for bringing me to my senses, Crosse. Vamp or not, getting it on with you would have been the stupidest move I ever made."

"Getting it on with me would have been the luckiest move you ever made," I informed him heatedly, "but you blew it, Rawls. The good ship Kat has sailed without you, and if you think you're ever going to get a chance at a second boarding pass, forget it. Now, dish—what makes you think I might not be turning vamp?"

He shook his head. "No, we're playing this my way. I want a confirmation of my theory before I talk to you about it."

"A confirmation from whom?" I demanded in exasperation. "Darkheart? Megan? Aside from Mikhail, they're the only vamp authorities in Maplesburg, and they don't—"

"I've got a contact in town who specializes in dealing with the dead…and the undead," he said with thin patience.

"A specialist?" My exasperation faded. "And you think he can take one look at me and know whether I carry Zena's curse or not?" I suddenly realized I was still clad only in my panties and bra and *Kama Sutra* garter belt. Hastily I crossed the room to where my dress lay on the floor. "What are we waiting for? Let's go see him now," I said, my voice muffled as I pulled the skin-tight sheath over my head.

"He's not a he, he's a she. She's a witch."

Something in the clipped tone of Jack's voice caught my attention, and as I shimmied the dress over my hips I darted a sidelong glance at him. The faint flush along his cheekbones that I'd noticed earlier had returned, and as he saw me watching him it deepened. He turned abruptly, averting his gaze from me.

I hid a small smile. Rawls had done his damnedest to convince himself he was immune to me, but just watching me get dressed was getting him all hot and bothered again. Maybe after we'd seen his old witch lady—warts, pointy hat and all—I'd change my mind about giving him a second chance. Until then, I didn't see any reason why I should make things easy for him.

"Be a darling and zip me, will you, sweetie?" I purred, presenting my back to him. I lifted my hair from the nape of my neck in a pinup girl pose and half turned my face to him. "What's the old dear's name? And how do you know her, anyway?"

My ploy was working, I saw. As Jack moved unwillingly toward me and his hands moved to the zipper of my dress, the hard color under his cheekbones deepened. He looked the very picture of a man who was trying not to let his erotic imaginings run wild, I decided smugly.

My smugness disappeared with his next words... and so did my assumptions as to whom he was erotically imagining.

"Her name's Esmerelda, and she's not old, she's in her twenties. As for how I know her, that's simple," Rawls said in a husky voice. "She's my ex."

Chapter 12

She was Jack's ex. She was also beautiful, passionate, sexy and still acted as if she had a claim on him. What else can I say about La Esmerelda, sweeties? Oh, yes— she was a jealous bitch.

And around her my junkyard dog turned into a big, slobbering puppy.

Of course, I didn't know all this when Jack parked the vampmobile in front of a dingy little storefront in a part of Maplesburg I'd never seen before, but even on the drive from my apartment I'd started to get a *trés mauvais* feeling about the upcoming encounter. As any experienced female knows, when a man talks freely about another woman, she's probably just a friend. It's when you have to drag every scrap of information out of him that your radar should go on high alert.

Getting Jack to talk about Esmerelda was like pulling teeth.

"Your ex-what, exactly? Ex-girlfriend? Ex-wife?" I asked as we got into his car. "Your ex-steady from high school?"

"Wife." He pulled out from the curb with a squeal of tires and clamped his mouth shut.

I pried harder. "So how long have the two of you been divorced?"

"Two years." In the illumination from passing street-lights I saw his hands tense on the steering wheel.

I felt a little tense myself. "*Merde,* Jack, stop acting as if you've got lockjaw and tell me about the woman who's going to give me a thumbs-up or a thumbs-down in a few minutes! Do you trust her? Does she know you're in Maplesburg? Is she really a witch?"

"She's really a witch," he said curtly, "and when it comes to her professional integrity, yes, I trust her. She knows I'm in Maplesburg because she followed me here. It's not the first time since our divorce she's shown up in the same town I'm in." He tromped down on the brakes as we came to a red light. "It's not how you think, Crosse. Esmie and I got married in a quickie ceremony in Vegas. Within a week we knew we'd made a mistake and got an even quicker Reno divorce. She doesn't show up where I am because she wants me back, she shows up because I'm usually where there's a lot of vamp activity."

For Rawls it was practically a speech, but I wasn't reassured. Two things struck me about what he'd said. First, he'd called her Esmie, and pet names are always a sure sign the ashes aren't dead. And if you're wondering why I cared, sweeties, the answer's simple: I didn't. As I'd told Jack, that ship had sailed, and I'd decided that Tash had had a point when she'd said she preferred men she could kiss at the end of a date to men she had to slug.

But in another way, I *did* care. For now, Jack was mine: my partner, my ally, my chance at a Get Out Of Hell Free card. I didn't want him distracted by a blast from his past—especially a blast from his past who presumably had the skills to toss together some eye of newt, a pinch of dried toad and a spoonful of graveyard moss to make a love spell that would bring her exhubbie back to her.

Because that was the other thing he'd said that didn't ring true to me. Rawls wasn't dumb. The way he'd read me a couple of times had actually been unsettlingly intuitive, for a mere male. But even the smartest men can turn into big lugs when it comes to women they once had a soft spot for, and I was willing to bet my newest pair of Manolos that's what was happening here. Esmerelda kept showing up where Jack was? I couldn't believe that was coincidence. I also couldn't believe it was because he was her vamp barometer. No, she obviously wanted him back in her bed again, I thought as we pulled up to the curb and Jack cut the car's motor. And since women *weren't* big lugs when it came to their exes, Esmerelda was going take one look at Kat Crosse and know I'd had my claws in the man she still considered her private preserve.

Which all added up to the *trés mauvais* feeling I've

already mentioned. I hadn't yet laid eyes on the woman,
and already I was probably her sworn enemy. I suddenly
wished I'd thought to strap a handy little flask of something alcoholic to my garter belt before we'd set out on
this doomed mission.

No sooner had the thought crossed my mind than
Jack reached past me, opened the glove box and retrieved a squat bottle. He uncapped it, put it to his lips
and took a healthy slug of its contents. The ambrosial
scent of bourbon wafted past my nostrils and I quivered
to attention like a gun dog scenting grouse.

"Just in case you've got the wrong idea, I don't drink
and drive," he said briefly. "But I don't always have holy
water in stock, and alcohol's the next best thing for
cleaning wounds. And there's always a good chance of
getting wounded around Esmie," he added with a
grimace, starting to cap the bottle.

"In other words, you need some liquid courage
before facing your ex-wife," I said, reaching for the
bourbon. "I'm totally down with that, sweetie. I could
use some, too."

Green eyes flicked my way. "Nix on that, Crosse. I
told you, I don't work with boozehounds, and from
what I saw tonight at that mausoleum, St. John kept the
drinks coming and you kept downing them. Ever
thought of quitting?"

Even as he spoke he dropped the bottle into the glove
box. He slammed it shut and chose a key from the ring
in his hand. As I watched, speechless, he locked the
small compartment.

My voice returned. "Quitting, Jack?" I repeated with

acid sweetness. "You mean as in pretending I have a problem and doing something about it? The only snag with that is I *don't* have a problem. A sociable cocktail or two with friends, maybe a teensy nightcap before toddling off to bed, occasionally some wine with dinner. That hardly makes me a card-carrying friend of Bill W, it just means I enjoy the finer pleasures in—"

"A friend of Bill W?" he cut in as he got out of the car and waited for me to do the same. "So you know the AA lingo. See, Crosse, that makes me think you've dropped in on a meeting or two in the past."

"So what if I have, sweetie?" I shot back. "Some of my best friends have taken the pledge, it's only natural I'd take an interest. But AA's for people who want to quit drinking and can't. If I wanted to, I could quit just like that."

We were standing in front of a tiny store's door. Dismissing the subject of my alcohol intake with an airy snap of my fingers, I peered through the dirty glass at the dark interior. I stood back and read the stick-on letters on the door.

"Herbal Remedies and Palm Reading," I said, unimpressed. "You sure this is the right place, Rawls? I mean, would a legitimate witch have to stoop to reading palms for a living?" I shrugged. "And whoever the proprietor is, she's obviously closed for the night."

"This is the place." He reached into the back pocket of his jeans and extracted a small piece of metal.

It looked oddly recognizable, and as he began to insert it into the door's lock I stopped him. "Is that my—" My hand on his wrist, I bent down to examine the object he was holding. I gave a delighted smile. "Why, Jack, you care. That's the hairpin you took from me the night we met, isn't it? And to think you've been carrying around a memento of that magical evening ever since!"

I released his hand. Without replying to my banter he slid the pin into the ancient-looking Yale lock on the door and started twisting it. Jude would have responded, I thought in irritation. Not only would he have responded, he probably would have handed me a cocktail while he traded quips with me. Vamp or not, he was a lot more fun than Rawls, and although I'd had second and third thoughts about keeping his information about Kane to myself, Jack's attitude right now proved I'd made the right decision.

The man was way too rigid. He'd never believe that a vampire might want to do the right thing and help take down a master of evil. He'd dismiss Jude's information about Kane's prediliction for abandoned churches as daytime hiding places, insist that it must be a trap, and before I knew it the two of us would be embroiled in one of our now-familiar arguments. Of course, if he was right and I wasn't in danger of turning vamp myself soon, I wouldn't have to stake Kane in order to save my own soul, I thought as I watched him maneuver the pin back and forth in the lock. But that wasn't a given. I wanted to believe Jack had found some loophole in the Zena curse, but the more I thought about it, the less likely it seemed. My flesh had started to burn in the sunlight. Staking vamps was torture to me. And Claudia's blood-soaked world had called to me with a seduction I'd barely been able to resist.

All of a sudden I needed a cocktail so badly I could almost taste the crisp jolt of vodka on my tongue, the complementary tang of some exotic fruit juice, the yummy splash of liqueur tying the whole scrumptious concoction together.

"Like hell you can, Crosse."

At Rawls's laconic comment my tantalizing vision of a glass brimming with something pale and frothy and delicious popped like a bubble. I ran my tongue across my lips and saw that he'd been successful in jimmying the lock. I frowned. "Like hell I can what?"

"Quit just like that." He slipped the hairpin into his back pocket. "You're hooked. You like to dress your drinks up with fancy names and recipes, but you'd chug down a bottle of Thunderbird if that's all you could get your hands on. Fool yourself if you want, Crosse, but don't try to con me. I know what you are." He swung the door open. "Esmie probably already knows we're here. She likes making an entrance. When she does, let me do the talking."

"Hold on a minute, Rawls!" I said, swiftly grabbing the nearest available part of him, which happened to be his upper arm. I felt his right bicep tighten like steel, but for once the feel of male muscle didn't conjure up a little thrill in me. "Get one thing straight—I'm *not* hooked. I happen to enjoy a cocktail once in a while, but if I decided to go on the wagon for whatever reason I wouldn't feel the slightest twinge."

"So prove it." Rawls's grin actually held humor for once. "Go cold turkey for three days, starting now. I'll bet you can't do it."

It was the grin that did it for me. "You're on," I said
coldly. "And just to show you how sure I am that I
won't lose this bet, let's make the stakes interesting. If
you win, I'll sign the club over to you. If I win, you
contact the Nebraska authorities and turn yourself in."

Rawls hesitated, but only for a second. "Fair
enough." He nodded at the darkened doorway. "Ready
to meet Esmie?"

I didn't move. "What's to stop me from taking a nip
or two on the sly?" I demanded. "There's a lot on the
line here for both of us and you're not with me twenty-
four hours a day, Jack. Aren't you worried I'll cheat?"

I was still furious he'd held back information from
me. I hadn't forgiven him for the throbbing tingle in my
arm. And now I had a fresh grievance against Jack—I
was beginning to suspect I'd been maneuvered into this
insane bet and I was already wondering how I was
going to get through the next three days without a teensy
pick-me-up now and then. But at his next action, all my
anger at him melted temporarily away.

He smiled at me. It wasn't one of his junkyard dog
grins, it was a real smile—faint, but real. And with a
movement so brief I might have imagined it, Jack Rawls
reached out and roughly touched my hair. "You play too
many games, you irritate me more than anyone else
I've ever known and you're a spoiled princess. You're
also honest enough to tell the rest of the world to go to
hell rather than violate your own code. Whatever else
you are, you're no cheat, Kat."

For a heartbeat our eyes locked. In his right iris I saw
the fleck of hazel I'd noticed before, like a flake of gold

on emerald. I opened my mouth to make some remark, realized I didn't want to hear my own voice and sensed his stance subtly shift toward me. I felt a strange fluttering in my stomach that wasn't anything like the usual lazy heat I experienced when I knew a man was about to kiss me.

I acted fast.

"Sweetie, you've finally broken down and called me by my first name!" I cried, stepping quickly back and slanting a come-hither look at him through my lashes. "I'll simply *have* to write this all down in my diary so I can remember it forever. First, however, there's the little matter of meeting the former Mrs. Rawls, no?"

I swept past him into the shadowy store, my heart pounding so loudly in my chest that I was sure he could hear it. What had happened to me just now? Was it possible that I'd actually been all a-tremble like some virginal schoolgirl, and over a possible *kiss?* A kiss, moreover, from a man whose hands had been all over me earlier tonight, a man I'd come this close to having rock-'em-sock-'em sex with?

I needed to get away from him, I told myself shakily. I needed to get away from him *now,* and damn the consequences. This mission was a bust, anyway. The woman we'd come to see obviously wasn't here and after a few minutes of blundering around in the dark even Rawls would have to admit—

A dim light at the far end of the room suddenly went on. I received a momentary impression of dusty glass containers on the shelves lining the cramped space and a counter in front of me jumbled with junk, and then a movement caught my attention. A few feet away from Rawls and me was a narrow staircase presumably leading to living quarters over the store, and at the top of the staircase stood a woman.

Now, it takes a lot to shake the fabulous Kat Crosse's self-confidence, sweeties. God and L'Oréal blessed me with gentlemen-prefer-blond hair, I still have all my own teeth and I fill out a Narciso Rodriguez bustier dress quite nicely, thank you. Add in my trademark simmering sexiness and you can understand why sudden attacks of insecurity aren't a problem with *moi*...or at least, they weren't before I met Esmerelda the witch.

She looked like one of those earthy Italian movie stars—all pouting red lips and tumbling black hair and flawless olive skin. Her crimson satin blouse was unbuttoned enough to show a tantalizing amount of spilling cleavage, and instead of being tucked into her low-riding jeans, the tails of the blouse were cinched around her nipped-in waist. Huge hoop earrings swung nearly to her shoulders, strappy Jimmy Choo sandals showed off carmine-painted toenails, and her dark eyes were made darker and more enormous with an expert lining of kohl pencil.

And then she opened her mouth and the Monica Bellucci image was immediately replaced by Adrianna—may she rest in peace—of *The Sopranos*.

"You effin' prick, Jackie! You borrow my Camaro, strip the damn transmission and leave me with the bill, and then you got the nerve to show up here where you're not invited? You got till I count to three to get the hell out of my store before I turn you into the snake you are, you bastard! One!" Swiftly she began to descend the stairs, her eyes flashing with fury. "Two!" She reached the bottom of the stairs and stood in front of Rawls, her hands planted on her lushly curved hips. "Thr—" Abruptly she broke off her count. "Who's *she?*"

She gave me a quick, suspicious look before turning her blazing gaze back on Rawls. To my surprise, he didn't seem put out by her attitude.

"Kat, this is Esmie. Esmie, Kat Crosse," he said laconically. "About the Camaro," he began, but the former Mrs. Rawls didn't let him finish.

"I know, I know," she said with a sudden sexy pout. "You didn't have a choice, it was either heist my car or those damn vamps woulda gotten you. But you still owe me for the tranny and the tow back to the garage after you ditched it in that Iowa field. You coulda dropped me a note, Jackie. I know we're not married anymore, but I still care."

Her pout became a kissy mouth. She twined her arms around Jack's neck and closed her eyes expectantly.

"You care because I'm a good source for vamp dust and you get big bucks selling it over the Internet to voodoo practitioners. Did you really have to pay to have the Camaro worked on?" Jack untwined her arms from around his neck and stepped away from her.

For a moment I thought Esmerelda was going to explode again, but then she turned with a flounce and walked behind the store's counter. She hit a key on the cash register that popped open the drawer, extracted a pack of cigarettes and shrugged. "Okay, so I used a spell on the garage guy to fix it for free. How come you're here, Jackie?" Sticking a cigarette between her lips, she popped her thumbnail against her index finger. I blinked in surprise as a bright yellow flame shot from her thumb. As she lit her cigarette she flicked a glance at me and then back at Jack. "Girlfriend trouble?" she asked, expelling a plume of smoke. "You want me to turn her into something?"

I waved the smoke away from my face and decided it was time I joined in the discussion. "I'm not your ex's girlfriend, sweetie," I told her, "and he doesn't want me turned into something. Just the opposite, in fact. I'm here because Jack's got a theory I might *not* be turning into what I thought I was turning into."

This time Esmerelda's gaze on me wasn't dismissively quick. She looked me up and down before taking another drag off her cigarette and stubbing it out in a glass dish shaped like a pentagram.

"You think you're turning vamp?" she asked, suddenly businesslike. "We're talking a curse here, right? I mean, it's not a case of you getting bitten a couple of nights ago, is it?"

"We're talking getting bitten by a queen *vampyr* when I was a baby," I said, finding myself liking her more now she'd dropped the attitude. "The curse was that I'd turn vamp myself in my twenty-first year." I tried to smile, but it felt more like a grimace. "And seeing as how I turned twenty-one a while ago and lately I've noticed symptoms of approaching vamp-hood, I think it's safe to say the curse is beginning to kick in. For some mysterious reason that he won't divulge, however, Jack doesn't agree."

"A reason he won't—" Esmerelda turned to Rawls like an avenging virago. "Whatsa matter with you, Jackie? If you know something, tell the girl! Can't you see she's falling apart, you jerk?"

"That's why we're here." Jack didn't seem to mind being reamed out by her. In fact, he seemed willing to cut Esmerelda a lot more slack than he'd ever done for me. He gave her a wry smile and his gaze held none of its usual hardness as he looked at her. "There's no use floating my theory until you tell us for sure whether or not Kat's turning, Esmie. I know you can do it, because you did it for me once."

"With Boots, after you got slashed by that vamp and needed to know whether you'd been infected." She bit her bottom lip. "But Jackie, Bootsie died a couple of months ago. He was a pretty old cat, you know. I've got a new familiar now, and I'm not sure it's such a good idea to try this conjure with Mabel."

I put up a hand. "Hold on, sweeties—a *cat's* supposed to give me a pass or a fail on this particular test? How does that work, exactly?"

"You lie on the floor and the cat explores your aura," Jack said with thin patience. "While it does, Esmie's mind is linked to its mind, and she interprets what the cat's reading from you."

"*If* you're using a cat," Esmerelda clarified. "The conjure works with any kind of animal, so the familiar isn't really the problem. Where you sometimes run into a snag is in the subject's reaction to the animal being used." She shrugged. "But Jackie's right, it's the only way to know for sure. If you want to go through with this, let's do it. Lie down and I'll whistle for Mabel. She's a little shy with strangers, so she's probably hiding."

I hesitated, not liking the sound of "shy with strangers." "She's not a scratcher, is she?"

Esmerelda's kohl-rimmed eyes rested on me. "After this is over, hon, remind me to loan you some pancake makeup to cover up that love mark on your chest. Your guy must be a wild man in the sack, huh?" she said thoughtfully. She seemed to recollect herself. "No, Mabel's not a scratcher. She'll probably take to you right away. Get comfortable and let me do my stuff now."

Reassured, I sat down. As Jack leaned against the wall, his arms crossed and his demeanor calm, I relaxed further and stretched out full-length on the floor. With her backfield-in-motion walk, Esmerelda had crossed to one of the shelves by the counter, and as I lay prone she came back to me, uncapping the glass vial she was holding.

A thin ribbon of purple smoke immediately began rising from the open vial. I opened my mouth to ask Esmerelda what it was and how she intended to use it, but as I looked up at her face my question died in my throat.

The sexy and garrulous Jersey girl had gone. In her place was a woman whose hard beauty shifted into cronelike ugliness and then to beauty again. Through the purple smoke I could still see her crimson blouse and jeans, but when the smoke wavered I thought I saw a torn and tattered black garment instead. The smoke wavered again and the jeans and blouse were back.

All of a sudden I knew I'd made a big mistake. Oh, I'd believed Esmerelda was a witch, all right, but I'd been thinking modern witch. I'd been thinking Wiccan and goddess power and female bonding, and I'm not sure I hadn't vaguely thrown in the Red Hat Society, as well. But the woman standing over me with the smoke-filled vial wasn't anything as benign or harmless as that.

Esmerelda was a witch. Her kind had once been burned at the stake and had filled fairy tales with real fear. Her kind definitely *weren't* to be screwed with...and I'd just put myself into her hands.

"Uh, you know what, sweetie?" Like her cigarette smoke had done earlier, the purple haze was drifting into my face and making it hard to breathe. "I've changed my mind about going through with this. Sorry for the inconvenience and I'll certainly reimburse you for whatever you've wasted out of that vial, but if you'll just put the cap on it and maybe crack open a window to let the smoke out—"

"Sssssss!" The sibilant hiss that came from Esmerelda's lips cut through my nervous little speech, but as I peered through the smoke at her I saw she wasn't trying to interrupt me. Her gaze was blank and directed toward a corner of the room. My fear did a quantum leap upward and I tried to rise to a sitting position.

"The thing is, I have this *teensy* allergy to cats—" My fear became terror as I realized that I couldn't move. I tried again, willing my arms to come unstuck from my sides and my legs to bend, but it was no use. I was as immobile as if Esmerelda had tied me up and, glancing frantically down the length of my body, I realized why.

I *was* tied up. A ribbon of purple wound around me like a shroud, starting at my feet and ending at my shoulders. I could move my head, but that was all.

"Jack, make her stop! Dammit, I'm not kidding, Jack—make her stop and get me out of this!" By craning my neck as far as it would go, I could see Jack, still leaning against the wall with his arms crossed. He was looking in my direction and his expression looked expectant, nothing more.

"Heee can't heeear you."

I jerked my gaze back to Esmerelda. Had those eerily drawn out words come from her? I didn't think so. She'd stopped moving around me, and her posture was oddly slumped. A gleam of white showed from under her partially closed eyelids, and alarm shot through me as I saw that her eyes had rolled back in their sockets. A trickle of spittle gathered at the corner of her mouth, and even as I watched it spilled past the slack red lips and fell to the floor.

"Whaaat are you? I shall reeead you and we will both have the ansssswer." This time I knew Esmerelda hadn't spoken. I whipped my head back and forth, trying to find the source of the voice as it continued. "Are you damned, human, or is your sssoul sssafe?"

"I don't know and right now I don't care," I said, my eyes stinging from the smoke. "Whoever you are, just get away from—"

The smoke parted. My voice turned into a dry rattle. The enormous python rearing up by my feet looked at me with brilliant golden eyes.

"I shall seee what lives insiiide you, human…and if

I like what I fiind, maybe I willl make my home there, too."

I didn't scream. I was beyond screaming. But as the smoke drew together in a curtain again, concealing the awful lidless eyes and the terrible swaying body, a bubble of pure horror rose in my throat. Make its *home* in me? What the hell did *that* mean? Surely not what I thought it meant, did it? Because if the choice was between becoming a vampire and being possessed by something that had scales and no legs, I was more than ready to take my chances with the undead.

This was all Esmerelda's doing. She'd let me believe her familiar was a cute little house tabby, damn her, and all the while she'd been planning to loose this abomination on me. Or wait—it was *Jack's* fault. He'd known she'd be able to tell with one glance from those overly madeup eyes of hers that her ex had been making whoopee with *moi,* and he'd still brought me here like a lamb to the slaughter.

My frantic thoughts skidded to a halt as I felt something heavy loop around my ankles. My legs were propelled slightly upward, and a second heavy loop coiled around my calves. A third coil wrapped tightly around my knees, and I found I wasn't beyond screaming, after all. Higher and higher up my body came the undulating loops of the python, and each time a new coil cinched around me the rest of its muscular length tightened like a vise. When it reached my chest and squeezed, I stopped using my breath to scream and concentrated on using it to stay alive.

Esmerelda's familiar dropped a coil around my neck.

It paused, its horrific head swaying on its nauseating stalk of a body, and seemed to study me. I opened my mouth to drag in a painful breath.

"Yeesss!" With a hiss that vibrated its forked tongue, the snake darted forward. The next second my world turned into a nightmare.

Yes, sweeties, I'm well aware of the symbolism here, and no, I don't want to dwell on it. Suffice it to say that I swallowed a frigging snake and the whole experience was as awful as you'd think it might be. It didn't taste like chicken either, if that was going to be anybody's next question.

My jaws were wedged open so wide that I thought they'd crack. I felt a flickering sensation, like a tickle at the back of my throat. The flickering sensation slid farther down my gullet and I felt my hold on sanity begin to slip.

And then something *really* strange happened.

Chapter 13

"Something really strange?" Dr. Liebnitz's pen stopped scritch-scratching across the page of his notebook. "You don't consider the other events of this dream you're relating 'really strange,' Katherine?"

For a moment I didn't answer him but just stared up at the ceiling of his office from my prone position on his leather couch. It was the day after the events at Es-merelda's store, and I still hadn't made sense of what had happened to me there. That was why I'd made this emergency appointment with the good doctor, but so far talking the episode out hadn't made anything clearer.

I roused myself from my study of the ceiling. At the hourly rate I was paying to relate my so-called dream to Liebnitz, I reflected, I couldn't afford to stare at plaster.

"By other events you mean meeting a witch, having a spell cast on me and the whole snake-down-the-throat thing?" I didn't give Liebnitz the opportunity to answer. "And please, Doctor, no more probing questions about that part. Believe me, this dream wasn't about my repressed sexual fantasies. To answer your question, yes, what had happened up till then was strange, but then the weirdness factor went off the chart. As I said, the damn snake was halfway down my throat and going deeper, when all at once I felt this electric rush surge through me." I frowned at the ceiling. "And I'm not using the term metaphorically, I really felt as if there was some immense electrical voltage using me as a conduit. I think if anyone had touched me at that moment it would have been like grabbing a downed power line."

"But the snake *was* touching you," Liebnitz said, his pen still for once. "What happened then?"

"All hell broke loose," I said flatly, my mind flashing back to the scene. "As soon as the power shot through me the snake loosed its coils around me and seemed to spasm. The next second it was out of my throat and rearing back, hissing and striking. I must have been in shock, because instead of fear I just felt an overwhelming awareness of sizzling heat building higher and higher in me. And then—" I paused, trying to put my impressions into words. "And then the heat seemed to explode from me," I said inadequately, "like an invisible fireball. Esmerelda—"

"The witch in your dream who had been in a stupor while her familiar dealt with you?" Liebnitz flipped back a page in his notebook.

"That's right," I confirmed. "Except now she wasn't. She jerked up like someone suddenly awakened from sleep, and when she saw what was happening to the python her eyes went wide and her face went pale. She spun around to the store's counter behind her and spun back holding a small mirror. There was an incredible flash of light, a sound that was somewhere between an explosion and a sizzle and then a thump as the snake fell to the floor."

Liebnitz was back to writing in his notebook again. He finished and looked up expectantly. "Go on, Katherine," he said encouragingly. "How did the dream end?"

I averted my eyes from him and looked up at the ceiling again. "Uh, I guess I just woke up," I said, justifying my fib by telling myself that if it had been a dream I probably *would* have woken up at that point. Of course, since it had been real life the scene had spun out a little longer, but I didn't think it was necessary to relate every minute detail to get an answer to the question I wanted to ask Liebnitz. "So what's your take on this, Dr. L? Obviously I was responsible for what happened to poor Mabel, and by causing her death I made sure Esmerelda's vamp litmus test on me couldn't proceed. Which is proof in itself that I *am* turning vamp," I ended, my voice rising.

I heard an unfamiliar clicking sound. Turning to look at Liebnitz, I saw he'd actually set his pen down on the small table beside him and was leaning forward in his chair. His face settled into concerned lines. "Katherine, these dreams you're relating to me seem to be becoming far too real to you. Vampires don't exist. Talking snakes

don't exist. These are all symbols from your unconscious mind. You need to remember that, for your own
peace of mind." He sat back in his chair again. "Unfortunately, our time's up. Would you like to make another
appointment for tomorrow, or just come in on your
regularly scheduled day?"

Neither, sweetie—I want you to tell me what the hell
happened *to me last night!* I felt like screaming at him.
With an effort I got myself under control. Liebnitz
thought he was dealing with a patient who had a vivid
dream life. It wasn't his fault that I hadn't had a blinding
flash of revelation during our session. "My regular appointment should be fine, Doctor. But if I have another
one of these disturbing dreams—"

"At any time of the day or night if you need to talk,
I'm available," he said firmly. Turning to his desk, he
extracted a business card from a drawer and scribbled
something on it. "This is my cell number. I don't give
it out to many patients, but I think you're on the edge
of a breakthrough, Katherine. Don't hesitate to call me
if you feel the need."

Despite the austerity of his features, his tone was
compassionate. I had a momentary impulse to tell him
the truth, but since being carted off to the local psych
ward would have conflicted with the lunch date I'd
made with Ramon, I squelched the desire. "Thanks,
Doctor, but I'm sure I won't have to bother you," I said,
slipping the card into my Lulu Guinness bag. "Now,
how much do I owe you for today? I know you had to
cancel another patient to see me."

Ten minutes later, still reeling from the size of the

check I'd written the good doctor, I entered Le Lapin Amourous, Maplesburg's only French restaurant. Ramon, wearing one of his trendy bowling shirts, tan slacks and with two-tone suede shoes completing his ensemble, was sitting at a table by the open windows. As I dropped into the chair opposite him I reached over and plucked the open menu from his hands.

"You've been looking a little chunky lately, sweetie," I informed him by way of greeting. "Have a salad."

"I'm having *biftek* and *pommes frites,*" he said, retrieving his menu as I signaled the drinks waiter, "with *gâteau au fromage* for dessert. Sorry, my friend didn't realize I'd already ordered a glass of wine," he added to the waiter as the man paused expectantly by our table. "She's not drinking."

"What do you mean I'm not drinking?" As the waiter glided away I tried to signal him back, but I couldn't catch his eye again.

"I mean Rawls told me about the bet you two have going," Ramon replied, setting down his menu and sniffing appreciatively as another waiter bustled past carrying something delicious-smelling. "I take it your bitchy attempt to persuade me to order something small means your shrink billed you big-time for your emergency appointment. Do you remember what I told you when you called to say not to expect you at the Hot Box this morning?"

"That you're cheaper than Liebnitz and with you I don't have to lie," I said with an edge to my tone. "Since when do you talk to Jack Rawls about me behind my back, sweetie?"

Just then the regular waiter appeared. Ramon waited until he'd left with our orders before replying. "Since he told me that you apparently took his car and left him without a ride home from wherever it was you two were last night. Jack warned me that if you showed up today you might not be in the best of moods because you'd gone on the wagon." He planted his elbows on the table and propped his chin on his hands. "Dish, girlfriend. What the hell happened between you two last night that you ended up stealing the man's wheels and making an emergency appointment with your shrink?"

In front of me was a glass of water with a wafer-thin lemon slice floating in it. I lifted it to my lips and took a less-than-enthusiatic sip before launching into a re-counting of the previous night's events. I got to the part about Mabel the snake falling dead to the floor, and shuddered delicately.

"Talk about gruesome," I said, taking another sip of the water and letting the faint lemon tang roll over my tongue. "The thing was practically barbequed, sweetie—all charred and black. I was so stunned by the whole horrible episode that I didn't even realize I wasn't bound by Esmerelda's purple smoke rings anymore until I found myself up and on my feet. I was just about to rip into her for what she'd put me through when she launched herself at Rawls."

"He was sporting a nasty-looking scratch across his cheek this morning," Ramon said with interest. "I thought maybe you'd done it."

I smiled thinly. "Believe me, when I have it out with him about involving me in his insanely jealous witch of an ex-wife's schemes, I'll leave more than a scratch on him. But last night I just wanted to get out of there. The woman was totally ballistic, screaming at him that she never wanted him to come near her again and that if he did she'd put a curse on him." I shrugged. "I'd had enough of both of them, so while she was trying to claw his eyes out I grabbed his car keys from the counter where he'd set them down earlier and left while he was still fending her off."

"Okay, that explains the grand theft auto," Ramon conceded, "but what's this about insanely jealous, *chica?* Seems like you left a big chunk of the story out, like what made the woman think she had to be jealous of you."

"You know, sweetie, if I had a cocktail or two giving me my usual alcoholic glow I'd assume your questions meant you were concerned for me, but dead sober I can see them for what they are—pure nosiness." I reached for the pitcher of lemon water and poured myself another glassful. "Since you must know, Jack and I had a little interlude at my apartment before we went to Esmerelda's. And before your imagination goes wild, let me add that he blew it before we actually did the deed."

"Madre de Dios." Ramon looked appalled. "He blew it? To look at him you'd never guess he had a problem with—"

"I don't mean *that,* I mean he screwed up his chances with me," I said hastily. "At a crucial moment he let slip that after seeing me with the gorgeous but undead Jude St. John, he'd revised his opinion about me turning vamp."

Ramon's mouth opened to ask another question, but

he was forced to wait as the waiter arrived with our entrees. As soon as the man wished us a *bon appetit* and left, however, he made up for the enforced delay. "Who's Jude St. John? What were you doing with a vamp? How come you ended up spending time with *two* gorgeous men last night while I ended up making popcorn and watching reruns of *CSI* after I got home?" His eyes narrowed suddenly. "And why do I get the feeling I'm about to learn the real reason why you invited me to lunch, *chica?*"

I busied myself with my *biftek.* "I don't know what you mean, sweetie," I said evasively. "I invited you because we're friends. The fact that while the rest of you were off on your wild-goose chases looking for Liz and her presumed kidnapper last night, I was quaffing cocktails with said kidnapper has nothing to do with it. And just because Jude was sexy and charming and altogether *trés sympathetique* to my quest to locate vamp zero, it hasn't got anything to do with it either." I popped a perfectly seared slice of *biftek* in my mouth, noting with satisfaction that Ramon was speechless for the first time since I'd known him. I swallowed my slice of steak and got to the point. "However, when the delectable Mr. St. John confided in me that he knew where I might find the daytime lair of Cyrus Kane, aka vamp zero, I immediately knew who I'd ask to accompany me on my little staking mission today."

Ramon found his voice. "Me, *chica?*" he asked in a hollow tone.

I gave him a tiny smile. "You, *chico.* Hurry up and eat your lunch. We don't want to be late for church."

* * *

"I got to tell you, girlfriend, if I were Kane I wouldn't be caught dead in a ruin like this even if I did have a thing for churches. I vote we call it a day and head back to the club in time for a couple of sundowners." Ramon looked at his once-spiffy bowling shirt and suede shoes, his expression woebegone as he took in their begrimed state. "And to think I could have spent today eating cookies and drinking tea with an assortment of sweet old ladies and the fabulous Tashya Crosse," he muttered darkly, "instead of poring through musty deeds at the county records office until my eyes felt like they were about to drop out of my head and then riding shotgun with a crazy woman while she tried to locate a bunch of buildings that don't exist anymore."

"The foundation and cellar of Bethel Zionist Congregational must be somewhere around here. This is where the deed says the church was until it burnt down in the 1890s," I said, ignoring his rant and using a fallen branch to push aside a mat of dead leaves on the ground in front of me. "And even forgetting for the moment that I can't indulge in a sundowner with you because of my temporarily teetotal state, it's only seven and the sun's nowhere close to setting. It just seems like it's getting darker because the trees are thicker in this part of the woods."

I started to push aside another clump of concealing leaves, but then I stiffened and looked over at Ramon. "Did you just say the fabulous *Tashya* Crosse, sweetie?" I inquired in icy disbelief. "And what's all this about tea and cookies with my bratty sister?"

He raised an eyebrow and sat down on a fallen and

hollowed-out tree trunk. Crossing his legs as if he was perched on one of the Hot Box's bar stools, he shrugged. "What, I got to check with you before I like someone? Sure, Tashya's fabulous. Maybe you don't see it 'cause she's your *hermana*, but she's the original girl with the strawberry-blond curls—when she's good, she's good, and when she's bad she's even more fun to be around. Jack tell you she tried out his nail gun?" Ramon grinned. "Man, he was one pissed-off bounty hunter. But Tash, she don't care, she just—"

"Tea," I said flatly. "And cookies. Explain."

My traitor of a manager uncrossed his legs. "You know, Kat, maybe you should think about going back on the sauce if this is how you're gonna be for the next two days. Tash said she told you she was paying a visit to Whispering Pines Retirement Home to ask Edith Hazlitt about that teenage vamp you couldn't stake. She asked me if I wanted to go with her, and now I'm beginning to think I should have taken her up on her invitation."

"I'm beginning to wish you had," I snapped. "*Merde,* sweetie, maybe you'd be happier working with the fabulous Tashya, too." I glanced at my watch. "It's seven o'clock, so I doubt anyone will be at the Darkheart & Crosse office, but you can trot along there tomorrow morning. I'm sure it won't be hard to find another gay guy with no real life of his own who'd jump at the chance to replace you at the Hot Box."

Even before I saw the color drain from Ramon's face I felt hot shame flood through me. The stick I'd been holding fell from my hand as I took a step toward him. "Oh, God, sweetie, I'm so sorry!" I said in a rush. "I don't know why I said such a horrible thing, but I swear I didn't mean it! You're right—I've been a total bitch today without my usual cocktail or two, but I never meant to take my mood out on—"

"This ain't a mood, *chica,* this is you," Ramon said, his tone distant as he stood up from the fallen tree trunk. "The real you, without the happy-hour buzz that deadens whatever it is inside that's tearing you apart so much you want to hurt everyone who cares for you. I don't know why you don't see it, because everyone else does—Megan, Tashya, probably Jack and now me. I'm just a dumb gay guy with no life of my own, so it took me a little longer to get the picture, that's all."

His sudden attack on me left me reeling. Then anger came to my rescue. "Everyone else sees the real me? Judging from the assumptions you've all apparently been sharing between yourselves, I don't think any of you know the real Kat Crosse. And guess what, sweetie—I like it that way just *fine!*"

My last sentence came out in a furious shout that echoed through the gloomy woods surrounding us. Ramon looked at me, his gaze steady and somehow unsettling. "I know you do, Kat," he said. "You make it obvious that you're not interested in really connecting with anyone. Maybe one day when the parties get boring and the cocktails stop tasting so good you'll figure out why you're so scared of letting another soul touch yours. Too bad you didn't figure it out before you threw our friendship away."

"I'm sorry you feel that way, sweetie," I said coldly. I glanced at my watch to break eye contact with him.

"It's seven and the crew at the Hot Box still has an hour and a half of overtime. I'll go there to lock up after I drop you off at—"

"Seven?" Ramon interrupted. "It was seven o'clock ten minutes ago. Now I think of it, your watch said seven almost half an hour ago, too."

I glanced at the diamond-encircled dial on my wrist and saw the motionless-sweep second hand. "The damned thing's stopped," I said, looking upward at the dense canopy of trees that cut off any sight of the sky and feeling a frisson of uneasiness feather down my spine. "There's no way of being sure what time it really is."

"We know it's after seven," Ramon said, his voice even hoarser than mine, "and there doesn't seem to be much light left. I don't know about you but I suddenly got a real *mala* feeling about this place. Let's make a run for the car."

"Since we're about half a mile from where the road petered out and we had to leave the MINI I think I'd better ditch these," I said through dry lips. Stooping quickly, I wrenched off my Manolos and left them where they fell. "Come on, let's—"

"We've really got to stop meeting like this, dear heart."

My heart slammed in my chest and I whirled around in panic as a voice that wasn't Ramon's came from behind me. At the sight of the golden-haired man brushing crumbled leaves from the sleeves of his white dinner jacket, shaky relief swept over me.

"Jude, you scared me half to death!" I chided to

mask my thankfulness at the sight of him. "Where did you pop up from, sweetie, a hollow log?"

"Actually, yes." He flashed his thousand-watt grin at me. "Roughing it in the bush isn't exactly my style, but sometimes one has to make sacrifices, don't you agree?"

"Not if one can help it," I purred, bending to retrieve my Manolos. "But where are my manners? Jude, this is Ramon, my friend and right-hand man at the Hot Box. Ramon, this is the decadently delicious Jude St.—"

"He's a *vampiro,*" Ramon cut in, his tone so terse it sounded strained. "I thought you told me he was one of the good guys, but he's a damn vamp."

I tried to cover his rudeness with a light laugh. "Of course Jude's a vamp, sweetie! That doesn't mean he's here to do anything so uncivilized as *kill* us."

"I think that's exactly why he's here," Ramon said in the same strained tone. "To kill me, at least. He might have other plans for you. Stop seeing him as your freakin' drinking buddy, Kat, and really look at him."

"You'll have to forgive Ramon," I said, turning to Jude. "We had a silly tiff before you showed up and he's still annoyed with me. I'm sure as soon as he understands you were merely waiting here for us so you could—" I broke off, frowning slightly at his handsome face. "Actually, sweetie, why *are* you here? I mean, you must have guessed I'd show up looking for the old church property, but…"

My voice trailed into silence as I did as Ramon had told me and looked into Jude St. John's face. Not the way I'd looked at him last night under the influence of his charm and his cocktails, but with eyes that saw past his sexy exterior to what lay beneath.

And what lay beneath was…

My breath froze in my lungs. Without taking my gaze from Jude, I rasped a command to Ramon a few steps away. "The stick I was using is by your feet. Grab it and break it off into a stake—"

Jude moved so fast that all I saw was the blur of his white-jacketed arm as he snatched Ramon by the throat. He lifted him off the ground, held him aloft for a split second and then threw him like a child would throw away a broken toy. Ramon flew through the air like a badly constructed kite and smashed to the forest floor with a sickening thud.

My limbs paralyzed with horror, I took in the twisted angle of his body and the thread of blood slowly un-spooling from the corner of his mouth. Desperately I tried to make sense of what I was seeing, but my brain didn't seem to be working properly. "I don't under-stand." My mouth was so dry I could hardly get the words out. "Why the elaborate charade when you could have killed me so easily last night?"

"Last night I still wasn't sure whose side you were on, and besides, I don't intend to kill you, dear heart," Jude said in a tone of faint surprise. "I intend to be the vamp who brings the fabulous Kat Crosse into the fold."

"Don't call me that," I said quickly. Mingled guilt and regret flooded through me as my stupid argument with Ramon replayed in my mind.

"Why not?" Jude asked with a trace of languid amusement. "You're a fabulous woman and you'll be an even more fabulous Queen of the Undead, if the whispers about you are right. And I'll be the one to earn your undying…" the amusement in his voice strengthened "…*literally* undying thanks for giving you the final nudge into what you were always meant to be. Admit it, dear heart, you've been going through agony wondering how it will happen. I'm simply saving you from a few more days or weeks of waiting." He began strolling toward me. "As to why I didn't make my move before now, let's just say that last night I wasn't completely sure which would prove stronger, your heritage or your destiny. I couldn't take the chance you'd—"

"You killed my *friend!*" While he'd been talking I'd allowed my gaze to surreptitiously scan the ground around me. Now I saw what I'd been searching for and I lunged for the sharply broken branch that lay between us. "You're right about me turning vamp, St. John, but you're wrong if you think I'll let you hasten the process! I'm going to nudge you toward *your* destiny, you bastard!"

As I spoke I obliterated the remaining distance between us and fisted the stakelike branch straight toward his heart. Whether or not I would have been able to carry through with the killing thrust was a question that was never answered, because Jude's reaction was faster than my attack.

With the same lack of visible effort he'd shown when he'd thrown Ramon, he brought his open left palm across his body in a slicing backhand that knocked my aim askew and threw me off balance. Before I could get back into position, his hand was blurring toward me again.

The fact that I was off balance probably saved me.

The heel of his palm connected with my jaw so solidly that I felt an agonizing wrench in my neck as my head snapped sideways. My feet weren't planted solidly enough for me to resist the blow and I crashed violently to the ground.

But not for nothing had I been Darkheart's star pupil during training. I hit the ground rolling. Coming to a sudden stop, I brought my knees to my chest before thrusting my legs out again and smashing my feet into Jude's knees with pistonlike force—except that one piston came equipped with a spike heel.

The sound that burst from him didn't resemble his usual languid tones, I noted with vengeful satisfaction. It sounded more like the roar of pained rage a wounded bull would make.

"That one was courtesy of Mr. Blahnik, vamp," I gasped as I threw myself toward my fallen stake. "The next round's on me." My fingertips brushed against the rough wood and my hand began to close on it, but before it was completely in my grasp I was yanked backward by the roots of my hair.

"I'll take you up on your generous offer," snarled Jude. He hauled me upright, and I felt as if my scalp was being pulled off. "I'm just *dying* for a drink, dear heart."

His right arm encircled my waist and pulled me close in a parody of an embrace while his left hand increased its cruel grip on my hair, arching my neck backward. He bent toward me, his fangs lengthening with shocking speed and his navy-blue gaze turning the red of spilled blood. If the charmingly debonair playboy of the previous night had ever existed, I thought in cold fear, he was long gone. In his place was a being who no longer possessed the slightest spark of humanity.

"You've got a choice, vamp."

As the toneless words came out of the gathering darkness from a few feet away, Jude jerked his head up. Out of the corner of my eye I saw Rawls, his nail gun in firing position and his expression unreadable.

"You can let her go and I'll hunt you down another day, or you can go ahead and turn her. Then I'll have no reason to try for a clear shot." Jack's teeth flashed white in the shadowy gloom as he went on in the same emotionless tone. "I'll just kill both of you."

Chapter 14

It was the eleventh hour, the cavalry had arrived…and I was in deeper *merde* than ever. Some men try to signal their lack of interest in a girl with the old, "It's not you, babe, it's me," speech. It was just my luck to have become entangled with a man who accomplished the same thing by declaring his intention of shooting a silver nail through my heart.

I should have given up all hope right then and there. In fact, I was in the process of doing so when I felt a tiny flicker of electricity deep inside me. The sensation was a cross between a period cramp and how I imagine swallowing a miniature stun gun might feel, and I'd last felt it when Esmerelda's hideous snake had been slithering down my gullet.

The hope I'd been in the process of giving up flared into desperate life again.

St. John shook his head. "Maybe you could have brought yourself to kill her a few days ago, bounty hunter, but I don't think you can now. Take my advice and start running, because in a moment it'll be two against one." As if Jack posed no more threat to him, he turned his attention back to me. "Ready for a rush, dear heart?"

His downward grip on my hair was so strong that my backbone felt as if it was about to snap in the middle and my throat was so parched that I was almost beyond replying. "You bet, sweetie," I croaked. "Are you?"

As I spoke I tried to control the electric surge building in me, but already the power seemed to have grown beyond my ability to handle it. Probably that was for the best, I thought grimly, since as Tash had so kindly pointed out, I sucked when it came to killing vamps. As a human lightning rod, however, my record was, Kat Crosse: 1, Bad Things: 0.

"Dammit, Crosse, fight back!" Jack's tone wasn't emotionless anymore, it was majorly pissed. "Get some space between you so I have a clear shot at the son of a bitch! *Hell!*"

Out of the extreme corner of my eye I saw an upside-down Jack—I was in a "Dancing with the Vamps" dip, remember—begin racing toward St. John and me, his nail gun now held in front of him in a two-handed bludgeoning position. Above me I saw St. John's gleaming canines descending swiftly toward my neck. I remembered the barbequed condition of Esmie's python after it had been zapped by whatever this force was that I'd somehow acquired, and my memory went further, dredging up a vision of a horrified Esmerelda snatching the mirrored ball from the counter behind her and directing its facets at her familiar.

The downed power line inside me was beginning to sizzle and spark. The heat was rapidly searing upward to flash-point level, but despite my awareness of it, I felt oddly insulated. What I'd told Liebnitz this morning was truer than I'd known, I realized suddenly—I was a conduit, nothing more. At any second, the force inside me would explode outward, destroying everything within reach, but the fabulous Kat Crosse would remain safely detached.

It was my modus operandi, after all. Thanks to Jack Rawls, however, cool detachment wasn't going to work for me this time.

Esmerelda had seen destruction racing toward her. It had come from me, passed through her familiar like electricity passing through water, and had been about to make the leap to her. She'd turned it back onto itself with the aid of the mirrored ball, but she almost hadn't been in time. I only hoped I would be, with Jack.

Moments ago I wouldn't have had a chance of breaking St. John's hold on me. Now as his fangs brushed against my jugular preparatory to plunging in, the growing power inside me gave me more than enough strength to make my move.

Several moves, to be exact, starting with jerking my head forward and to the side so that my hair pulled from his grasp and his fangs snapped on empty air instead of the pulsing vein he'd been anticipating. He was fast, though. With an outraged snarl he lunged at me, forcing me to execute a quick side step before I turned my attentions to taking care of Jack.

"Stay away!" I said harshly as he ran toward us. "I'm capable of destroying you, Rawls! Get away *now!*"

I didn't expect him to listen to a word I said, and he didn't disappoint me. As St. John's hands clamped around my neck and his thumbs pressed viciously into the tender skin under my jawbones, forcing me to bare my neck to him again, Rawls went for him. I assume that was his intention, anyway. But just as he lifted the stock of his nail gun to smash it into St. John, I drove an elbow deep into his solar plexus.

It was another of the dirty-fighting tricks Darkheart had taught my sisters and me. "Feels like pile driver in stomach," he'd assured us. "Will make strong vamp go down like sack of beets." He hadn't been exaggerating, I realized now. Jack went down, if not like a sack of beets, at least like a man who was suddenly fighting to replace the oxygen that had just left his lungs.

"How very Sydney Carton of you," St. John said inches from my neck. "But your misguided attempt to save him from being destroyed by you won't work. In moments you'll be drinking his blood faster than you ever tossed back a cocktail, dear heart."

I didn't reply. I couldn't. It didn't feel like there was a miniature stun gun inside me anymore, it felt like there was a nuclear reactor and it was going into meltdown. *It's already way stronger than it was last night,* I thought. *If it's increased this much in twenty-four hours, what will it be like tomorrow?*

But I didn't have time to worry about that now, just like I didn't have time to wonder where the force was coming from and why I was its conduit. I knew the answer to that, anyway, even though I hadn't wanted to face my suspicions. Jack had been wrong. I was turning—not merely into a vamp but a queen *vampyr,* one whose powers would totally eclipse those of the late, not-so-great Zena. What was happening now was just a preview of the destruction I'd be capable of unleashing when the change in me was complete.

Preview or not, however, it would be enough to take my revenge on St. John for killing Ramon.

Almost delicately, the twin razor blades of his canines sliced the skin over my jugular. His muscles clenched, and I knew I wasn't imagining the sexual greed I could feel coming from him. As if he'd been holding himself in check only to prolong the pleasure, he suddenly drove his fangs deep into me…and at the exact same moment, the power in me went nuclear.

I'd told Liebnitz that touching me would have been the same as touching a high-voltage wire. From the jolting spasm that ran through St. John's body, it seemed my comparison hadn't been far off. He jerked his head up, his fangs dripping with my blood and his red gaze fixing on me in shock.

"No!" The single word of denial exploded from him. "I heard you went over to the dark side last night! You *can't*—"

"Can't what?" In a reversal of our former positions, my arms snaked around him as he tried to put more space between us. I pulled him close, pressing myself against his chest and feeling the searing heat surge from me to him. "Can't destroy you the way you destroyed Ramon? Can't watch you scream in agony all the way to hell? Think again, sweetie—I can and I will. Ramon was right, you're a *vampiro,* with nothing human about you!"

Even as I spoke I saw a thread of liquid fire run up the sleeve of St. John's white dinner jacket. Another thread of fire joined it, and then another as he struggled to get away from me. A few feet away, Jack was on his knees, shielding his face with a raised arm. I saw that the force pouring from me had become visible; a glaring light that bleached the tree trunks around me to a deathly white and lit up St. John's contorted face.

The threads of fire spreading over him were now fissures, and it wasn't just his clothes that were burning, it was his flesh. Flame hovered in a sheet over the left side of his face, but through it I could see his eyes had turned a to-die-for navy again and his fangs had retracted. He looked human, but he wasn't, I thought coldly. He'd lost any chance he'd once had for mercy and redemption the night David Crosse had damned him.

The same way David Crosse paved the way for your *damnation,* a small voice suddenly whispered in my mind. *Take a good look at the vamp you're sending to hell, sweetie…and ask yourself what makes him so different from you.*

It was the thought I'd been trying to push away since I'd seen St. John kill Ramon. If I looked past the callous cruelty that had grown around him over the years like scar tissue over a suppurating wound, would I connect for an instant with a tiny spark of humanity? Buried deep in the vampire, was there a trace of the man he'd once been?

A jolting shock ran through me. A thread of flame jumped from Jude's chest to my arm. I felt a pain more terrible than anything I'd ever known, and suddenly I was completely ablaze…while the flames that had been covering him were gone as if they had never been.

Everything happened with confusing speed after that, but one thing stands out with terrible clarity: the look of terror-filled hatred in Jude's eyes as he realized he wasn't burning anymore and I was totally sheathed in flame. Then he tore his gaze from me and wrenched free of my arms.

"I don't think so, dear heart," he rasped, backing away from me. "I'm going to hell in my own way. I'll burn for eternity before I let you touch me again!"

Through the envelope of fire surrounding me I saw him turn swiftly to pick up something on the ground behind him. He straightened, holding the branch I'd dropped during our fight. Wrapping both hands around it, he drove the sharply broken end straight into his own heart.

"No!" My scream ripped my throat like broken glass, but as painful as it felt it didn't compare to the agony of the flames that were now consuming me. I took a stumbling step toward Jude, but before I could take another I saw him implode into a scattered drift of ashes and dust.

He'd staked himself. He'd done what he'd said he would—send himself to hell rather than stay a moment longer in a world that had me in it. As the realization tore through my stunned thoughts I felt the force that had been streaming in flames from me suddenly rise to a towering crescendo.

"Jack, get *down!*" My desperate warning was just in time. Jack hit the dirt as the fireball of white light racing from me passed over him. It streamed like an earthbound meteor into the tree that Ramon had smashed into earlier and exploded in a blinding shower of sizzling whiteness.

And then everything went black and I followed the blackness down into unconsciousness.

"If anyone's gonna take off her dress to check her for injuries, it better be the gay guy is what I'm saying. But I'm warning you, man, she don't come out of this pretty soon, she's going to the hospital."

"And what do we tell the doctors when we get there? That she suffered massive burns all over her body, but she doesn't have a mark on her now and her damned clothes aren't even singed? While you're at it, why don't you add the part about you being dead and then coming back to life when that fucking fireball exploded all over you?"

I opened my eyes, not surprised to see Rawls's angry face above me but finding it impossible to believe Ramon was beside him. They were facing each other, unaware I was watching them.

"I told you already, I wasn't dead, I must have been knocked out when that *vampiro* threw me onto the ground," Ramon said stubbornly. "Nothing's going to make me believe Kat brought me back to life. If I was a dead straight guy and she was doing the fan dance in front of my corpse, maybe, but this shit about her being some kind of healer just doesn't jibe with the Kat I know. And another thing—"

"Healer?" I said flatly. "As in angel of mercy, soother of fevered brows, carrier of bedpans? I'm with the man in the bowling shirt—that isn't my style at all." I looked hopefully up at Rawls. "Please tell me I've been out for forty-eight hours and I've won our bet, sweetie. I'd *kill* for a vodka martini right about now."

"You've been out for an hour," he said unsmilingly. "How do you feel?"

I sat up, felt the room revolve around me—they'd brought me to the Hot Box, I realized, and laid me on the office couch—and managed a teensy nod. "Like I've gone over my limit by about two and a half cocktails," I conceded. I looked at Ramon. "Of course you must have been knocked out, sweetie, but I'll admit that when I saw you lying there so crumpled and still, I imagined the worst. All I could think about was that stupid argument we had and what an absolute bitch I was. Forgive me?"

"I always do, *chica*," Ramon answered with a too-quick smile. I frowned, but before I could say anything more, Rawls spoke.

"Crosse, we've got to talk about what happened tonight. And about what happened last night, too," he added, "at Esmerelda's. If you'd stuck around long enough to listen to what she had to say about—"

I stood up abruptly. The room did its merry-go-round impression again but I managed to stay upright. "Oh, I stuck around," I said in a sweetly icy tone. "Let's see—

I stuck around for the purple binding spell, I stuck around for the snake, I even stuck around for round one of the Jack versus Esmerelda prizefight. And then I didn't feel like sticking around any longer, so I left. Your ex must have known what would happen when she let loose her damn python on me, and you can tell her from me—"

"I can't tell her anything," Jack interrupted. "She's gone. I went to the store today and the whole place has been cleaned out to the bare walls. I've got a feeling Esmie's going to make sure her path and mine never cross again." He paused. "While I'm around you, at least," he added. "She's terrified of you, Crosse."

I gave a mirthless laugh. "Guess what, Rawls. I'm terrified of myself." Walking past him to the small bathroom adjoining the office, I filled a paper cup with water. Returning to the couch I glanced at Ramon, who was sitting at my desk. "There's a bottle of headache tablets in the middle drawer, sweetie. Toss them over, would you?" I waited until he complied before turning to Jack again. "You told me once that the word was I would be one of the most powerful vampires ever unleashed on the world. I didn't want to believe you, but now I have to." Palming a couple of tablets, I popped them into my mouth and chased them down with a gulp of water. "You saw what happened to that damned snake. You saw what was happening to Jude before he broke free of me, and you saw him use a stake on himself rather than let me finish him off. The thing is, I'm still officially human, Jack. If I can cause this much destruction now, what am I going to be like when I make the final transition to vamp and learn how to use this hellish force I've been cursed with? And who am I going to use it against—Megan? Tashya?" I swallowed the rest of the water and crushed the paper cup in my hand. "You or Ramon?" I gave him a thin smile. "I've got one chance and one chance only—to find Cyrus Kane and stake him before I turn. As a safeguard, I want you with me 24/7, with your nail gun locked and loaded in your hand at all times."

"Nice theory," Jack said dismissively. "It blows. Which drawer of the desk do you keep the bottle in, Crosse? And don't tell me you don't have one stashed away, because I'd bet the farm you do."

"Back of the first drawer, under some folders in the second drawer, and there's bourbon in the filing cabinet," Ramon volunteered. He looked at me unrepentantly. "I was looking for stamps one time, okay?"

I ignored him and concentrated on Jack. "After you've finished supplying yourself with my liquor, sweetie, maybe you could elaborate a little on what you just said?" I said with an edge to my voice. "God, Rawls, how much more proof do you want? Even to other vamps I'm the big evil!"

He was standing in front of the filing cabinet with his back to me. Under the black T-shirt he was wearing, his deltoids and trapezius muscles flexed as he lifted the mickey of bourbon and took a long pull straight from the bottle. He capped it, dropped it back into the filing cabinet and turned to face me with the enthusiasm of a man turning to face a firing squad.

"You're not the big evil, you're the big good," he said tightly. "You're something I've heard stories about but never believed in, which is why I needed confirmation from Esmerelda before telling you what I suspected. You're a Healer, Kat. That's why Esmerelda's so terrified of you and that's why St. John committed vamp suicide."

I stared at him for a moment. Then I looked over at Ramon, who was wearing the same carefully expressionless expression on his face that I was sure was on my own.

It had been a long night, okay, sweeties? And yours truly had been on the wagon for a grand total of twenty-five hours, eighteen minutes and some seconds, not that I was counting. What I'm trying to convey here is that I was under a *teensy* amount of strain, and given the circumstances it's understandable that I needed a few minutes of relief from the Wagnerian opera that had become my life.

I saw the corner of Ramon's lips twitch slightly. I felt a giggle rising uncontrollably in me and tried to turn it into a cough. It came out as an inelegant snort and at that point both Ramon and I lost it.

"Sorry, sweetie," I howled as I caught sight of Rawls's stony expression. "We're not laughing at you, it's just…" Another wave of laughter overtook me and I bent over weakly, holding my stomach. "…it's just…a Healer? *Moi?* I don't know exactly what that is, but it sounds dauntingly selfless, sweetie. Are you sure you've got the right girl?"

"Of course he has, *chica,*" Ramon said, wiping his eyes and attempting to fix a look of mock-seriousness on his face. "I always knew that inside that bad-girl exterior there was a saint just crying to be let out." His expression crumpled into giggles again. "St. Kat of the Bar Stools? St. Katherine of the Broken Hearts?"

"St. Kat the Ball Breaker, sweetie," I said, taking the pocket linen he held out. "I'm the Healer, I get to choose what I'm called."

"Healers have the ability to turn vamps back into the humans they once were," Jack said tersely. "Your powers seem to work against anything inhuman, judging from what happened to Esmerelda's familiar. And judging from what happened to Ramon, you can even fight death and win."

I mopped my eyes and tried to get myself under control. "I hate to squelch your fascinating theory, Jack, but if I can turn vamps into the people they once were, why was Jude going up in flames like a match to gasoline? Why did the fire leave him for me? And if you're brave enough to take on the sixty-four-thousand dollar question, why did he stake himself instead of letting me Heal him?"

"That one ain't the sixty-four-thousand-dollar question, girlfriend, it's the one with the easy answer," Ramon said, sounding suddenly sober. "You spend a whole bunch of years killing innocents and turning other people into damned souls like yourself, would you choose to have a conscience again? If Healers really exist, they must be a vamp's worst nightmare."

"You started to put your arms around St. John during your meeting with him at the mausoleum," Jack said, still in the same clipped tones he'd been using throughout the discussion. "I saw the expression on his face as he avoided you. He looked like—"

"Like I was Typhoid Mary," I said, the last of my humor dissipating, "or yes, his worst nightmare. And as it turned out, he was right. He knew I had this latent force or power or whatever you want to call it, that could be turned against him. He didn't want to be torched." I looked away, remembering the feel of the fire on my own skin. "I can't say I found being a human bonfire one of my favorite experiences, either."

"If he didn't want to be torched, then why'd he set you up tonight?" Ramon asked with a frown. "It *was* a setup, right? You were at a place he'd told you to look for, except he said this vamp zero you've been trying to find would be there."

"Kane," I said impatiently. "Cyrus Kane, the Master who turned Zena, and therefore the vamp whose death can release me. Of course Jude set me up, since Kane wasn't there and he was. Obviously he thought he could turn me before I went all lighter-fluid on him. He said he hadn't been sure whether my heritage or my destiny would prove stronger, but I guess he came to the conclusion that the destiny I was cursed with would override any resistance I might have as a daughter of a Daughter." I gave Jack a cool glance. "What strikes me as a trifle more important is that right after he said that, you appeared on the scene and announced your intention of shooting me if you had to. You were bluffing, weren't you?"

Jack met my eyes. "No. If he'd managed to turn you, I would have been doing you a favor by releasing you to death before you made your first kill as a vampire."

His matter-of-fact tone caught me off-guard and I

retaliated with flippancy. "You're forgetting your Healer theory, Rawls. What's to keep me from turning vamp, being as bloodthirsty as I want, and then performing a Heal on myself when I'm ready to put my wicked, wicked ways behind me?"

"This is just something I'm throwing out here since we three aren't all on the same page about you being a Healer, but when you're over there on the dark side, you probably don't want to come back," Ramon offered. "Even if you're a Healer who got turned vamp," he added sagely.

"Thanks for clearing that up, sweetie," I said, standing from the couch. "I hope you're as helpful tomorrow when we resume our search for Kane. Now, what are we doing about sleeping arrangements? I'm absolutely wrung out and I'm sure you boys are, as well, so I think the best solution is to bunk down here at the Hot Box for the night. I get the couch," I informed them as a yawn overtook me.

Jack took two swift steps from the filing cabinet to me, planting himself in my path. "Why?" he demanded.

I raised my eyebrows. "Because I'm the girl."

A spasm of irritation crossed his features. "Why are you trying your damnedest to push this away? This is one inconvenient subject I won't let you avoid, Crosse, because if you don't learn fast how to control your Healing gift, you're going to get killed. It almost happened a few hours ago." His jaw tightened. "I'm no expert on Healers but none of the stories mention anything about vamps they're trying to save being burned alive. Something went wrong between you and

St. John tonight, and we've got to find out what it was before you try your powers out on another vamp!" As if suddenly aware he was shouting, Jack paused and took a ragged breath. "We can start with Darkheart. He's made vampires his life's study; he's got to know something about Healers."

"That might not be such a bad idea, Kat," Ramon said slowly. "I still don't buy Jack's theory, but family's family. It's about time you came clean with your sisters and your grandfather about your fears."

His expression was earnest. Ramon cared about me, I saw. And he was right—despite the recent rift between me and my sisters and the distance I'd allowed to grow between me and Darkheart, my family did, too.

But I'd just seen something else. I'd seen it in the concern Jack tried to cover with anger, in what he'd said to me outside Esmerelda's store and the way he'd been about to kiss me last night before I'd turned away. He didn't have patience with my games and my teasing evasions, like Jean-Paul and Terry and a score of other males had in the past. He didn't see the fabulous Kat Crosse when he looked at me.

He saw the woman he'd begun to care about.

He saw Katherine Crosse, damn him.

Chapter 15

I went into full-blown ball-breaking-bitch mode. After all, a girl should stick with her strengths, no?

"Come clean with my family?" I widened my eyes at Ramon. "Why in the world would I want to do that, sweetie, when I have you to tell them my secrets behind my back? For all I know, you and your new best friend Tash have already had a juicy dish session about my worries over turning into a vamp."

I turned to Rawls. "And as much as I appreciate your concern about what went wrong between me and St. John tonight, Jack, maybe you should be more concerned about what went wrong with *your* vamp-fighting skills. I seem to remember that I was shouldering all the burden of taking him down, while a big bad bounty hunter stayed well clear of the action."

"This is what she does," Ramon said to Jack as if I weren't in the room. "She throws up a big friggin' smokescreen whenever she doesn't want to face the truth. Only trouble is, lately she's started slashing around with a knife behind that smokescreen, and she don't seem to care who she cuts with it or how much blood she draws."

"Oh, *please,* sweetie," I said in an edged drawl. "Could you be any more melodramatic? I know what my problem is and what I have to do to fix it, but if the price I have to pay for your help in finding Cyrus Kane and staking him includes constant apologies for who I am and how I act, then I'd rather go it alone." I gave Ramon a bright smile and Jack an even brighter one. "And since there's no time like the present, I might as well start looking for the elusive Mr. Kane tonight. Jack, I assume you retrieved your vampmobile from where I left it in my building's parking lot last night and drove it out to the scene of this evening's excitement. Which means you must have driven my MINI back, Ramon." I held out my palm. "Keys, please. And by the way," I added coolly, "did Jack just take a wild guess at where to find us tonight, or was that another confidence of mine you felt compelled to share?"

Ramon dropped the MINI's keys into my outstretched hand. "I phoned him from the county records office and gave him a heads-up on the places we were going to, *chica,*" he said with a spurt of anger in his voice. "You want to see that as a betrayal, go right ahead."

"You're not hunting Kane alone and you're not hunting him tonight." Jack folded his arms across his

chest and moved to the door. "I agree he has to be destroyed before he gains a foothold in Maplesburg, but
as a master vamp he's too dangerous to confront after
nightfall."

I kept my bright smile pinned to my face to hide the
outrage seething inside me. This was my own fault. I'd
broken my own rules and let Rawls get further into my
life than I should have, and now he was showing his true
colors. He'd reverted to his junkyard dog persona,
standing in my way and expecting me to back down
from his alpha-male display of control. I gave him what
he expected and batted my lashes at him.

"Oh, okay, Jack. I guess you know best." With a disappointed pout I walked away from the door and to the
couch, where the object I wanted was lying on the floor.
I scooped up his nail gun and turned swiftly back to face
him, my finger on the trigger. "Or maybe you don't,
sweetie," I exploded. I jerked his weapon at him, letting
it stray for a moment in the general direction of Ramon,
as well. "After all, I'm the one with the power, and I
don't just mean I've got the drop on you right now, I
mean I proved tonight that I can kill vamps with the best
of them. If anyone's capable of taking out Kane, I am,
and that's exactly what I intend to do." I gave him the
same humorless grin he'd given me so often. "Move
away from the door, Rawls. I'm just pissed enough at
you to pull this trigger if I have to."

"You didn't kill St. John, he killed himself," he said,
not moving. "I still haven't figured out why he did,
because by then you'd screwed up somehow and your
power had turned against you."

"It turned against me because I lost *focus,* dammit!" I yelled at him, my fury boiling over. "That's when it all went to *merde*—when I forgot for a second that I was dealing with a vamp and saw some human connection between us! I let the power get away from me, but I won't make that mistake again," I said fiercely. "Now, are you going to step away from the door, Rawls, or do I have to nail you to it?"

A few minutes later I was in my MINI heading for town. I'd left the nail gun in the Hot Box's parking lot, but not before I'd used it to seriously hinder Rawls's chances of following me. The vampmobile was sunk on its four nail-punctured tires like a fatally wounded rhinoceros, and besides feeling positively Hemingway-ish, I felt a warm glow of satisfaction when I imagined how long it would take Jack to get mobile again.

I needed a plan, I told myself as I slowed the MINI to the town's speed limit and turned onto the street that led to my apartment. It was all very well to declare my intentions of dusting a master vamp before sunup, but there was the teensy snag of finding Kane first. Under different circumstances, I might have considered tagging along with Megan on her nightly patrol to be the most likely way of running into a vamp stoolie who would rat on his master's whereabouts in exchange for a chance to walk away from my sister's stake, but buddying up with Megan was out of the question. She'd made it plain enough last night that her opinion of me had sunk to an all-time low.

I frowned as I brought the MINI to a halt in an empty parking space by my apartment. How had it all gone so wrong between Megan and me? Between Tashya and me, too, for that matter. We'd had our disagreements in the past, but when the chips were down we'd always known we could count on each other. Family was family, as Ramon had said, and my sisters still cared about me, but there was a rift between us that hadn't been there before.

In my apartment a few minutes later, I stripped off the tan Missoni trousers and ecru sweater I'd put on this morning for my doomed vamp-finding mission with Ramon. From my closet I selected a black Chloé knit top and my favorite Rogan hip-skimming jeans. I hesitated for a moment in front of my shelves of Manolos and Jimmy Choos and Louboutins, but then selected a pair of Kate Spade skimmers. I was going hunting, after all. It was the one situation where flats were more appropriate than heels. It was while I was slipping them on that the solution to my problem came to me. It was so drop-dead simple it was knock-'em-dead elegant, I thought as I surveyed myself with approval in the closet's full-length mirror before flying out of the door and downstairs to my waiting MINI.

Really, vamp-hunting has a lot in common with fashion, no?

The good news was that Mikhail didn't seem to be anywhere around. The bad news was that Tash had picked tonight of all nights to accompany Megan on her patrol. Or maybe Tash's presence wasn't bad news, I thought as I peeked around the corner of a brick wall and watched them walking slowly by a vacant lot. Who better to distract an eagle-eyed Daughter from the fact that she was being followed than the most irritating sister in the universe?

As I said, my plan was simple. Megan's favorite vamp-drawing-out ruse was to pose as a dumb civilian who would strike a vamp as easy prey. When fang boy or fang girl struck, their last conscious thought would be something along the lines of, "whatthefuck?" as their anticipated victim revealed herself as a lean, mean staking machine and sent them to hell.

So as I say, it was simple: by hanging back far enough to spot the undead jackal who would eventually pick up the tantalizing trail of two presumably innocent gazelles, the lioness who was heading up the rear of the procession would spring into action and take out said jackal without the gazelles even realizing what had happened.

Said lioness being me, of course. And said jackal being the hulking biker type I'd just spied slipping out of the shadows of the vacant lot behind Megan and Tash.

He was a vamp, all right, and not an ordinary stalker looking to have some sadistic fun with two women walking the streets alone. As he passed under a street-light I saw the gleam of his canines extending far past his lower lip. The setup was perfect for my plan. Megan and Tash were approaching a corner. When they turned it and were temporarily out of sight, I'd rush the vamp, do my nifty fire-and-live-current thing with him until he talked, and then melt back into the night without the Daughter posse being any the wiser.

The only trouble with perfect plans, I've since learned, is that they so seldom work out perfectly.

The first part went like clockwork. Rounding the side of a dilapidated building that immediately hid her from my view, Megan turned the corner a few feet ahead of Tash. Then Tash disappeared around the side of the building, too. The vamp was a couple of yards away from doing the same thing when I burst from the shadows and launched myself at him.

This time the power rose up in me immediately. I felt the now-familiar sensation of a live current building to a tremendous flash-point and hung on to the vamp as he struggled to get away from me. The first thread of liquid fire appeared on the greasy leather of his Harley jacket and then everything began to go wrong.

"Let go of my sister, you undead creep!" Tash exploded from the shadows and threw herself at us, her strawberry-blond curls bouncing wildly. Her baby-blue eyes blazed with righteous fury. "You want to pick on someone, pick on someone who can fight *back,* you coward!"

"Tash, no—" I began, but that was all I had time to say before the force boiled out of me. I felt the biker vamp being wrenched from my grasp. Out of the corner of my eye I saw Megan efficiently dispatching him, driving her stake through his leather jacket and the filthy T-shirt he wore underneath it and deep into his chest. Tash gripped me by the shoulders and peered worriedly into my face.

"Kat, are you—"

The floaty top she was wearing burst into flames. The curls nearest her face were suddenly alight, and as

I shoved her violently from me I saw threads of fire running rapidly up the legs of her jeans. I stumbled backward, trying desperately to bring the force under some kind of control.

I couldn't, so I did the next best thing. As I felt the power about to burst from me in a destructive climax I turned swiftly to face the dilapidated building on the corner. The next moment it exploded like a fireworks factory being hit by a bomb. Bricks shot into the sky, glass dropped in shards to the sidewalk and a massive cloud of dust and small debris rose to cloak the whole scene in a choking cloud. I swayed on my feet, struggling against the undertow of dizziness that was trying to drag me down into unconsciousness.

"What the hell was *that?*"

Megan's sharp question cut through my fogginess like a splash of ice water. I blinked to clear my vision, and her angry face came into focus. She was kneeling beside Tash, using her bare hands to beat out the last fiery sparks glittering like evil jewels on her jeans. Tash's eyes were closed. Her face was dead-white, except for the black smears of soot near her hairline. As I watched, Megan pressed her thumb firmly to Tash's neck.

"Owoooo!" I'd seen Mikhail in the very act of shapeshifting only once previously, and at the time I'd decided to avert my gaze in the future. Now I barely registered the sight of the howling black wolf that had loped to Megan's side undergoing a rapid transformation to human male. His howl turned into words as the transformation became complete. "...have a pulse?" he asked tersely, dropping to one knee beside Tash.

"Yes, thank God," Megan answered with an uncharacteristic tremor in her voice. "It's weak but it's there. We've got to get her to a hospital, Mikhail." She fumbled in her jeans pocket and tossed him a set of keys. "I left the truck in a parking lot a block back. *Hurry!*"

As if the sight of Mikhail sprinting away nudged my limbs into working again, I managed a shaky step forward. "Is—is she going to be okay, Meg?" I said in a whisper. "The burns...are they bad?"

"They were worse a moment ago," she said, not looking at me as she gently stroked a frizzled curl from Tash's white cheek. "They seem to be fading, I don't know why. But I'll bet you do, Kat." She rose to her feet, and although I knew I topped her by an inch and a half, I suddenly felt small as she turned her furious gaze on me. "You've got some kind of unholy power, don't you? How long were you intending to keep it a secret from us, Kat, and how the hell could you end up using it on your own *sister,* damn you!"

"I didn't mean—"

"Of course you didn't mean to hurt her! That's your problem, Kat—you never mean it! You don't mean to hurt people, you don't mean to insult Mom's memory by calling your club The Vampire's Kiss, you don't ever mean to take that one last drink that tips you over the edge. You don't mean *anything!* Nothing about you is real! It's all a stupid, shallow facade and the only reason I used to find it amusing, *sweetie,* is because I thought there was someone real underneath it!" She dragged in a breath. "Are you turning vamp, Kat? Is that where this force you have is coming from?"

I froze at her question. Then I forced my stiff lips open to say the first thing that came into my mind. "You're behind the times, sweetie, the fabulous Kat's gone on the wagon. I haven't had a drink all day."

She stared at me. "You're unfuckin' believable, you know that, sis?" she said in a low tone that throbbed with anger. "If anything happens to Tash because of—"

Whatever her threat was going to be, she never completed it because at that moment Mikhail brought the pickup truck to a screeching halt at the curb. He leapt out, his wolfishly good-looking features tight with concern. "Cops on the way," he said tersely as he lifted Tash by the shoulders and Megan got a grip on her legs. "Fire trucks, too. Apparently even in this area of town an actual explosion is something to phone the authorities about. Kat, you'll have to ride in the truck bed. It's not legal, but—"

"Kat's not coming with us," Megan said as they hoisted Tash onto the front seat. She swung herself up into the truck and supported Tash's limp body as Mikhail ran around to the driver's side. *"Go!"* she snapped as he hesitated.

A moment later I was left standing alone in the street by a burning building with the wail of approaching sirens getting closer. Something fluttered on the sidewalk. Still feeling frozen inside, I stiffly walked over to it and picked it up.

It was a once-pink ribbon, now charred and smeared with soot. I folded my fingers so tightly around it that my nails dug painfully into my palm.

Then I opened my hand and let it fall away into the night.

* * *

"Natashya Crosse," I said into the receiver of the bar's pay phone. "With a *Y-A* at the end and an *E* on *Crosse*. She was brought in a couple of hours ago. Has she regained consciousness yet? Yes, I'm family, I'm her sister. She hasn't? No, there isn't a number where I can be reached right now. I'll phone back in an hour to see if her condition's changed. Thank you, nurse."

Sagging against the pay phone, I closed my eyes tightly. As soon as I did I saw Tash, her hair on fire and her blue eyes wide with terror. I pushed the vision away, only to have it replaced by a picture of Megan looking at me with fury.

"We need to talk, Katherine, *da?*"

My eyes flew open and I saw Darkheart standing in front of me, his eaglelike gaze probing. "How did you know where to find me?" I asked. Then fear flooded through me and I clutched his arm. "Oh, God, the nurse was lying. Tash is dead—"

"Natashya is not dead," he said firmly. "Is still not awake, but doctors are hopeful. As for how I found you, was simple. Megan told me you had interfered with ambush and this in some way led to Tashya's accident. She refused to say how, but is evident she is angry with you. I ask myself where you would go if feeling guilt and sorrow, and I decide you are at tavern."

"Well, your guess was right," I said dispiritedly, "I hit the taverns. I went tavern-hopping. I decided to go on a tavern crawl—"

"How much vodka?" Darkheart asked sternly. With his accent it came out *wodka*.

"No wodka," I replied with a sigh. We'd left the corridor where the pay phones and washrooms were, and I nodded at an unoccupied table in the corner with a glass on it. "That's my drink. You can do a sniff-test if you want, but it's plain club soda."

"I believe you," he said as we made our way to the table and sat down. It was far enough out of the way of the bar's main action that no one could hear our conversation. When his thick salt-and-pepper eyebrows drew together in a meaningful scowl at me I guessed he intended to take advantage of the semiprivacy, so I spoke first.

"Whatever you're about to say, please don't. I'm worried sick about Tash and I can't take any more lectures tonight."

His eyebrows drew together even closer. "Was not going to lecture, Katherine, was going to offer help. Something is wrong, *nyet?* Perhaps I can fix."

For a moment I was tempted. Then I shook my head. "I don't think so, Grandfather. This is something I have to fix by myself, and as soon as I hear that Tash is all right that's what I plan to do." A thought struck me. "Is there anything I can do to help you? A couple of days ago you said you'd tried to call me on my cell because you needed some advice. Did you clear up your problem?"

"Da." To my astonishment faint color tinged his cheeks. "Had long talk with Liz on night she came back from kidnap. All is okay now."

"Oh, no, you don't get away with the *Reader's Digest* version. I want the total skinny, the real dirt—" I saw the confusion on his face and went on "—the whole story, Grandfather. You and Liz had a fight and you made up, is that it?" I remembered his hangover the day I'd seen him in the Darkheart & Crosse office. Now I knew why he'd hit the wodka bottle.

But he was shaking his head. "No fight. I make decision not to see her again and when I tell her she cries. That is when I try to talk to you, because I think perhaps I do not know right way to explain things to an *Americanic* woman."

I blinked. "Okay, first there's no good way to dump a girl, *Americanic* or Russian or whatever she is. Second, why? I thought you were blissfully happy with Liz. You're back together again now, aren't you?"

"*Da,* we are together again," Darkheart said. "But I thought was not fair to expose her to danger of being with me. Night we thought she was kidnapped, I blamed myself for not breaking off relationship sooner. When she came home and I saw she was not harmed, I was so filled with relief I told her everything I had been thinking."

"And what happened then, did you two kiss and make up?" I probed with interest.

"Not first thing." Darkheart's cheeks went a ruddier shade. "First she slaps my face. Then she tells me I have big nerve thinking I have to protect her from my life, and that she will never forgive me if I dump her again. *Then* we kiss."

His cheeks were flaming now, and I decided not to probe further. Not only didn't I want to think about my own grandfather doing the horizontal mambo with his attractive middle-aged girlfriend, but I didn't need to know that his love life was probably hotter than mine was at the moment.

"So new rule is now that Liz knows everything about cases we are working on," Darkheart admitted. "No hiding anymore. She has already helped solve problem of vamps that were in Maplesburg before Zena."

I'd been about to take a sip of my club soda. At his words my hand jerked and soda splashed onto the table. "She found out who turned AC/DC?" I asked, dreading his reply. "Who was the vamp? Was it—"

"Was man called St. John," Darkheart said, obviously unaware of my tenseness. "Liz said he was son of rich family in town. He came to drugstore late one night and asked her for date, but he was older than boys she went out with so she turned him down. Also she had AC/DC for boyfriend already."

I shook my head to clear it. "Wait a minute. Liz is Bitsy? *Was* Bitsy, I mean? And she was AC/DC's girl-friend before he got turned by St. John?"

"*Da,*" Darkheart agreed. "But not his girlfriend for long. After they break up, she sees him one night talking with St. John. After that she only sees AC/DC once more, when he climbs up drainpipe to her bedroom window when she is asleep and taps on her window for her to let him in. She tells him to go away or she will call her parents."

I repressed a shudder. "And all these years Liz never knew what a narrow escape she had from being turned vamp by an ex-boyfriend?"

"*Nyet,* family moved to New York soon after and she only came back to Maplesburg last year," Darkheart said.

"But—" He broke off with a puzzled look. "What is that?"

"What's what?"

"Music I can hear, like being played on tiny instruments. Is coming from you?"

I listened. Very faintly I could hear a cell phone's personalized ring signal playing a tune. I pulled my Nokia from the back pocket of my jeans and shook my head. "It's not mine. Maybe someone at that table over there—"

But already Darkheart was slapping the pockets of his jacket in a distracted manner. He grimaced. "I am fool. I forget Megan gives me Tashya's cell phone so she can reach me if she has to." His hand dove into an inside pocket and came out with Tashya's pink cell phone. Inexpertly he flipped it open. *"Da?"* he barked into it.

I kept my eyes on his face, trying to read his reaction to whatever Megan was telling him, but I couldn't. Had Tashya come to? That had to be it, I thought with shaky hope—she'd regained consciousness and Megan was phoning to put Darkheart's mind at ease. I watched as he nodded once. *"Da,* granddaughter," he said gruffly. "Is good you called."

Slowly he closed the pink clamshell case. He dropped it into his jacket pocket. His hands were old man's hands, I realized suddenly, heavily veined and knuckled. Why hadn't I ever noticed that before? And why hadn't I ever seen the tremor in them that was now so visible?

I knew what he was going to say before he opened his mouth, but the words he spoke made it all too terribly real.

"Is bad news, granddaughter," Darkheart said unevenly. "The worst. Natashya did not become conscious again. She died a few minutes ago."

Chapter 16

I stood in the basement morgue of Maplesburg Hospital and looked for a long time at the red gold curl. It was peeking out from under a gray plastic sheet, and the rest of the sheet was pulled up over a body. In a minute I would work up the courage to pull the sheet away, I told myself numbly. It wouldn't be Tashya's body I uncovered, of course, because Tashya couldn't be dead. But still, I wasn't ready to take the sheet off just yet.

It had been an hour since Darkheart had received Megan's call. I'd gone with him to the hospital, but I'd refused to go in. Sometime later as I lurked in the shadow of a tree by the building's entrance, I'd seen him come out with a sobbing Megan, supported on stumbling legs by Mikhail. I'd watched them pass and when

I was sure they were gone I entered the hospital to see Tashya one last time.

A long-ago fling with a student doctor had given me a sketchy knowledge of hospital procedure. Better yet, our heated and clandestine meetings while he was supposed to be saving lives had familiarized me with the layout of the place. So I knew that Tashya's body would have been removed from the room where she'd died just as soon as the grieving family left, and I knew how to get to where she would have been taken.

The morgue was in the basement. I'd taken the stairs, not wanting to alert the attendant on duty with the clang of an elevator door opening, and when I saw I was in the right place I looked for a handy broom closet or electrical room to hide in, prepared to wait all night if necessary for the chance to see my sister in private. But while I was looking for one, the double-swing doors of the morgue swished softly open and an old man dressed in orderly's whites shuffled out with a magazine in his hand. Watching from around a corner, I saw him head for a door marked Men's.

Despite the magazine, he wouldn't leave his post unattended forever, I told myself as I stared at the red gold curl that couldn't belong to Tash. It was time to pull the sheet back.

I did…and looked through a sudden spill of tears at Tashya's closed eyelids, her cupid's-bow lips, the dusting of freckles across her nose that she'd always hated.

"My beautiful, bratty little sister," I whispered as I let my gaze fill with every detail of her. "*Such* a pain in the butt, sweetheart. Always borrowing my clothes without asking, hogging the phone when I was waiting for a call, flirting with my boyfriends. How did you manage to do all that and still make me love you so much? Was it because sometimes just looking at you made me feel like the sun had come out? Was it because I knew under that bratty exterior was someone who'd fight to the death for me if she had to? Or was it because I always knew how much you loved me?"

I heard the sound of a door shutting somewhere outside the room and the weary shuffle of the morgue attendant's feet as he walked slowly back to his post. I bent down and pressed my lips against Tashya's cool brow, pain beyond measure burning my heart. "I love you, sweetie," I whispered through my tears as they spilled hotly onto her. "I love you."

I pulled the sheet back over her, this time covering the curl. Then I left the room and climbed the stairs and exited the hospital, stumbling like a drunk from the place where my dead sister lay. I found myself in a Dumpster-lined alley behind the building and reached for the cell phone in my back pocket.

I'd hit rock bottom. I'd killed my own sister. If ever I needed professional help it was now, before I gave into the selfish desire I had to put a sudden and irrevocable end to everything. Whatever she felt toward me, Megan would be destroyed if she lost both her sisters within hours, and she wasn't the only one who would pay the price of pain for my cowardice. Darkheart, Grammie, Popsie—I didn't have the right to do this to them, but alone I wasn't going to make it through the night. With shaking fingers I hit the speed dial I'd entered yesterday morning when Dr. Liebnitz had given me his cell number

I heard the buzz as it rang on the other end and my stomach clenched. What if he didn't pick up? What if he was at the opera or a movie or with friends, and he'd turned his cell off?

From somewhere a few feet above and behind me in the dark I could hear a sound like music being played on tiny instruments. Slowly I turned, raising my eyes, but my pounding heart and my prickling spine already knew with sick certainty what I was about to see.

Cyrus Kane, master vamp and sometime psychiatrist under the pseudonym of Dr. Liebnitz, hung in the air in front of me. I closed my cell phone, and in one of his pockets, his stopped ringing. He smiled at me with the detached concern he'd shown so often in his office—*his office that always had the drapes tightly shut,* I thought insanely—and dropped to the ground.

"So, Katherine," he said with calm confidence as he came toward me, "are you finally ready to let me help you?"

I wasn't, not then.

But a little while later, I found that I was and stopped fighting him.

As I'd expected, the Hot Box was in darkness. I slipped through the door of my establishment and made my way through the public area to the private rooms customers never saw, my hair drifting around my shoulders as I walked the unlit corridors. Forcing back the dark hunger that had been building in me since my encounter with the master an hour ago, I paused for a moment, stripping off my knit top and my jeans and unhooking my bra. My panties came off last and then I was naked, the air a sensual caress on my bare skin. It felt sinfully delicious…but it was only a prelude to the real delights of this night.

And they were about to begin now.

Jack was asleep on my office couch, with the crocheted throw that was usually thrown over the back of it pulled inadequately over him. Although he was wearing his jeans, he'd removed his T-shirt, and the faint moonlight streaming through the window delineated the hard muscles of his torso. He really was a *most* attractive man, I mused as I stood in the doorway and let my gaze roam over him. In a rough-hewn and dangerous way, of course, with that short-cropped black hair and those strong angles of his face. A con, I thought with a secret little smile playing around my lips. A con who killed vamps. It was like playing with fire.

I suddenly saw that his eyes were open and he was looking at me, framed in the doorway. A tiny chill ran down my spine, but the flicker of fear aroused me even further. I walked unhurriedly toward him, stopping when I was a few inches from the couch and lazily running my hands along the flare of my hips up to the fullness of my breasts. I paused, cupping them in my palms so that they looked as if they were being forced upward by the tight lacings of a bustier. Still watching him through my lashes, I bent my head and ran the tip of my tongue over the swell of one breast, then the other. I raised my head and smiled at him.

"You and I started something the other night, Jack," I said in a husky purr that seemed to hang in the air between us. "Do you want to finish it, sweetie?"

For a moment he didn't respond. Anger sparked in me, but it subsided as Jack pushed back the throw and swung his bare feet to the floor. His hands went to the fastening of his jeans. His smoky green gaze, sexy even with the flaw of gold marring the emerald of his right iris, held mine as he unzipped his fly.

Heat spiraled swiftly through me. Under his jeans Jack was as naked as I was…and as fully aroused. With that one downward tug of his zipper he was ready, willing and impressively able to satisfy my most urgent cravings.

I closed the distance between us with a step, parting my legs so they flanked his thighs. As I did, Jack leaned slightly back with one hand behind him on the couch and the other settling on my waist, his gaze darkening with an unspoken demand I had no trouble reading.

"You like it slow, don't you, sweetie?" I breathed as I placed my hands on his shoulders and began to lower myself tantalizingly against him. "And you like to be teased, too, I can tell." While I spoke I brushed the tight buds of my nipples against his mouth and gave a low laugh as I heard him draw in a quick breath. I slid farther down him, letting my hair fall like strands of silk across the tanned column of his neck. "You owe me a kiss, sweetie," I said softly. I was kneeling on the edge of the couch now, my thighs straddling him like a bareback rider's thighs might straddle a stallion. The analogy was deliciously apt, I thought as I moved close enough that my lips whispered against his. "You were going to kiss me outside the witch's store, but somehow it never happened."

A muscle tightened at the side of his jaw. My junkyard dog was straining at the leash, I noted in satisfaction. His gaze was still focused on my face and except for the unsettling fleck of sun-gold I avoided looking at, the green of his irises had shadowed nearly to black. I lowered myself a fraction more and his lashes dipped briefly to his cheekbones. "Show me what I missed, Jack," I murmured against his mouth. "Give me the kiss you were going to give me then."

Slowly his palm moved from my waist, past my rib cage, brushed against the side of my breast. He pushed aside a swath of my hair and cupped his hand around the back of my neck. Then he spoke for the first time since I'd entered the room, his voice pitched so low that he might have been talking to himself, not me.

"I should have given it to you that night, Kat. It might have changed everything."

His mouth parted on mine. I waited for his tongue to tease me, to invade me, to bring me to a fever pitch of desire, but all I felt was a lingering warmth as he pressed a kiss to the corner of my lips.

And then his mouth withdrew.

I stared at him, fury and disbelief warring inside me. "Is that it?" I demanded, my grip tightening on his shoulders. "Is *that* what I lost when I turned away from you that night?"

"No." His tone was flat. "That's what we both lost."

Our gazes locked. Slowly I let my lips curve into a cold smile. Then I lowered myself onto him completely.

Even as I heard his ragged gasp mingle with my own moan of pleasure my mouth was at his neck, my canines poised and ready to strike. I lifted my hips, felt him inside me, let myself move slowly down his length again as I spoke into his ear. "Guess what, Jack? I've got a surprise for you."

He inhaled unevenly as I moved upward, but his voice was steady when he answered me. "I know, Kat. And I've got one for you."

I froze as I heard the unmistakable click of a firing mechanism lock into position. Slanting my gaze downward, I saw the muzzle of Jack's nail gun aimed at my heart.

"You had it under the throw all the time," I murmured. "You were prepared for me to show up here. I suppose that's why I saw no sign of Ramon when I walked through the club?"

"That's why," Jack confirmed.

I was silent for a moment. Then I smiled, the tension leaving me. "This is what they call a standoff, no? My fangs at your neck, your gun at my heart. But a standoff only works when both antagonists are prepared to make their move." Lightly I touched the tips of my fangs to him and two beads of blood, like red pearls, instantly welled up on the tanned skin of his neck. "I'm prepared to open your vein, Jack. The question is, are you prepared to drive a silver nail through my heart?"

For what seemed like an eternity I waited for his reply, but just as I was wondering if I'd misjudged him I heard him give the tight exhalation of a man finally facing a hard reality. Setting the nail gun down on the couch, Jack wrapped his hands around my waist and pulled me to him.

And when I drove my fangs into his neck a few minutes later…it was very, *very* good for both of us.

Chapter 17

"The bounty hunter lost more blood than I would have liked you to spill from him, but I realize how hard it must have been to obey my order and restrain your impulse to drink from him. After his day of recuperation he should be fully restored," Cyrus Kane said as I rose from the luxurious bed of quilted silk in which I'd spent the previous twelve hours. As my satin-slippered feet sunk into the Persian carpets covering the floor, he closed the polished mahogany lid of the coffin I'd just awoken in.

Masking my eagerness, I let my gaze stray around the high-ceilinged room, taking in the opulent furnishings and the attention to detail before turning to him with a smile. "Then tonight can proceed as planned?"

Behind his ascetic demeanor was an echo of my own

excitement. "The preliminaries have already begun, Katherine. As we still have a few hours before you're needed for your part, perhaps you would like to use the time to ready yourself?"

He stood aside to let me pass ahead of him through the resting room's doors to a large hall as elegantly appointed as the room I'd just left. I shook my head in wonderment. "If you had told me when I saw you at your brownstone office that all this was beneath the building, I wouldn't have believed you, Cyrus. And in answer to your question, yes, I would like to use the time to get ready. If the outfit you've selected for me is as lovely as the sleep attire you provided, I can hardly wait to see it."

"The dress I've chosen doesn't show off your considerable charms as obviously as your present one." Kane paused, his cool gray gaze taking in the see-through gauze gown I was wearing. "But I don't think you'll be disappointed in the label."

"It's a designer gown?" This time I didn't bother to hide my pleasure. "Who, Cavalli? Valentino?"

"Charles Worth," he answered as we entered another room, this one smaller but still spacious. Delicate gilt tables and richly upholstered couches were dotted here and there around the room and gilt-framed paintings lined the dove-gray walls. Looking closer, I saw that the paintings all concealed doors. It was a dressing room, I realized as Kane continued. "He's before your time, but his creations are in keeping with the era of this house. Naturally the gown's been altered enough that it doesn't look too modestly old-fashioned."

He pressed the edge of one of the gilt frames and the door behind it swung open to reveal a closet with a single garment hanging on a velvet-covered rod. Lifting the dress free of the rod, Kane laid it on a couch. "This is the gown you'll be wearing for your initiation kill, Katherine."

A spill of black silk tulle frothed across the couch, its midnight color glinting in the lights from the overhead chandelier. The glints came from black cut-glass beads and sequins, I saw as I reverently touched my fingertips to the fabric. Point de Venise lace and black silk ribbons dripped from the deeply plunging neckline and the even more scandalously deep dip of the back. Not only was it the most exquisite gown I'd ever seen, but the unrelieved black would show off the new alabaster of my skin and the unlipsticked ruby of my lips to perfection.

I met Kane's inquiring look. "It's beautiful," I said simply. "And you're right, Cyrus, anything more modern would have been out of place in this sanctuary of elegance and luxury you've created here."

"Sanctuary?" Kane's tone was sharp. He saw my startled look and softened his tone with an obvious effort. "I'm sorry, Katherine. I found your choice of words an unsettling one, given the fact that a church stood on this site long before this building was erected."

"Oh, no, you're wrong," I said without thinking. "When St. John told me the most likely place for your daytime lair was a disused church, I searched the town's records. This site didn't show up as ever—" I stopped, appalled at myself. "I contradicted you, Cyrus," I whispered. "I shouldn't have."

"No," he agreed with a dangerous chill in his voice. "Neither should you have brought up the name of Jude St. John when I've already explained to you how his ill-fated attempt to turn you was part of a larger plan to seize power from me. Since you've done both, maybe I should clarify our respective positions. You have all the makings of a legendary queen *vampyr.* I have no doubt that after a few years under my guidance that title will become yours, just as it once was Zena's. I, on the other hand, have never coveted a title and have turned down any that have been offered to me. I want only one thing. Can you guess what it is, Katherine?"

I shook my head, not daring to speak.

"Maplesburg." His gray eyes flashed. "And if you ever try to stand in the way of my possessing it, I'll destroy you."

"But *why?*" As soon as the incredulous question left my lips I was terrified I'd overstepped a boundary again but the sudden rage in Cyrus's reply wasn't directed at me.

"Because I founded this town! And then I was driven out of it!"

"I don't understand," I said faintly. "You founded *Maplesburg?*"

"I and my congregation," Kane said, reining in his anger with a visible effort. "Yes, the church that once stood here was mine. The night I was forced to flee, it was razed to the ground and the name of Cyrus Kane was erased just as completely from the history of Maplesburg. Do you understand now what I plan for this town?"

Slowly I smiled. "You plan to do the same thing to

it that its citizens did to you. When you're finished here, it will be as if Maplesburg never existed."

He nodded in approval. "Very good, Katherine. Those who do not come over to my side will either leave town or be killed, starting with the Daughter and her supporters. New residents will move in, but their fate will be the same. Eventually buildings will fall into disrepair, whispered rumors will spread and without anyone admitting that they believe in vampires, the town will be shunned. It won't be the first time a once-thriving community withers and dies without any official explanation. And finally I will have exacted justice for what was done to me three hundred years ago."

His eyes clouded with memory. Then he gave me one of his wintry smiles and moved to the door. "I'll send attendants in to help you bathe and dress," he informed me. "You prefer males?"

The thin gauze of my sleeping shift suddenly felt hot against my skin. "I may experiment in the future, but for tonight I'd like men."

He nodded briskly. "I'll send someone to escort you to the ceremony on the stroke of midnight. I expect you to be dressed and ready, so don't disappoint me."

"I won't." I met his cold gaze, anticipation fluttering darkly inside me. "I intend to exceed all your expectations of me tonight."

Cyrus had called it a dungeon and the assortment of chains and lashes and manacles on the stone walls bore his description out, but like every other part of this

underground sanctuary, the room I was in had touches
of decadent luxury. For the observers that was, I
thought. Those unfortunates who provided the enter-
tainment weren't as lucky.

Jack, for example, was manacled by the wrists to an
iron bolt set into the wall, and he'd had to seek what
comfort he could in unconsciousness. Even that would
soon be taken from him, however, when the drugs Cyrus
had ordered took effect and aroused him. I frowned, ir-
ritated by the delay and wishing Cyrus hadn't left me
here alone while he took care of some last-minute arrangements that required his personal attention. As an
unblooded initiate I was not allowed to mingle with the
sumptuously dressed guests I could see in the open area
of the room—most of them acquaintances from Europe
and South America, Cyrus had told me, although a few
were American vampires. Above them a rococo chandelier, its crystals sparking with shards of brilliance from
the hundreds of wax tapers burning on it, hung from a
ceiling so far above that even the blaze of candlelight
didn't illuminate it. An airy framework of iron stairs and
walkways descended from the darkness of that unlit
area, its delicate strength an exercise in *fin de siècle*
elegance. As I saw a late-arriving group of guests step
from the staircase and join the rest of the crowd who
were quaffing flutes of champagne and laughing among
themselves, I stirred with restlessness.

I quelled my impatience by recalling the tidbits of
information Cyrus had provided when I'd first entered
the dungeon and expressed my admiration for it. It *was*
worth admiring, I thought as I looked around me. The

cavernous room had been blasted out of the green and gray New York granite bedrock that underlay most of Maplesburg, an achievement that impressed me even more when I'd learned that Cyrus had commissioned his special renovations to the house when he'd bought it a hundred years ago.

"After two centuries away I felt it was time to end my exile and gain a foothold in Maplesburg again," he'd explained. "It was safe enough for me to do so by then. Even the oldest inhabitant who might have known me was long dead, and when the wealthy and free-spending Cyrus Kane arrived in Maplesburg from Europe, no connection was ever made to my former incarnation here. And of course, the money also stilled the tongues of those who might otherwise wonder aloud about my eccentric desire to do all business at night," he'd added with a rare chuckle.

My impatience vanished as I contemplated how long a wait Cyrus had endured to get what he wanted. From the start he had known how he intended to take his vengeance, but he had laid his plans with infinite patience in order to ensure their success, just as he had patiently waited for the perfect time to bring me into his fold. The flame of hatred in him had never weakened, I mused, wondering what circumstances had surrounded the igniting of such a strong fire. He had been silent on the details and I hadn't had the courage to ask him, accepting that if he wanted me to know, he would tell me.

"It's time, Katherine." Lost in my thoughts, I hadn't seen Cyrus approach. Taking me by the arm, he inclined his head toward the figure in the middle of the room. "The bounty hunter is conscious and I've been assured that he will remain that way." He looked at me, his eyebrows slightly raised. "You're trembling. Are you nervous?"

"A little, but only because I want you to be proud of me, Cyrus." I hesitated, hoping my next words wouldn't offend him. "You know how I feel about my father from our sessions in your office—that he was always an absence in my life, and that when I learned he'd become a vampire and taken sides with Zena against his family I felt betrayed. I understand his choices now and I'm honored that you were the one who turned him, but it's hard to think of a man I've never known as being my father." I bent my head to hide the flush I could feel on my cheeks. "What I'm trying to say is that I want to make you proud of me the way a father feels proud of a daughter who's pleased him, Cyrus. You've filled the hole in my life that David Crosse left empty."

I'd gone too far, I realized when I raised my eyes to his and saw the icy displeasure in them. I opened my mouth to stammer an apology but Cyrus cut me off before I could speak.

"My confidence in you was badly misplaced, Katherine," he said, removing his hand from my arm as if the very touch of me repulsed him. "I thought I saw astuteness behind the vapid mask you showed to the world, but it seems I was wrong. Where did you get the notion that I turned your father?"

"St. John," I said tremulously. "He said you turned David Crosse and then Crosse turned him. That's not true?"

"How could it be? I turned Jude, a mistake I'm glad to have behind me now, but I didn't turn Crosse. No one did. He was a Healer, never a vampire. I'm disappointed enough that you could be taken in by a man whose intelligence was so far exceeded by his disloyalty. What appalls me more is that you couldn't put the pieces together even after your powers began to emerge. Whom did you think you had inherited your gift from?"

His words seemed to be coming to me from far away. I closed my eyes to shut out the illusion of the room whirling around me, and a thick fluid rose in my throat. I choked it back. David Crosse, a Healer? Zena's dying statement that David had gone over to her dark side, a lie?

No. I opened my eyes. "I saw him in hell. That's proof positive that my father was a vampire and was staked. I saw him in hell suffering the agonies of the damned."

"You saw him in hell *experiencing* their agonies," Cyrus said, his tone cutting, "just as he experienced their symptoms and their memories when he connected with them during a Heal." His mouth thinned to a line. "Willful blindness is more despicable than stupidity, Katherine. The people of this town refused to relinquish their blindness even though I tried to show them the light, and in the end I realized they were unworthy. I've come to the same conclusion about you."

Abruptly he turned from me. As he walked away I understood what my foolish questions and doubts had cost me, and terror sliced through me like an ax.

"Cyrus, no!" Hampered by the length of my gown, I stumbled after him and grasped his arm. He stiffened, and immediately I let my hand drop. "I've lost your confidence," I said unsteadily. "Let me earn it back. Let me go through with my initiation and prove myself worthy to you."

David Crosse wasn't a vamp.

The thought tore through my mind as if it belonged to someone else. I thrust it away as Kane turned to face me.

"As you say, I've lost confidence in you. I've made my decision."

He was a Healer.

Again that sense of someone else's thoughts in trying to claim my mind! Had the champagne I'd enjoyed during the pleasant interlude I'd spent in the bath chamber muddled my senses? I realized Kane was about to turn away again, and I forced an iron control on my thoughts. "I'm not asking you to reverse your decision, Cyrus, I'm begging you to postpone it. After my initiation you can banish me, punish me, whatever you think I deserve, and I'll accept it willingly."

I was a Healer.

Cyrus was saying something. With an effort I ignored the alien voice in my head and concentrated on listening to him.

"…hear you right, Katherine?" There was chilly amusement in his voice. "Did you just say you were begging me?"

He was a master, I told myself, and I had displeased him. He was right to force me to acknowledge my subservience to him. "Yes, Cyrus, I'm—"

Kiss ass much, sweetie? Merde, *just grow yourself a pair, girlfriend, and tell that jerk to go to—*

"—I'm begging you, Cyrus!" To my horror I realized that in my effort to drown out the voice in my head I'd shouted the words at him. I waited for him to order me from his sight, but instead he nodded in faint approval.

"I can't fault your zeal, Katherine—"

The name's Kat!

"—or your willingness to take chastisement," Kane went on as the intruder in my head fell silent for a moment. "Very well, your initiation will proceed as planned. Come, we're keeping the spectators waiting."

"Just one last quick question." Terror shot through me as I realized that the intruder had graduated from mental communication to control of my voice. I tried to bite back the words I could feel forming on my tongue, but they were already being directed at an impatient-looking Kane. "When you jumped me in the alley, what did I do wrong? Why couldn't I Heal you before you turned me?"

Cyrus's thin lips curved slightly up at the corners. "But you weren't trying to Heal me, Katherine, you were trying to kill me. Your power was driven by such hatred that I wonder you didn't burst into flames on the spot. You'd crossed over into the dark side before my fangs even touched you."

His smile disappeared. With a curt gesture he motioned me to precede him toward the middle of the floor where Rawls stood manacled. For a second I hoped the intruder had gone for good, but then I heard her whispering in my head.

Oh God, Daddy, is that what happened to you? With every whispered word the intruder was getting stronger.

I tried to force her from me but to my shock her whisper continued as unhesitatingly as if my efforts didn't deserve her attention. *When you realized you and the family you loved were under attack by a queen vamp, did you lose control of the power and attack Zena with hatred? Is that how she knew she'd won against you— because she saw you'd entered her world of hate all by yourself?*

She was overwhelming me! Who *was* she? Could she *be* me—one last, despicable fragment of the woman I'd been before the master had transformed me? Revulsion and fear filled me at the thought. As if sensing my momentary weakness, she surged forward, and I realized in sudden terror that I was losing the battle. I made a final despairing attempt to regain possession of myself, but she was too—

"Oh, Daddy, I'm so sorry," I said out loud, coming to such an abrupt halt that Kane almost ran into me.

"Why have you stopped, Katherine?" he asked icily. "Please keep walking. This is a ceremony, and as such deserves to be conducted with a certain dignity."

The fabulous Kat Crosse was *back,* I thought with relieved triumph. I was back in control of my mind and my body and my emotions, and the vamp personality who'd taken over the moment Kane had turned me was fading. Not permanently, and maybe not for very long, but right now the essential spark of humanity that was the real Kat—the real *me*—was holding the reins.

But that could change at any minute. I'd clawed my way up from the limbo I'd been shoved into, so Bitch Girl might be able to do the same. And I had the unpleasant feeling that if she did, I might never reemerge again.

If I wanted to save Jack, I had to do something fast. Unfortunately, when I saw the state he was in, the only thing I could think of to do fast was faint from horror. I forced myself to stay on my feet and looked at him the way I imagined Kane expected me to—part cold stare, part salivating hunger.

His face was encrusted with dried blood and his left eye was completely swollen shut. His arms were suspended above his head, the iron manacles biting deeply into the flesh of his wrists. There was more—lots more, including raw lash-marks on his bare back and burns on his chest—but it's a picture I don't like remembering.

"At this point I must join the onlookers, Katherine," Kane informed me. "Conduct yourself as befits a future queen vampire and restore my faith in you."

His stern command echoed in the large chamber. Even the luxurious tapestries hanging against the granite walls couldn't deaden the sound and I swallowed dryly, my gaze darting around the room looking for inspiration and finding none.

Cyrus noticed my glance and misread it. "Beautiful, isn't it?" he said, nodding in the direction of the staircase. "For that I didn't use local workers, but instead brought in the most talented craftsmen from Europe. I almost regretted having to kill them when it was finished."

I couldn't tell him that my interest was fixed more on the pinpricks of red light shining from the shadowed corners of the room. Eyes, dozens of vamp eyes, and they were all trained in my direction waiting for the action to start.

A slight gesture from Cyrus brought a beautiful woman forward. She approached me, carrying a long case covered in rubbed black velvet. Her dark eyes sparkled as she lay it down carefully in front of me, as though she was giving me a precious gift.

"You must choose your instrument," she informed me. "Of course," she gave me a small, hungry smile, "you can choose more than one."

She leaned forward and I could feel her warm breath on my cheek, see the ruby flicker behind the liquid gaze. "Welcome, sister," she whispered. Open-mouthed, she kissed me.

For a moment, sweeties, it was touch and go. I felt control slipping away from me, felt myself being pushed aside by a dark hunger, seemed to see a yawning, lightless vortex opening in front of me as the female vamp's soft lips held mine.

Just over the woman's shoulder, I saw Jack. His eyes were open and what I saw in them yanked me back from the brink.

"Thank you…sister," I said pleasantly, backing up a step. The passion in the woman's beautiful face was replaced by confusion and then with quick suspicion.

"Master—" she began, but Cyrus cut her off with a curt nod.

"Enough. It is time to begin."

He motioned for me to open the case. I knelt down, eased back the heavy lid, and gazed down at various instruments. Some were so ornate that I couldn't even imagine what their function could be. Others were brutally simple in construction and their promise of pain. All of them looked as though they'd been well used and well taken care of.

I took a deep breath. Somehow I was going to have to put on the performance of a lifetime if I was going to save Jack's life—and my soul. Despair caused my hand to tremble as it hovered over an ivory-handled whip.

Right epiphany, wrong time to have it, I told myself shakily. Forcing myself to raise the whip, I advanced on Jack and leaned close to his bruised and battered face as if I was taking an initial moment of pleasure in surveying the damage that had already been done to him.

"Okay, sweetie, here's the scoop," I whispered rapidly to him. "I'm not feeling so vamp—well, not right at this minute, anyway—and I'm going to get us out of here as soon as I figure out the teensy problem of how I do that. I know you probably don't believe me, and that's okay. All I want is for you to buy me some time by pretending that you're unconscious again. Then when—"

"I should have killed you when I had the chance, vamp," Jack said in a low, slurred tone. "I don't know why the hell I didn't."

I glanced over my shoulder nervously before turning back to him. "Jack, listen to me!" I hissed. "You were right, I *am* a Healer, but when I went up against Cyrus he—"

"Go Heal yourself, then," he said, his tone grimly defiant. "Better yet, vamp, why don't you just go fu—"

Stepping back swiftly, I brought the whip down with a resounding *crack!* on the stone floor. At the same time

I did something that I still shudder over whenever I can bring myself to think about it.

Deliberately putting all my weight on the delicate heel of one of the gold kid shoes hidden beneath the long skirt of the Worth gown, I wrenched it sideways. I felt the heel snap off immediately. I raised the whip again, this time over Jack, and took a quick stride forward as if I wanted to add the force of momentum to my blow.

I tottered sideways on the broken heel and the whip fell from my hand. I heard what I'd guessed I'd hear from the onlookers—a ripple of amusement, swiftly suppressed—and spun around, my face a mask of frustrated fury as I reached down and yanked the broken right shoe from my foot and hurled it from me.

Then I went into full-blown diva mode.

"Was this *planned,* Cyrus?" I screamed in rage as I saw him move from the edge of the crowd toward me. "Is there someone among your followers who wanted to make me look foolish during this most solemn of ceremonies, who was so jealous of my destined role that they thought to humiliate me by tampering with the shoes I was to wear?" I swung my gaze around the room, my gaze terrible with anger, or so I hoped. "Who did this? Who deliberately sabotaged my moment of initiation?" Kane reached my side and I turned to him, hoping he'd assume that I was trembling with outrage. "You were right. My initiation won't take place. I refuse to shame you by hobbling around like a court jester, instead of carrying out the rites with the dignity they deserve. I've failed you, Cyrus. Do with me what you will." I hung my head, and mumbled into the lace of my neckline, "Unless you just want me to go change my shoes."

"Katherine, look at me." His hand was under my chin, tipping it up—God, I thought, the man was so patronizing it was pathetic. I kept my thoughts to myself and looked with burning devotion into his eyes. "Fire," he said softly, "fire and spirit. That bodes well for your future, Katherine. The ceremony will be delayed for a few minutes while I send someone to fetch another pair of shoes for you. Take that time to compose yourself while I inform our guests of what is happening."

Without waiting for my thanks—which would have been *trés* sincere, sweeties, believe me—he strode away. I darted a look at Jack and saw him regarding me with stubborn suspicion. Bending down and reaching beneath my gown to remove my left shoe, I said under my breath, "I'm going to insist on starting the ceremony all over again and ask for the weapons to be offered to me again. Did you see anything you liked?"

For a moment he didn't answer me. I kicked at the lace of the gown's hem, as if it was in the way of the shoe I was trying to take off. "*Merde,* Jack," I whispered, "I don't have much time here. Like it or not, there's a vamp inside of me trying to get out, and if I don't—"

"Ask for a pike, Crosse." His voice was a rasp, but it gained strength as he went on. "I didn't see one but these bastards are bound to have one."

"A pike?" I couldn't delay any longer. "What does a pike look like?"

"It looks like an iron pole with a sharpened end," Jack said grimly, "and it's the only thing I can think of that might break open one of the links of this chain."

"Then I'll insist they find one. I have to go, I can already see some suspicious gazes looking our way."

"Just one more thing, Crosse," Jack grunted as I began to stand. "You know we're not going to get out of here alive, don't you? Best case scenario is we go down fighting, so what I've got to say I better say now." His battered gaze met mine. "You're fabulous, Kat Crosse," he said hoarsely. "I wish I'd given you that kiss when I should have." He smiled wryly and jerked his head. "Go. And give 'em hell before they take us down, babe."

"You, too, sweetie," I said unevenly. I let my eyes linger for a final moment on him, wondering just how it would have worked out between a junkyard dog and a slightly bitchy Kat if we'd had the chance.

Then I forced myself to turn from him and walk away. I'd never know the answer to that question, I thought as I hurried to the corner of the room I'd waited in earlier. The only question that would be answered in the next few minutes was the one that had come to me when Jack had thought I was a vamp.

He'd told me to go Heal myself. He'd meant something else, of course, but was it possible that I could? And if I couldn't, would Katherine take over when Jack and I started fighting against Cyrus's guests?

I shut my eyes against the vision of her fangs sinking into Jack's neck, tearing the flesh from him even as the last scrap of humanity that was my soul disappeared forever. I *had* to do it, I told myself tensely. I had to try, at least.

I wrapped my arms tightly around myself the way I'd wrapped them around Jude. I was responsible for Tash's death, I thought hopelessly. I'd betrayed Jack. I'd failed at everything I'd tried to do, so why did I think I could—

The explosively destructive heat came up in me so quickly I almost couldn't push it down. It wasn't working, I realized in despair. I couldn't Heal myself. This was just one more Kat Crosse screwup in a long line of similar screwups, and I'd been insane to think that I could—

Abruptly I stopped berating myself, my eyes widening in belated comprehension. "Oh, *no*," I whispered in appalled denial. "Forget it, sweetie. After twenty-one years, it's far too late to try loving yourself as you really are."

But Tash had loved me, I admitted slowly. And despite everything, I knew Megan still did. I'd behaved abominably to Ramon and he hadn't washed his hands of me—what was that, if it wasn't love? My grandparents, Darkheart, my father…

They all loved me. And Jack did, too. Was it really so impossible for me to accept the person they loved?

Warmth began to build inside me, and although my arms were wrapped tightly around myself I knew who I was really hugging close. At long last I was comforting the child who'd believed herself abandoned, reassuring the young girl whose disgust with her reflection in the mirror had led to a sickness, forgiving the frightened, lonely woman who'd fled from everything real and masked her pain with temporary diversions.

The warmth filled me—healing, forgiving, loving warmth, and with it came a long-overdue peace. Kat Crosse wasn't always fabulous. Sometimes she was a bitch, sometimes she fucked up, sometimes she needed a good kick in the butt. And that was okay, because she was just human.

But she wasn't a vamp anymore.

I opened my eyes, only to find they were wet with tears. Maybe the fabulous Kat never cried, I thought with a watery smile, but it seemed I did.

A terrible, tinkling crash sounded behind me. I spun around, hearing the echo of shattering crystal continue to resonate around the great granite-walled chamber as two women scrambled from the smashed shards of the massive chandelier that had hung over the room. More figures raced down the iron steps, but I hardly saw them.

"Heads up, Megan! Behind you—vamp creep at six o'clock!"

Megan whirled and drove her stake into the vampire that had been about to attack her, but my burning gaze was fixed on the woman with the red gold curls who'd shouted out the warning.

It was Tashya. She was alive.

Chapter 18

When you realize the sister you thought was dead is alive and well and staking vamps like crazy, any other questions you might have fly right out of your head. So it wasn't till a day or so later that I thought to ask Megan how the Darkheart crew—and the few dozen tough-looking Russian comrades from New York that Mikhail had called on for help—had known where Cyrus's lair was.

"Thank Grandfather Darkheart for that," she said. "He went looking for you and when he found your cell phone in the alleyway behind the hospital, he realized something bad had happened. The first thing he did was phone the Hot Box, but Jack said you hadn't returned—and by the way, don't you think leaving him with *four* flats to fix was a little harsh, sis?" she asked. "The poor guy had just finished repairing them when he got Darkheart's call."

"And assumed the worst," I said wryly. "So he told Ramon to take the vampmobile and leave, while he waited to see if a certain sexy vamp paid a midnight visit on him. Which I did, so I guess I can't blame him," I admitted. "But you still haven't said how you found the connection to Liebnitz's office, sweetie."

"That part was easy enough," Megan said. "I checked your cell to see if you'd had time to call 911, but it showed your last call went through to a Dr. Liebnitz. After that we started digging—and found the good Dr. L was a *very* shadowy figure, who didn't come up on any computer database, not even the medical registers."

"But Dr. Hawes recommended—" I stopped, putting the pieces together. "Kane covered all the bases," I said slowly. "He guessed I might be conflicted enough to seek help from my old therapist, and he *glamyred* Hawes into providing his name as a substitute. To make it less obvious, he prompted Hawes to suggest two women, as well, knowing full well I'd pick the lone male on the list."

There was more, like how they'd found the original blueprints for the brownstone's renovation and how they'd learned that the place would be swarming with vamps that night, which led to Mikhail calling in his buddies. But as I say, on the night in question I wasn't worrying about details.

I was too stunned by the sight of Tashya.

I battled my way through the confusion toward her, pushing vamps and Russians aside and trying to keep my skirt from tripping me up, but when I finally got to her, all I could do was stand there.

Then I burst into tears and threw my arms around her. "But how—what—" I said incoherently before I stopped trying to talk and just held her as if I'd never let her go.

Tashya was holding me just as tightly, but when a vamp stumbled into us and nearly knocked us down, she released my grip on her. "Just a sec, sis," she said, turning swiftly and ramming her stake into the vamp. She waited until he turned to dust and then smiled at me. "I'm not a ghost," she said softly. "I know it's a shock, but I'm really alive…thanks to my Healer sister. Yes, we all know," she added, forestalling my next question. "Ramon told us Jack's theory about you…but by then I already had proof."

"Sweetie—" I waited while she dusted another vamp that had raced toward us, and then went on. "When I saw you in the morgue I didn't even know I was a Healer. All I knew was that I'd lost you." I swallowed back a fresh batch of tears. "I didn't perform a Heal on you, I swear. I just cried my eyes out over you and told you how much I loved you."

"I know," Tash said, her voice suddenly as uneven as mine was. "Because when I opened my eyes and saw you slipping out the door, my face was still wet with your tears. I didn't understand why, of course, all I knew was that one moment I'd been standing on a sidewalk with you and the next I was lying on a cold metal table in a room that smelled totally yucky," she added, wrinkling her nose in distaste.

I think that's when I knew she was really back with me, sweeties—when she pulled a face and looked for a moment like the bratty sister I'd known and loved and fought with all my life. I was just about to tell her that when the fighting heated up around us and we both got busy—Tash with her vamp staking and me with my own priority, which was making my way through the chaos to Jack and unchaining him.

But before I'd taken more than half a dozen steps I felt a powerful arm wrapping around my throat from behind and Cyrus's voice was in my ear.

"It seems I was right to be disappointed in you, Katherine," he said, tightening his grip until my windpipe felt as if it was being crushed. "Instead of accepting the destiny I held out to you, you allied yourself with those who have no chance against me."

Suddenly the pressure on my windpipe released and I felt his arm withdraw from my throat. I spun around and was disconcerted to realize he didn't mean to attack me. His fangs weren't in evidence. His face was as composed as it had been during our sessions in his office. He even managed a wintry little smile at me.

"Megan will die screaming," he said coldly. "She will be my first target and by the time I finish with her she will welcome death as a friend. The old man will be next. Before he is broken I will make his every nightmare come true. Tashya—"

"It won't work, Cyrus," I interrupted him. "I know what you're trying to do, but you can't corrupt my power anymore."

"Tashya," he continued as smoothly as if I hadn't spoken, "will find and embrace the darkness that could have been yours, and when she has sworn eternal allegiance to me I will send her after the bounty hunter."

His threats were based on fear, I realized. Cyrus Kane wasn't a stupid man. He knew he had run out of all his options, except for the one he was trying to use now. His threats were a desperate attempt to goad me into the only emotion he understood, the only one he could accept—hatred.

And he wanted me to hate him, not just to cripple my power, but because he hated himself.

"It can end, Cyrus," I said softly. "You just have to let me take it away from you and all the evil will end. Then you can start the long journey back to peace."

I moved toward him and saw a flash of fear behind his icy gaze. I took another step and saw a flicker of something else.

Was it hope?

I stopped moving and opened my arms to him, readying myself for the pain I knew had been corroding him for centuries. Cyrus Kane hesitated.

I went forward and accepted the legacy of pain and love that David Crosse had bequeathed to me. Everything that Kane had seen in his long life, everything he'd done—horrors and death and despair—it all poured over me, and only the light and the warmth burning deep within me kept it from overwhelming me. As I felt the connection between us begin to fade at last , I closed my eyes in exhaustion.

When I finally found the strength to open them again I almost didn't recognize the man who stood before me.

Vampaholic

He looked somehow smaller, less substantial. Cyrus Kane the vampire had been a master, and his power had been almost visible. Cyrus Kane the man was middle-aged, his posture slightly stooped, his features nondescript.

Except for his eyes. In them was reflected all the anguish and regret a man with a conscience would feel after reliving the memories we had both just shared.

"Katherine." His voice was a thread. "You spoke of a journey toward peace. My first step must be to ask your forgiveness."

I shook my head. "Your first step is to forgive yourself, Cyrus."

"Watch your back, Crosse!" The shouted warning came from a few feet away and I turned just in time to see Jack fire his nail gun at a vamp charging toward me. It dusted instantly, and Jack gave me a tight grin before bringing his weapon to bear on a new target.

"Cyrus, I'm needed—" My words broke off as I turned and saw he was no longer standing where he'd been. My gaze swept the room, and I caught a glimpse of him moving away through the crowd.

He'd started on his journey, I realized. It was time for me to do the same.

"Kat, you okay?"

Jack had made his way to my side, and as I looked into his bruised face and saw the concern there, I gave him a slow smile.

"You know what, sweetie? For the first time in my life, I really think I am."

I looked past him. My sisters were staking vamps like

it was going out of style. Mikhail and a bunch of husky Russian-looking types were doing the same, and as my glance strayed beyond them, I saw Darkheart—Ramon and Liz covering his back—wielding a stake with all the vigor of a man half his age. Looking again at Jack, I saw that although his gaze was still on my face, his finger had unconsciously tightened on the trigger of his nail gun.

Killing vamps was my sisters' and Mikhail's and Darkheart's job, and it was Jack's job, too. But mine was saving them. I could foresee a *teensy* amount of conflict between my junkyard dog and me in the future over our differing roles.

"Go do what you have to do, sweetie," I said, leaning forward and planting a kiss at the side of Jack's mouth. "I've got a feeling I'm going to be busy for the next hour or so, too."

And with any luck, I thought as Jack grinned and kissed me back, along with the conflict we'd have a rousing session of makeup sex after every one of our arguments. I mean, sweeties, just because a girl finds out she's a Healer doesn't mean she has to put *all* her naughty ways behind her, does it?

I watched my guy wade into battle. Then I turned to the work I'd been born to do.

Epilogue

The letter arrived a month later. The weeks following the fight at Kane's lair had been chaotic, what with the Hot Box's grand opening—a smashing success, by the way—an increase in cases for Darkheart & Crosse, and the usual nightly vamp patrols. I'd been right about the conflict. Meg wasn't thrilled by me trying to Heal the vamps she was about to dust, especially since most of them snarlingly chose the Way of the Stake over reawakening their souls, anyway. Jack was even less happy. During one delectable interlude that followed our arguments on the subject, he confessed that his real problem was with his fears for my safety—which touched me so much that I brought out my velvet-lined handcuffs and silk Hermès blindfold, and drove him crazy all night long.

Call me old-fashioned, but I just *love* when a man goes all protective and malely-male on me, even if I don't let him stop me from doing what I need to do.

But as busy as things were, I couldn't forget how close I'd come to losing both my sisters—Tash to death, and Meg because of the wedge I'd driven between us—and I insisted the three of us meet one afternoon a week, *sans* men, at the Hot Box for drinkies and a girl gab session. These days, drinkies for me meant Shirley Temples, so when Ramon dropped by our table and handed me the letter, I was completely sober.

As it turned out, I needed to be.

"Is that postmarked India?" Megan asked. "God, Kat, don't you ever get tired of all your lovelorn ex-swains fleeing to the four corners of the earth to forget you, only to bombard you with heartbroken letters—"

"It's not from an ex-swain," I said, scanning the first few lines of the letter. "It's from Cyrus."

"Kane?" Tash's tone was loaded. As I set the pages of the letter on the table so she and Megan could read with me, however, I found myself hearing not her voice, but Cyrus's, as if the inked words in front of me were eerily audible.

"Dear Katherine,
You told me I needed to forgive myself before asking it of others, but I fear that the former will take more time than I have left. Hence this letter which, although it can never erase the wrongs I did, may repay in some small measure the debt I owe you.
As a Healer, you saw me as the man I once had

been, so please bear with me if you already know some of what I'm about to tell you. As I told you, I founded Maplesburg with the intention of leading a community of God-fearing citizens, but the pride I had as a vampire was already at work in me then. I ruled my parishioners with a rod of iron, arrogant in my own infallible righteousness. In the end, my overweening pride was my downfall.

With the Colonies still some eighty years away from breaking with England, when the lovely young widow Lady Jasmine Melrose arrived to take up residence in Maplesberg, even my somber flock were flattered she had chosen to live among us. Their excitement was dashed when it became clear she intended to live a life of seclusion, not socializing or even attending church. God forgive me, I took this as a challenge to my arrogant belief in my own powers. I called on her, and was turned away at the door by a manservant. For most of that winter of '92, while my brother preachers in Salem were condemning innocent women as witches, I pursued my own particular path to damnation. Each rebuff from the elusive Lady Jasmine fueled my determination, and when the night finally came that the manservant told me she would see me, unholy triumph shot through me.

An equally base emotion filled me at my first sight of her. Not only was she shatteringly beautiful, with her alabaster skin, red lips and silky blond hair falling to her waist, but she was dressed in a loose robe secured by a single tie at her waist. When she slipped the robe from her shoulders, I willingly cast my soul away in my hunger to sink into her exquisite flesh...but as it turned out, it was she who sunk into mine when she pierced my neck with her fangs.

The rest you can guess. As a vampire, I had the same zeal to convert others as I had when I'd been a man of the cloth. Even after my dark Mistress left Maplesburg, her work here done, I stalked my former flock, turning some and killing others. In the end, those who remained came for me with stakes and crosses and I barely escaped with my undead life.

As to what relevance this old story holds now, I fear history is about to repeat itself. From the postmark on the envelope, you will see I have made my way to a Tibetan monastery-in-exile in India. My health has suffered during my journey to this mountainous retreat, although if anyone can pull me through, the good monks can. But their herbs and wisdom may be no match for my injuries, and my warning to you cannot wait. The night before I reached the monastery, Katherine, I was set upon by a group of bandits. Just when I thought that the next blow from their cudgels would be the fatal one, they scattered and fled, screaming in fear. As I lay there on the ground I saw a beautiful blond woman—"

"That's *it?*" As I turned the obviously unfinished letter over, Tash gave a scornful snort. "I just *knew* a

Heal wouldn't work on a Master like Kane. He's obviously still a vamp and this is one of his mind-games. He wants us scared—"

I read out loud from the other side of Cyrus's letter.

"Dear Friend,
It is my sad duty to inform you that Brother Kane died before he could complete his last communication to you. It may comfort you to know that he was not alone in his final hours upon this earth. His sister arrived when his fever was at its height and sat with him until his death, and I am sure that the sight of her, so angelic an oothing, helped ease him over the threshold into the unknowable."

I raised my gaze to Megan and Tashya. "It's signed by the Lama of the monastery," I said unevenly. "Are either of you thinking what I'm thinking?"

"That Kane's angelic sister was the same blond apparition who sent a bunch of bloodthirsty bandits running for their lives?" Megan said, her tone as unsteady as mine. "And that both of those women are really the notorious Lady Jasmine, his former vamp mistress? I'm also thinking Kane was trying to warn us about her, which means he thought she intends to make a return engagement in Maplesburg, no?"

"Gawd, I don't *believe* the two of you!" Before I knew what she meant to do, Tashya jumped from her chair and snatched the letter from my hand. "It's a trick!" she insisted, her voice rising. "A stupid trick, meant to scare us into believing it's starting all over again—a big bad vamp blows into town, one of us thinks Zena's curse is still valid and we're about to turn vamp, and the three of us end up at each other's throats. Well, I'm not playing the game this time!"

She ripped the letter in two, then ripped it again before defiantly tossing the torn pieces into the air. I saw quick anger in Megan's eyes and put my hand on her arm. As paper fluttered down like confetti, she followed my glance, taking in Tash's trembling lips, her stark white face, the tears glazing the baby blue of her eyes.

"You're right, brat," she said swiftly. "We're jumping to conclusions. Kane was feverish when he wrote this, so maybe—"

"So maybe nothing," I said hollowly, holding out a scrap of paper that had fluttered into my lap. It was covered with a bold yet somehow formal scrawl, and the ink it was written in looked thick and fresh. "Take a look at this. This wasn't on the letter before Tash tore it up," I added shakily.

Meg read out loud in a voice of dawning dismay.

"Felicitations, ladies! After having such a delight-ful visit with my old friend, I have decided to make the acquaintance of some new ones. You may expect me soon, but pray do not put yourself out with preparations for my visit, since I assure you that they shall prove to be of no avail. Yours cordially, Jasmine, Lady Melrose."

She looked at me. "Did you read the P.S. she tacked on at the end?" she asked hoarsely.

I forced a nod, then saw Tash's scowl of

incomprehension. "It simply says, 'David Crosse lives,'
I told her, tears flooding my eyes. "I don't care if a
hundred Mistresses are on their way to Maplesburg,
sweeties—if what this Lady Jasmine says is true and
Dad's really alive, this if the best news we could ever
have gotten!"

"I agree," Megan said, her own eyes swimming. "I
know I'm a tough daughter of Lilith, but I feel a major
blub coming on. Sister hug, anyone?"

"You're on," I said with a hiccupping laugh as I put
my arm around her and turned to Tashya. "Come on,
brat, let's bond."

My fingertips touched her shoulder and I started
to draw her into Megan's and my embrace. What
happened next turned my blood to ice.

"Don't touch me, Healer!" Tash hissed, wrenching
violently from me and backing away a few steps. Her
face looked so bloodless that her freckles stood out like
blotches. She took another step backward, fear and confusion in her eyes. Then she turned and ran.

David Crosse was still alive.

And so was Zena's curse, I realized sickly as Megan
and I watched our vamp sister flee from us.

* * * * *

*Look out for the next DARKHEART & CROSSE
adventure DEAD IS THE NEW BLACK
by Harper Allen. Available January 2007
wherever Silhouette Books are sold.*

New York Times *bestselling author*
Linda Lael Miller is back with a new romance
featuring the heartwarming McKettrick family
from Silhouette Special Edition.

SIERRA'S HOMECOMING
by Linda Lael Miller

On sale December 2006,
wherever books are sold.

Turn the page for a sneak preview!

Soft, smoky music poured into the room.

The next thing she knew, Sierra was in Travis's arms, close against that chest she'd admired earlier, and they were slow dancing.

Why didn't she pull away?

"Relax," he said. His breath was warm in her hair.

She giggled, more nervous than amused. What was the matter with her? She was attracted to Travis, had been from the first, and he was clearly attracted to her. They were both adults. Why not enjoy a little slow dancing in a ranch-house kitchen?

Because slow dancing led to other things. She took a step back and felt the counter flush against her lower back. Travis naturally came with her, since they were holding hands and he had one arm around her waist.

Simple physics.

Then he kissed her.

Physics again—this time, not so simple.

"Yikes," she said, when their mouths parted.

He grinned. "Nobody's ever said that after I kissed them."

She felt the heat and substance of his body pressed against hers. "It's going to happen, isn't it?" she heard herself whisper.

"Yep," Travis answered.

"But not tonight," Sierra said on a sigh.

"Probably not," Travis agreed.

"When, then?"

He chuckled, gave her a slow, nibbling kiss. "Tomorrow morning," he said. "After you drop Liam off at school."

"Isn't that…a little…soon?"

"Not soon enough," Travis answered, his voice husky. "Not nearly soon enough."

HARLEQUIN *Romance*®

**From the Heart.
For the Heart.**

Get swept away into the Outback
with two of Harlequin Romance's
top authors.

Coming in December...

Claiming the
Cattleman's Heart
BY BARBARA HANNAY

And in January don't miss...

Outback Man Seeks Wife
BY MARGARET WAY

TAKE 'EM FREE!

2 FREE ACTION-PACKED NOVELS PLUS 2 FREE GIFTS!

Strong. Sexy. Suspenseful.

Silhouette®
BOMBSHELL™

COMING NEXT MONTH

#117 DAUGHTER OF THE BLOOD—Nancy Holder
The Gifted

For New Yorker Isabella de Marco, serving as Guardienne of the House of Flames in New Orleans was a birthright she still hadn't come to terms with. The ancestral mansion was in the midst of dangerous transition, and powerful demonic forces were aligning against her. With her partner and lover both wounded, Izzy comes to rely on a mysterious new ally for help...but does he have a hidden agenda to bring about her eternal damnation?

#118 VEILED LEGACY—Jenna Mills
The Madonna Key

Adopted at birth, Nadia Bishop never knew her roots—until she came across what seemed to be her own photo on the obituary page! Was this the lost sister who'd appeared in her dreams? Tracing the murdered woman to Europe, Nadia discovered the key to her own life—her blood ties to an ancient line of powerful priestesses made her a target...and her child's father might be part of the conspiracy to destroy her.

#119 THE PHOENIX LAW—Cate Dermody
The Strongbox Chronicles

The biggest threat in former CIA agent Alisha MacAleer's new life was babysitting her nephews—until an ex-colleague showed up on her doorstep, dodging bullets and needing her help. Suddenly she was thrust back into the world of double agents, rogue organizations and sentient AIs, while also helping men who'd betrayed her before. As avoiding death grew more difficult for Alisha, could the phoenix rise from the ashes once more?

#120 STORM FORCE—Meredith Fletcher

Taken hostage by a gang of escaped prisoners during one of the worst hurricanes in Florida history, Everglades wilderness guide Kate Garrett was trapped in a living nightmare. Her captors were wanted for murder, and though one of them might be the undercover good guy he claimed to be, it was up to Kate to save her own skin. For the sake of her children, she had to come out alive, come hell or high water...or both!

SBCNM1106